Love on the Rocks

OTHER BOOKS
BY JAMES L. DICKERSON

Colonel Tom Parker
The Curious Life of Elvis Presley's Eccentric Manager

Faith Hill
The Long Road Back

That's Alright, Elvis
The Untold Story of Elvis's First Guitarist and Manager, Scotty Moore
(with Scotty Moore)

Ashley Judd
Crying on the Inside

Just for a Thrill
Lil Hardin Armstrong, First Lady of Jazz

Scotty & Elvis
Aboard the Mystery Train
(with Scotty Moore)

Creature from Reelfoot Lake
(novel)

Legend of the Soul Eater
(novel)

Someone is Trying to Kill Me
(novel)

LOVE ON THE ROCKS

Romance to the Rescue

James L. Dickerson

Love on the Rocks

CHAPTER

1

Katherine Summer had everything in life that a woman could possibly want. Once, on a particularly fragrant spring day, she sat in the shade near her garden and made a checklist of all the things that made her life wonderful:

- ✓ A husband that loved her.
- ✓ A precocious five-year-old daughter.
- ✓ A soaring career as a landscape artist.
- ✓ An island home that was positively dreamy.

Most days, Katherine woke happy and went to bed happy. Life had been that way for a long time. She married at twenty-one. She had her daughter Dedi at twenty-five. Everyone said that she and Roger were the perfect couple. Considering the time and effort that went into building their storybook romance, its end came with mind-numbing suddenness.

She was slammed from nowhere.

The day had begun like any other—a bright, sunny Saturday. Dedi was first out of bed, and she wasted no time bursting into the master bedroom, energetically reaching for sleepy hands and arms to drag into the waking day. In an irresistible voice, she pleaded, "Don't you know it's Saturday?"

Bessie, their blond cocker spaniel, was right behind her, yelping and twisting in three directions at once. It didn't take much to get her going. That morning they had breakfast on the deck, from which they had a panoramic view of the river.

The cool water was crystal clear. The sky was deep blue, with fluffy white clouds that tip-toed past, in no hurry to move along.

Occasionally, an ocean freighter passed by their island. Eight-story steel monsters that looked much too large for such an easygoing, people-friendly river populated with slow-moving fishing boats and water-splashing swimmers.

Dedi loved the ships. She always waved at them. She couldn't tell if anyone waved back from the tiny windows, where anonymous men and women piloted the ships through a fifty-mile nautical minefield of floating logs and hidden rocks; but every once in a while her wave was answered with a china-rattling blast from a ship's foghorn.

Toot! Toot! Toot!

Dedi took it to be a special gift, meant only for her. Sometimes it was. The river was magical in that way.

After breakfast, Dedi asked, "What are we going to do now, Mommie?"

Katherine leaned back in her chair, still nursing her coffee, enjoying the rich aroma.

"Dear, I need to put a few finishing touches on a painting," Katherine explained. "Then I'll do whatever you like."

"But I want to do something now!" she protested.

Katherine studied her daughter, who by that time was kneeling at her chair, her enormous eyes pleading for capitulation. So earnest. So innocent. Katherine was tempted, she really was, but she had a strong work ethic. She just couldn't see going out to play when there was so much work to be done.

"Why don't you ask your father if he'll take you out in the boat until I finish my work? Then you can come back and get me."

Dedi walked on her knees over to where Roger was seated, her tiny shoulders rocking back and forth. She reached out for his hand, her fingers sticky with peanut butter. "Will you, Father—will you?"

Roger looked at Katherine and grinned. He admired Katherine for her ability to say no to Dedi when the occasion merited it, but he didn't have it within himself to disappoint those saucer-sized green eyes that looked so innocently at him.

Sometimes he called her his big-eyed girl.

"Oh, I think we might work something out."

"Oh, really?" asked Dedi, her voice trembling with excitement.

"Why don't you go put on your swimsuit?" said Katherine.

"I will!" squealed Dedi. She jumped to her feet and ran into the house.

"You don't mind, do you?" asked Katherine.

"Of course not. We'll explore for a while. Then we'll come back and get you. It's not a big deal."

"Can you give me about an hour?"

"You got it."

When Dedi returned from the house, she was decked out in a mint-green, one-piece swimsuit, with orange-framed sunglasses and a floppy hat.

"Let's go," she said cheerfully.

Roger took her outstretched hand and walked her over to Katherine. "Give Mommie a kiss," he said.

Dedi reached up and put her arms around Katherine's neck and pecked her on the cheek with a moist kiss.

"Thank you," said Katherine. "Be sure to mind your father."

"I will."

Roger leaned over and kissed Katherine on the mouth. His lips were morning soft.

"Take your time and get it the way you want it," he said. "If you're not ready when we get back, I'll keep her busy until you're ready."

"You're just too good to be true," Katherine beamed.

Roger and Dedi walked down the walkway to the dock and boarded the twenty-eight-foot mahogany runabout, a classic speedboat built in the 1950s and lovingly restored to its full glory. It had a rebuilt Chevy engine that gave it enough juice to overtake anything on the river, except the ultra-speedboats built for racing.

Roger got Dedi into her life preserver and cast off, aware of Katherine's watchful eye as he started the engine and pulled slowly away from the dock. He waved to her, without turning around, sort of a "see you later" gesture.

Dedi spun in the seat so that she could see her mother as she waved goodbye with that peculiar quiet deliberation possessed by all five year olds. Katherine watched until they were out of sight.

Then she resumed painting.

For the next hour, the air seemed unusually sweet, scented by the red, pink and white flowering shrubs that encircled the cottage. She loved to work when the days were so nice. It added something special to her brush strokes, made them more nuanced, more optimistic—two qualities essential for an effective landscape.

Once an hour had passed, she found herself glancing every few minutes at her watch. Fifteen after the hour. An hour and a half. Two hours.

Where are they? she wondered, continuing to paint, although she wasn't terribly focused. Every time she attempted a fine detail, her eyes wandered to the river, searching for something familiar headed in her direction. Often she faltered, lost her place, and had to refocus.

Finally, three hours passed! It felt like nine hours.

Katherine put her painting away.

She cleaned her brushes and scrubbed her pallet.

Then she walked down to the dock and gazed at the river, watching the boats come and go, some more quietly than others. Some had children that screamed and waved at her. She waved back. She tried to smile . . . sat on the edge of the dock, her legs dangling only inches from the water, the sun stinging the side of her face. Where were they?

As the fourth hour approached, she heard a boat motor behind her. She turned and saw a boat headed in her direction from the Canadian side of the river. She shielded her eyes from the sun with her hand, but she couldn't make out any details of the boat.

As the boat purred closer, she realized that she'd never seen it before. Her heart skipped a beat.

Once it was about a hundred yards away she realized that it was an Ontario Provincial Police cruiser. A Canadian flag fluttered on the stern. The word "police" was written in large letters on the side of the boat. *Oh, this can't be good* she thought.

She rose to her feet as the boat neared the dock.

There were two uniformed men inside the boat, both grim-faced. She argued with herself, making the case that their facial expressions meant nothing.

She tried to recall if she'd ever seen an OPP officer smile. She couldn't recall a single instance. Even the female officers presented a stern countenance.

There, that settles it! They're just on routine patrol.

As the boat pulled up to the dock, she said, "Hello," her voice sounding surprisingly hollow, like it had risen from the depths of a deep well.

One of the men leaped out of the boat and secured it with a line. The other man cut the engine. From the time they pulled up, until the time one of the men spoke, seemed like an eternity.

"Are you Mrs. Summer?" asked one of the officers.

The other officer looked down at his shoes.

Katherine nodded, forcing out a soft, "Yes."

The officer coughed.

"I'm afraid I've got some bad news."

"Oh," she said, feeling her knees tremble.

"Yes ma'am," said the officer. "There's been an accident."

At first the words barely registered. It was as if she was overhearing a conversation taking place on a television in another room. Everything seemed out of focus—distant and sort of blurred.

There was a long pause as the officers looked at her, patiently waiting for a response. She held her breath, afraid to inhale or exhale.

Finally, she came to her senses and released her breath. Her eyes widened and she excitedly asked, "Are they all right?"

She reached out and touched an officer's arm.

"My husband and daughter—are they all right?"

The officer shook his head.

"No ma'am. I'm afraid your husband and your daughter both drowned."

Almost immediately, he winced, wishing he'd said it better. But is there a good way to say those words?

Katherine stared at them, wondering if she'd heard correctly. Time stopped still. She replayed their words, hoping to hear something different. When that didn't happen, she sank to the dock, dropping straight down, hard.

The men sat next to her, their normally jaded eyes watery with tears.

"Are you sure?" she asked.

"We're sure."

"What . . . tell me what happened?"

"They were in that runabout of yours when they struck some rocks just beneath the surface. Your husband and your daughter were thrown into the water"

"But she had on a life preserver. I saw her put it on!"

"Yes ma'am, she did. Unfortunately, the boat turned upside down and her life preserver got caught on one of the lights and held her underneath the water."

Katherine grimaced, aging ten years on the spot.

"And my husband?"

"Well . . ." The officer paused, struggling to find the rights words. "We couldn't find your husband. He must have been knocked unconscious and swept away. We looked for him."

"But maybe . . ."

The officer interrupted. "No ma'am there's no chance he survived."

"How can you be so sure? Maybe he's stranded on a rock somewhere."

The officer shook his head, slowly and respectfully.

"I know this river. I know its currents. In all the years I've done this, never once have we found anyone if they didn't end up on the rocks. We looked everywhere for him. Did everything we possibly could do. I'm so sorry."

Katherine covered her face with her hands and wept.

The two officers sat beside her, saying nothing.

Her sobs came and went like great waves, rising and falling in intensity. She'd sit still for a minute, soundless, and then the sobs started all over again.

After a while, one of the men said, "We'll need you to come into Brockville to identify the remains."

"The remains?" she sputtered.

"I mean . . . to tell us for certain that it's your daughter."

"Can't someone else do that?"

"No ma'am. I'm afraid you'll have to do it."

One of the officers started to put his arm around her, but then thought better of it. His natural instinct was to comfort her. To hold her the way his mother had held him when he was upset. But his training was that he shouldn't touch females under any circumstances, unless it was to keep them from hurting themselves or others.

"Do I have to do it now?"

"You don't have to do it now, but I think it'll be easier on you if you do."

"Very well," she said, coming to her feet.

The officers helped her into the boat and headed back into open water. They avoided looking at her as she watched her island slowly recede into the distance. Her arms were crossed in anxious anticipation. She had a forlorn expression on her face that neither man would ever forget.

*   *   *

Brockville didn't have a full-time morgue. Those duties were performed in a special section of City Hospital. After the OPP officers docked their boat, they drove Katherine to the hospital and took her in to meet the morgue official, a part-time pathologist whose morgue duties took up only about ten percent of his time at the hospital.

Dr. Van Zant was in his early seventies and had thick bushy gray hair that was long in the back. Some people thought he looked like Albert Einstein. Others thought he resembled one of the Three Stooges.

Taking long steps, he escorted Katherine and the two OPP officers into a sterile-looking room that was bare except for several metal chairs, a lamp, and a table containing numerous back issues of various glossy travel magazines. With a vague hand gesture, Dr. Van Zant indicated the chairs.

"Please wait here. I'll be back in a few minutes."

Katherine sat in one of the chairs, but the OPP officers said they preferred to stand. She looked around the room. She and Roger had been in the hospital several times. The time she gave birth to Dedi. The time he had a hernia repair. The time she broke her leg in a rock climbing accident on one of the islands. On each occasion they walked past the morgue, not really noticing that it was even there.

The room was windowless. Its pale-green walls were devoid of any photographs. The floors were immaculately clean. The sweet-and-sour scent of pine cleaner filled the air. Katherine sat in silence, the OPP officers restless on their feet, as they shifted their weight, sliding their feet, first one way, then another. Although she was seated she somehow felt as if she was slipping away. From what she did not know.

"Would you like a glass of water?" asked one of the police officers.

"No thank you."

"If there's anything you want, just let us know."

"Yes, I will. Thank you."

Katherine's mind wandered, taking her back to the day she entered the hospital to give birth to Dedi. The river was frozen solid. Mid-January. A snow storm was blowing into the area. Roger had difficulty starting the iceboat, but once he had it going, he locked the throttle on high and returned to the cottage for Katherine, who was bundled up in two coats and an Indian blanket they'd once purchased on a trip to Arizona.

They made it across the ice without any problems, but it seemed to take forever to get the car started, even with an electrically heated engine block. By that time, there were already three inches of snow on the ground. It took an hour to get to the hospital, what with the slipping, and sliding and the frequent pauses to frantically brush the snow from the windshield, but the doctor was waiting for them when they arrived.

Roger barely got comfortable in the waiting room when the doctor appeared

"We've had some problems," the doctor explained in a monotone. "Your wife has a condition called toxemia. Right now, her blood pressure is 210 over 130. There's a possibility that she could have a stroke during delivery, though we'll do everything we can to keep that from happening. I thought you should know."

"Thank you. I understand."

The following hour was the longest in Roger's life.

The next time the doctor burst through the door he flashed a broad smile.

"Your wife is fine—and your baby girl is fine."

Roger hugged the doctor and asked to see Katherine.

"Just don't stay very long. She's been through a lot."

Katherine was so heavily sedated that she couldn't speak. She did manage a smile, though. Roger kissed her on the lips and held her hand for a while. Then he told her that he was going to see their precious little girl, Dedi.

This time, Katherine winked.

Roger was speechless when he saw Dedi in the incubator. She weighed less than six pounds. She was as pink and wrinkled as a crumpled rose. The nurses said it would be a day or so before he could hold her, because of her low birth weight, so he was disappointed about that; but looking into her tiny face through the glass, seeing glimpses of Katherine on her face—and marveling at her reddish hair—made him happier than he'd ever known he could be. It was below zero on the day Dedi was born, and by the time they left the hospital there was eighteen inches of flaky fresh snow outside.

In the morgue, Katherine folded her arms, chilled by the constant stream of cool air from the air-conditioner that blew into the room with a low hum, the coldness reminding her of the day she saw Dedi for the first time. The silence unnerved her. She wished the OPP officers would say something, say anything.

Suddenly, the double-door that led to the next room banged open. Dr. Van Zant pushed a sheet-covered gurney into the room. There was a small bundle beneath the sheet, hardly more than three feet in length.

Katherine felt panicky inside, totally unaware of the tears on her cheeks.

Dr. Van Zant hesitated before he pulled back the sheet, the way you would hesitate before reaching into a fire. It was a brief hesitation, hardly measurable, but it was long enough for Katherine to notice it and to see the pain in his eyes.

"It's all right," she said, speaking in an intense, tight little voice that came from deep inside a twisted place. "Please do it now."

As long as she lived, she knew that she'd never forget the sight of Dedi stretched out lifeless on that gurney. Her eyes were closed, but she had a slight smile on her lips. Her face was unblemished. It was as if she had died in the instant it takes to leap into the air to reach for a butterfly.

So perfect did she look that Katherine found it difficult to believe that she was truly gone. Katherine leaned over and kissed her on the forehead, taken aback by the cold roughness of her skin. In life, her skin had always been so warm and clammy.

"Is this your daughter?" asked Dr. Van Zant, his voice cracking.

"Yes—that is definitely my daughter."

Dr. Van Zant nodded politely and covered the child's face with the sheet. Then he wheeled her out of the room. Katherine started for the door, shadowed by the OPP officers, both blinking with watery eyes.

The three of them drove back to the island, first in the patrol car and then in the boat, without a word being spoken. The silence was brittle. Once they reached the dock, the OPP officers helped Katherine out of the boat.

"Is there anything you need us to do?"

Yes, she thought. *Make it back the way it was. Give me back my life!*

But instead of speaking her mind, she shook her head. "You've done plenty already. Thank you for everything."

She reached out and hugged each man. Then she went into the house.

Three days later, Katherine boarded one of the triple-deck cruise ships that took sightseers on tours of the islands. Clutched to her chest were two clay jars that Dedi had made for her in pottery class. One of the jars had flowers painted on it. The other jar had three stick figures—a mother, a father, a child.

Katherine remained on the first deck and went to the stern, where she leaned against the rail, the jars still held close to her chest. Most of the ship's two hundred passengers gravitated to the bow side of the three decks so that they could see where the ship was headed.

Katherine didn't want to know where it was headed. She wanted to see where it'd been. She was alone except for a young couple who had lingered behind so that they could have privacy to snuggle and kiss.

They gave Katherine an ugly look, the intent of which was to shoo her away to the other end of the boat.

She stood her ground.

As Brockville receded into the distance, Katherine stared at the water, mesmerized by the purr of the ship's engines. Because of all the time she'd spent on the river with Roger and Dedi, it was a sound that brought back pleasant memories.

The river was something that the three of them shared, each of them reveling in its sights and sounds.

Katherine and Roger had never discussed burial plans, so she was at a loss when the funeral director called her to ask what she wanted done. She wasn't sure. She told him she'd have to sleep on it. Roger and Dedi would've loved to be buried on the island, but Katherine was hesitant to do that since such a burial place would have no guarantee of permanency. After she was gone, the new owner of the island might have the graves relocated. Fifty years down the road the river authority might decide to blast the island away to make a wider channel in the river.

The only burial that could have permanency would be cremation. That way Dedi's ashes could be spread across the river they loved. The second jar, meant to represent Roger's ashen remains, was filled with rose petals.

Katherine refused to budge from her spot at the rail. She knew where she wanted to say goodbye to Roger and Dedi, and she knew it'd take about thirty minutes to get there.

Frustrated by her refusal to take a hint to go elsewhere, the young man said, "You must have been young once. Give us a break."

"What?" she answered. "What did you say?"

"You must have been young and in love. Can't you see that we want privacy?"

The words stung her to the quick. *What in the hell do you know about being young and in love? You want to cop a feel. I know exactly why you want privacy.*

"I'm sorry—I was here first."

Both the man and the woman cursed and walked away, disappearing on the starboard side of the ship.

Katherine watched the markers of her life recede, growing smaller and smaller, finally disappearing. She inhaled the sweet wetness of the river, savoring the memories that spun through her head on fast forward.

Finally, she saw the buoy she'd been waiting for.

"Goodbye, sweet loves," she said. "I'll see you in my dreams."

She uncorked both jars and held them at arm's length over the water and gently poured ashes and rose petals in a steady stream until both jars were empty. Then she tossed the jars into the river, where they were swallowed up in one gulp.

Several minutes later, she knew that she'd timed it perfectly, for she saw their island as the ship moved past. She'd left them where she knew they'd both want to be. Where they could be near her and the island they loved.

CHAPTER
2

One year after the accident, Katherine had coped with losing her husband and daughter reasonably well, at least she no longer cried every night, but she hadn't reached the point where she saw much of a future for herself. When she daydreamed, it was always about the past, never about the future.

Frankly, she was a mess. Who would not be?

As a psychologist, Dr. Jason Montclair understood that. Katherine had come to him for grief counseling after the accident, at the suggestion of her minister, an insecure man who thrived on ceremony more than counseling.

The first year of therapy went smoothly enough. He encouraged her to talk about the accident and to express her feelings. Recovery was a building process.

"There are no instant cures," he repeatedly told her. "It takes time."

"It just seems so odd," she said, "—the idea that talking about something can have a healing effect. Intellectually, I buy into the premise. But emotionally I struggle with it. You would have to experience my feelings to understand what I go through every single day of my life. Are you saying that I have the power to heal myself?"

"Yes, that's exactly what I'm saying. But your point is well taken. There is no way that I can understand what you are feeling. But I believe in the process and I believe that you already possess all the tools that you need to heal yourself."

Katherine felt enormous guilt that she hadn't been in the boat with her husband and daughter. One emotionally paralyzing thought she kept returning to, time and time again, was, "If I'd been there, maybe I could have done something."

She had fantasies about resuscitating her husband and using super-human strength to untangle her daughter from the overturned boat.

"If I'd been there, I know I could've saved them. I was a fool to put my work ahead of my family. I should have put them first."

It wasn't easy, but Jason eventually convinced her that she bore no guilt for the accident. He explained the difference between healthy grief and self-loathing, and he encouraged her to confront the sadness and helplessness that she felt over her loss.

Two months after the sessions began he saw a marked improvement in her ability to cope with her grief. She was able to discuss her feelings without assigning blame. Unfortunately, he encountered an unexpected problem during her therapy.

Instead of listening dispassionately to her descriptions of her feelings, he hung on every word. Instead, of searching her face for subtle indications of masked emotions, he gazed into her eyes, dazzled by their effervescent green beauty. His heart raced whenever she was in his office and he laughed at everything she said, even when it wasn't funny. He noticed when she wore stockings and he noticed when she didn't have on a bra.

Dr. Jason Montclair had done the unthinkable. He'd fallen in love with his patient. Once he realized that, he suffered through a string of sleepless nights as he struggled with the ethics of treating a woman for whom he had romantic feelings.

Since he was a man of unquestionable ethics, the debate that raged inside him was not over what to do—there was no question about that, he had to terminate their professional relationship—but rather over how to explain his decision to her. He struggled with that dilemma, right up until the moment she walked into his office, the beginnings of a smile on her face.

She thought it odd that he avoided eye contact with her.

"That's quite a drive, isn't it?" he said as she settled into a chair on the other side of his desk. His office was in Ogdensburg, New York, across the river from Brockville, several miles to the east.

To get there, Katherine had to pilot her boat to the Ontario shore and then get in her car and drive to the Seaway Skyway Bridge, a fifty-year-old suspension bridge that connects New York with Ontario—and then drive over into Ogdensburg.

"Oh, it's not too bad," she answered. "It gets me off the island."

"Too bad you can't come by boat. That'd probably save you an hour or so."

"Maybe."

Jason swiveled in his chair, presenting her with his profile.

"I've been wondering . . ."

His voice trailed off and halted.

Before he spoke again, he tugged at his earlobe.

". . . if you might not find it more convenient to see a therapist in Brockville."

Katherine felt a surge of anxiety.

"Dr. Montclair, what do you mean?" she asked. "Are you dumping me?"

"No, no. It's just that . . ."

"Then what are you saying?"

Jason shook his head the way he'd always done when he was frustrated. "I'm only suggesting that you'd find it more convenient to see someone closer to your home."

"Isn't that for me to decide?"

"Yes, it is, but . . ."

"But what?"

Jason paused, searching for the right words.

"Ethically, I can no longer be your therapist."

Katherine released a long sigh.

"Nothing you're telling me makes sense. I was a wreck when I first came to you. You saved my life. You made everything make sense again. Why would you, out of the blue, tell me I have to go somewhere else?"

"Because the ethics of my profession require me to refer you to another therapist. I'm not dumping you, as you put it. I'm doing what is in your best interests."

Katherine looked at him as if he had lost his mind.

"Do you have any idea how ridiculous that sounds?"

"Yes, I know exactly how ridiculous it sounds."

"I'm not leaving this office until you tell me what's going on."

She folded her arms, a determined look on her face.

"Seriously. I'm not leaving."

"Sometimes it's better not to talk about some things."

"If you don't start making sense, I'm going to report you to the psychology board. You have one of those in New York, don't you?" Jason nodded.

"Yes . . . when you report me to them, please explain that I referred you to someone else because . . . because . . . well, because I think I'm falling in love with you."

Katherine looked stunned.

"You what?"

"I don't want to discuss it."

Katherine came to her feet, feeling a sudden urge to run from the room.

"You don't know me well enough to fall in love with me."

Jason stared at her, not sure what to say. He wasn't the first therapist to fall in love with a patient, but surely he was the most inept at explaining it to the patient.

She started for the door.

"I'm going to leave now. We can talk about this later."

"Maybe we can both go to the same therapist in Brockville," he said lamely, instantly regretting the comment.

"What! The two of us go to a therapist! What do you mean? Like we are a couple? That's crazy!"

"Just an idea."

"Let's talk about this another day."

"Another day?"

"Not today."

She went out the door, taking great care to close it quietly behind her, walking backward, as if she were closing the door on a sleeping child.

Outside the office, she looked at the receptionist and smiled politely. Then she straightened her skirt and burst into tears that had absolutely nothing to do with Dr. Jason Montclair, or so she thought.

CHAPTER
3

After telling Katherine that she should be counseled by another psychologist, Dr. Jason Montclair had a rough few days. That had never happened to him before. He'd never felt attracted to a patient.

In retrospect, he should have discussed his problem with his peers, sought their advice; but that would have involved telling them more than he wanted them to know about his private life and so he didn't.

He foolishly made it up as he went along, which was why Katherine reacted the way she did in his office. He should have been more tactful, more understanding of her feelings. *What an idiot I am*, he thought.

When several days went by and he didn't hear from her, he called, his heart skipping a beat when she answered the phone. After she said hello, it took him a full three seconds to respond. When you've got dead air, three seconds is a long time.

"Katherine, this is Dr. Montclair," he said, finally.

"Yes," she answered, drawing that one word out into three unlikely syllables.

"I'm calling to follow up on our last meeting."

Meeting! she thought. *I go to him for counseling and he tells me he has feelings for me. Now he's describing our last encounter as a meeting!*

Another long pause.

"So what would you like to know?" she said, coolly.

"Well . . ." It was a total mistake to call. He knew that now. ". . . did you contact the psychologist I referred you to."

"Not yet."

"Do you plan on doing that?"

"Haven't decided."

Long pause.

"Why don't we have lunch tomorrow and try to straighten this out?"

"See—that's what makes me angry! Is this lunch you want me to go to a counseling session or a date of some kind? I'm getting mixed signals."

"No, it's not a counseling session—and it's not a date, I don't think. I'd like to have lunch with you as a friend."

"As a potential friend, you mean?"

"I suppose."

"Well, fine. I'll meet you at noon tomorrow at Grady's."

Before he could respond, she hung up.

Jason clicked off his cell and took a deep breath. He'd never been very good with women on the telephone. That'd created problems for him his entire life, because nine times out of ten, social meetings between men and women are initiated by telephone calls.

As a psychologist, he understood that telephones are effective interview tools because they establish a one-on-one relationship that is difficult to duplicate in a face-to-face interview; but as a man he found that type of one-to-one directness in his social life intimidating to the point of making him feel foolish.

The following morning he counseled a couple who had issues over the wife's desire to work outside the home. Tensions had escalated to the point where they were ignoring the needs of their three-year-old son and talking about separation. Sitting in the office with them was like watching competing tornadoes tear up the landscape. Jason didn't see much hope for them as a couple, but he tried to impart a sense of urgency for them to understand their son's needs.

The last patient he saw before lunch was a thirty-two-year-old bed wetter who had unresolved anger issues with his mother. He actually had hopes for this patient, though discussing urination frequency before lunch was a real appetite suppresser. After the patient left, he went into his private bathroom and washed his hands. Then he splashed water on his face and dried off with a couple of paper towels.

The scenic drive across the river to Brockville was relaxing. It was one of the oldest developed areas in Canada and it had a laid-back, easygoing atmosphere that wasn't too far removed from Andy Griffith's fictional Mayberry, North Carolina. Without the deep-fried Southern accent, of course. People actually stood on street corners and spoke to each other. They waved to passing cars.

Once he completed the short, riverside drive from the bridge to Brockville, Jason made his way down King Street and then turned onto a narrow street that led to the docks. Grady's was a trendy restaurant located on the water between two docks that catered to yachts. It had atmosphere to spare.

Since the largely unpolluted, clear-water river ran so deep there was very little gas-producing algae around the docks. That provided the restaurant with a fresh smell that was punctuated by a host of sweet fragrances that wafted from the many varieties of brightly pedaled flowers planted in the vicinity.

Jason parked his car and started up the walkway to the restaurant. From a distance, he saw Katherine standing outside the building, gazing out at the river. He could guess her thoughts. He approached her from behind, feeling halfway guilty about interrupting her line of thought.

From about ten feet away, he cheerfully said, "Katherine," ending with a question mark.

She turned and faced him for the first time since the bad day in his office.

"Dr. Montclair," she said coolly. "I didn't see you coming."

Jason started to respond, but hesitated. Seeing her in what turned out to be a romantic setting, took his breath away. Outside in the sunlight, she was more beautiful than she'd ever appeared in his office. Perhaps it was the light reflected from the river. Perhaps it was because whenever she went to his office, she dressed like a person going to see a doctor— conservative, neat, simple, wearing as little makeup as possible.

Standing before him now, her hair seemed ablaze with vibrant colors of rust, and her clothing—a green sweater, worn with khaki pants—seemed smart and stylish, like something you'd see in a glossy magazine. Her eyes sparkled in the bright light.

"I . . . ah . . . I wasn't trying to sneak up on you."

"Oh, I know that," she said.

She's smiling he thought.

He didn't respond, so she continued, "Have you eaten here before?"

"A couple of time, but it's been a while."

"It's one of my favorite restaurants. I was surprised that you wanted to meet here. Did I mention during our sessions that I liked eating here?"

"No, no," he responded. "I just thought it would be more convenient for you than some other places. Why don't we go inside and order?"

"I think I'd rather eat outside on the deck, if you don't mind."

"Sure," he said. "That'd be great."

If their meeting had been a sports event, she'd be ahead two to zip. He hadn't made a strong start—and he knew it. He wondered if she was deliberately keeping him off balance. No sooner did he accept that as truth, than he realized that she was just being herself. That realization made him feel like a scheming fraud.

Maybe I'm out of my league with this woman he thought. *Maybe she's too good for me.*

Once they were seated and ordered lunch, Katherine looked him directly in the eye and said, "When I came to you for counseling, you gave me advice—and I followed it. I haven't found a new therapist yet because I'm not sure I need one at this point."

"Why do you say that?"

"Because I agreed to meet you here for lunch. That says something about me, doesn't it? About the way I'm handling my grief? Am I wrong?"

Jason nodded and smiled. "No, you're not wrong."

Katherine put her elbows on the table and raised her hands up to her face, interlocking her fingers to form a scaffold upon which to rest her chin. She gazed at Jason with bemused intensity. "So what's the deal with lunch? Do you want to counsel me—or is there something else you want from me?"

Jason wasn't sure he heard her correctly. He paused, looking like the proverbial deer caught in the headlights of an oncoming eighteen wheeler.

"I'm afraid to answer that question."

"Why? Because you think it might get you in trouble?"

"I knew I was in trouble the moment I met you."

"Oh," she said, smiling. "It's going to be like that?"

"What do you mean?"

"You are going to misdirect my questions. The way a therapist would do."

"No, no. That's not my intention at all."

"So answer my question."

Katherine lowered her hands to the table, so they were resting flat on either side of her salad plate. Jason reached out to put his hand on top of hers, but she moved her hand away.

"I don't hold hands on a first date," she said.

"I'm confused," he said.

"Welcome to the club."

"I don't know what to say, I really don't."

"You could start by answering my question."

"You mean as to whether this is a counseling session or a date?"

Katherine nodded.

Appearing from nowhere, the waiter arrived with the entree. They sat in stone silence as he put their plates on the table and then asked if they needed anything else.

"I think we're fine," said Jason.

Before the waiter left, he turned to Katherine and—in the most sincere voice imaginable—said, "I was so sorry to hear about your tragedy."

"Thank you," she said, fighting back a sudden rush of tears.

CHAPTER
4

It was not until he'd already started college that Jason Montclair developed an interest in psychology. In high school in Altoona, Pennsylvania, he'd been an all-star quarterback on the football team. On the day he and two other students signed Penn State football scholarships, the halls of Altoona High School buzzed with reporters.

Even Jason's parents got caught up in the frenzy.

"I know we've always emphasized academics, son, but there is some serious money in football," said his father. "We just want the best for you."

Jason enjoyed a splendid first season at Penn State, where he was heralded as the team's Golden Boy. Unfortunately, one week into the second season, he suffered an extensive injury to his right knee. He underwent surgery to correct the problem, but within weeks it became clear that his football career was over.

His first year he took all the required courses, but he didn't feel a sense of direction until the second year, when it became obvious that his future would not be in football. He enrolled in Psychology 101 pretty much as a lark. He didn't pay much attention in class and he seldom took notes.

To his astonishment, whenever he got his test results back, he always scored in the top five percent. He had a natural knack for the subject, and a deep interest in learning what makes people tick. The following semester he changed his major from business to psychology— and he never once looked back.

Jason wasn't the most popular student at Penn State, but he had a large circle of friends and the female students found him attractive. He was tall and well built, with dark eyes and hair. Unlike most student athletes, he never pumped himself up in an effort to be bigger and stronger. When he first arrived on campus, everyone was surprised how ordinary he looked when he wasn't suited up.

One of his female classmates, after learning that he'd been on the football team, turned to him during class one day and whispered, "Did you really play football?"

Jason nodded.

"You don't look like you played football. I don't believe you."

He grimaced.

People always told him that he was a dead ringer for Al Pacino, a comparison that left him with mixed feelings. It was nice to be compared to someone famous. But why couldn't it be someone like Brad Pitt? That was the story of his life. Something was always a little out of focus, a little out of kilter. Nothing was ever perfect.

"Looks can be deceiving," he told the inquisitive classmate, who promptly told him that her name was Margaret. They met for coffee after class, and before either of them knew what'd happened they were a couple.

Jason's height was emphasized by Margaret's petite build. Their differences seemed to garner constant attention. Margaret's perky, fresh look, with her blonde hair and light-blue eyes, offered a contrast to Jason's dark hair and olive skin. Their personalities were also different. Margaret was driven. There was only one way for things to be done—her way. Jason was much more open to differing viewpoints. In the beginning, he found Margaret's independence attractive, mistakenly thinking that it was a reflection of her free-spirit approach to life; but, as time went by, he discovered that there was nothing "free" about her.

In the fall of their senior year, Margaret was adamant that she did not want to wait until after graduation for a wedding. She seldom let a day go by without talking about how she planned to decorate Smith Chapel for her wedding.

The chapel would only hold one hundred and fifty guests, so Jason feared that his family and friends would be left off the invitation list. This time he had her parents on his side. They, too, wanted an Altoona wedding in their home church. In the end, all succumbed to Margaret's charm and persuasiveness, agreeing to a small campus wedding to be followed by a large reception at the Altoona Country Club.

No one was surprised that the newspaper described the wedding as the most elegant and exquisitely decorated Smith Chapel had ever been. As the last carillon bell music rang out from the tower, signifying 6 o'clock, the massive doors of the chapel opened to reveal Margaret and her father. The Martin Ott Pipe organ dwarfed the organist with over 1,200 pipes bellowing out the Wedding March fanfare, the music demanding that the guests rise to their feet for the bride's entry.

As Jason and his the guests watched his bride stroll down the aisle beside her father, the evening sun created a golden hue around them, the result of hundreds of famous Smith Chapel daffodils planted just beyond the chapel doors. Jason's eyes filled with happiness as he watched the haloed silhouettes approach.

The wedding and reception could not have been more perfect. Friends and family had a wonderful time celebrating and dancing late into the night. Margaret was right. Their April wedding captured the crisp beauty of spring, while occupying the first position of the traditional wedding season. When Margaret's bridesmaids told her, "No wedding this season will ever match this one," she passed the comment along to Jason, who laughingly responded, "No wedding this season will match the cost either."

Margaret didn't appreciate the humor.

Unhappily, the couple had to forgo an extensive honeymoon to return to their classes. Jason was required to spend hours in the psychology lab each evening, much to the disappointment of Margaret, who often skipped her last class to get a head start on preparing dinner. Not certain what kind of cake that he preferred, she once baked four different cakes so that he would have a choice.

When he arrived late for dinner, he saw a side of her that he hadn't seen before. Asked which cake he preferred, he said it didn't matter. It truly didn't.

In a rage, she poured the dinner into the trash and smashed each of the cakes with a large flatiron skillet.

"I skipped class to make you a wonderful dinner," she ranted, waving the skillet over her head. "And you ruined it by being late and dissing my cakes!"

"I'm so sorry," he said, stunned by her outburst. "I thought you knew I needed to get this research wrapped up before the end of the semester."

"Psychology, psychology, psychology," she mocked. "You'll spend six years in graduate school to become a psychologist—and earn no more than a paralegal—when you could become a physician. Medicine. That's where the real money is."

"But I like psychology," he protested.

"Okay, so prove to me that a psychologist can keep me in the life-style that I so richly deserve."

"I'll do my best."

Graduate school had its ups and downs. Margaret didn't miss any opportunity to tell anyone who'd listen that she wanted Jason to go to med-school instead of psychology. She didn't interact with the other wives and her unhappiness soon became apparent. By the time that Jason received his Ph.D. Margaret had a long list of things she wanted, though she insisted they were things that she "needed."

Jason received an offer from a large practice in Pittsburgh, but he chose instead to start up a practice of his own in Ogdensburg, New York.

Margaret was livid.

"No one important lives there," she complained.

"But it'll be a great place to raise a family."

"Family is important, but it's not everything."

"I know, but . . ."

"But what?"

"Nothing."

"You shouldn't start a conversation if you have nothing to say."

Six months into their new life, Margaret seemed happier when she wasn't spending time with Jason. She got involved in several civic organizations and played tennis daily, making little time for Jason. They argued about it, but she told him that her community involvement would help his referral base.

"I'm doing it for you, silly!"

December that year was unusually cold. Margaret hadn't made it home in time for dinner in weeks. Tonight she had a meeting across town and Jason worried about an approaching snow storm. He called to see if her meeting had been cancelled, but her cell phone was turned off. By 10 o'clock that evening, he was pacing, worried that she could be stranded somewhere in the storm, unable to reach him.

Suddenly, there was the sound of a key in the lock.

Margaret was ashen and appeared disconcerted as she walked through the door around midnight. As Jason approached her, fearing that she had been in an accident, Margaret put her arm out to stop him.

She hardly looked at him as she blurted out, "Jason, I'm sorry. I just don't know how I feel about things anymore."

"What do you mean?"

"What do you think I mean?"

"I honestly don't know. You don't know how you feel about what?"
She grimaced.

"You can be so dense sometimes. What I'm trying to say is that I've fallen in love with my tennis partner, Dr. Blaine."

"The urologist?"

"He's going to get a divorce and marry me. He can take me places you can't go."

Three weeks later, Jason signed papers for a no-fault divorce. In the lawyer's office, he wanted to say something grand, such as "Call, if you ever need me."

Or "Please keep in touch."

But the closest thing to a grand gesture that he could muster was to hand her one of his business cards.

"Hmmm," she mumbled. "Looks a bit frayed."

CHAPTER
5

After Jason and Katherine left the restaurant at the marina, they went their separate ways. Jason returned to Ogdensburg, and Katherine went back to her island, more than a little perplexed by their meeting.

Katherine felt badly that their lunch had ended with her in tears, but she couldn't help it. It wasn't her fault. If the waiter hadn't said anything, everything would have been all right. Unexpected memories remained a constant threat to her recovery. She never knew when they would appear.

The lunch with Jason had not gone well. Why was she so oppositional? Why was she so eager to pounce on his every word? Perhaps she should give him the benefit of the doubt. What did she have to lose?

When she arrived at the island, she delayed going into the house because it was such a lonely place without Roger and Dedi, whose voices had always filled the rooms with hopeful expectations. She walked around the island making a complete circle, frequently pausing to look out at the river. She loved being surrounded by water.

Growing up in Toronto, she lived with her family in Downsview, a suburb that was far removed from Lake Ontario, where lakeside residents liked to pretend that they were surrounded by water, when in fact it was only a one-dimensional southern exposure.

As a child she went with her parents, Donald and Jean, to the lake to play in the water. She was intrigued by the stories that she heard about the lake emptying into the St. Lawrence River and meandering past hundreds of islands on its way to the Atlantic Ocean. The river became a fanciful place for her, an *Alice in Wonderland* adventure that she thought and dreamed about all the way into adulthood.

Katherine saw the river as a metaphor for life: To stay alive, it has to keep moving. Understanding that helped keep her sane.

She was watching the waves gently lap against the rocks that surrounded her island, when her cell rang inside her purse. She took the cell out and looked at the caller ID. It was Dr. Jason Montclair.

Oh no she thought. *I wish he'd waited a day or two!*

"Hello."

"It's Jason Montclair."

She noticed that he didn't say Dr. Jason Montclair.

"Hi."

"Where are you?"

"On my island."

"Can you talk?"

"Sure."

"I feel badly about the way our meeting ended. I hope I didn't say anything . . ."

Interrupting him, Katherine said, "No—no, when the waiter said what he did, it just hit me kind of hard. People try to be kind. I think they sometimes want to share my grief. What they don't understand is that sometimes I simply don't want to think about it."

"In the waiter's case, I think he was simply trying to make conversation."

Katherine sighed.

"I think you're probably right. I probably scared the hell out of him."

Jason wanted to laugh, but he didn't dare.

"I think he will get over it. He didn't impress me as someone who would go home and obsess over having said something inappropriate."

"That was unkind."

She chuckled beneath her breath.

Jason could tell by the tone of her voice that she agreed with him, but didn't want to admit that, for whatever reason. Jason could hear the river in the background. It pulled at him like a magnet. She must have been caught up in the river sounds as well, because there was a long pause in their conversation.

Whatever moment they both clung to somehow slipped away.

Finally, Jason said, "Do you think we can be friends?"

"I don't know why not."

She didn't pause before responding. A good sign.

"There was an area of your life that we never made it to in therapy. Do you mind if I ask you a question?"

"I don't think so." She paused. "Well, I guess I should ask if it is a question that is any of your business."

"It is appropriate, I think—both for a therapist and a friend."

"Okay."

"You haven't mentioned your parents. Have they been supportive?"

"I wondered why you didn't ask about my parents during our sessions. I was an only child. I was very, very close to both parents. I never hated my mother like a lot of my girlfriends hated their mothers. She taught me things that her mother taught her. And I wasn't afraid of my father, the way a lot of girls are. He treated me more like a son than a daughter. He took me on fishing trips with him, and he talked to me about his work."

"What did he do for a living?"

"He worked for Exxon Canada. In logistics. Traveled a lot. He got a pilot's license so that he could fly the company plane."

"Did you ever fly with him?"

"Several times. I loved it."

"So were your parents there for you when you lost Roger and Dedi?"

Katherine took a deep breath. Of all the things in life that can potentially cause pain, it's odd, isn't it, that the chief instigators of pain are usually innocent questions?

After a moment, Katherine continued: "When I was a freshman in college, Mom and Dad flew to Quebec City on business. It was just the two of them. Dad figured he would combine work with play. They hadn't had a vacation in almost a year. They asked me to go with them, but I couldn't because I had classes."

"Quebec City is a wonderful city."

"Yes, it was one of Mom's favorite places. They left early in the morning. It was mid-spring, so the weather was really nice. Sunny skies. Temperature in the sixties. After a long, cold winter, it seemed just the cure for cabin fever. . . Anyway, they had engine problems going into Quebec City—it was a one-engine Cessna and didn't have much glide capacity—and they went down."

Jason felt his heart skip a beat. Why did he always ask this woman the wrong questions? Why didn't he just keep his mouth shut?

Katherine continued: "I was worried when I didn't hear from them by noon. They were fanatical about checking in with me. I think it was their justification for asking me to check in with them on a regular basis. I didn't get the call until mid-afternoon."

"Oh, God—I'm so sorry."

"They had no family to speak of. Just me. At the funeral, there were lots of friends, and Dad's co-workers turned out by the hundreds. Everyone was so nice to me. Dad's secretary took me home for the weekend and took care of me. Later, Dad's coworkers raised enough money for me to finish college. Like I said, everyone was wonderful to me, but within three months all that outpouring of love and sympathy pretty much trickled away to nothing. Losing my parents hurt more six months after they died than it did at the time of the accident."

"I hope you understand that I only ask you these questions because I want to help you deal with your pain."

There was a long pause.

Finally Katherine said, "Would you like to have dinner with me tomorrow night?"

CHAPTER
6

Katherine blended into the shade on the western side of her cottage. It was the perfect place to paint early in the morning. Not until the sun moved directly overhead would it be necessary to move to the other side of the cottage, where the afternoon shade blossomed with pastel evenness until the close of day, when the soft, evening light gradually tapered off into pitch-black darkness.

The summer morning air was crisp and cool. It'd be at least four hours before the sun bore down hard enough to cause beads of perspiration on her forehead. Her morning coffee was on a flat rock within easy reach. She was in a happy place.

Bessie, her five-year-old cocker spaniel, lay curled at her feet.

Katherine preferred watercolors, but today she was working in oil. The portrait was nearly done. A young girl with high cheekbones and vibrant green eyes. She twirled her brush onto her paint pallet, creating a mixture or rust and raspberry for the girl's hair. It was an elegant shade of red that reflected strength and courage.

Suddenly, the gentle murmur she'd heard in the distance, but hadn't paid much attention to, crackled with urgency. She turned and saw a speedboat brazenly plow through the gently rolling waves near her dock. Eyes flashed. Temper flared.

"Too fast!" she shouted, waving her paintbrush above her head.

Bessie ran to the water's edge and barked, glancing back at Katherine for assurance.

The man in the boat cracked a broad, rakish grin and waved. Thirty-something handsome. Muscular build. Longish blond hair curled every which way by the wind.

Katherine frowned.

I despise men like that.

She wanted to do something dramatic, perhaps shake a raging fist at him, but the boat was gone in a flash, great plumes of water arching in its wake. Instead, she returned to her painting, touching up her subject's hair with quick flicks of her wrist.

Bessie ran back and sat at her feet, a satisfied look on her face.

She laid her brush on the easel and reached for her coffee. As she sipped her favorite beverage, she looked out across the St. Lawrence River, which flowed on all sides of her home in that section of the waterway known as the 1000 Islands, a fifty mile stretch of nearly two thousand islands that extend from Brockville to Kingston.

Katherine was midway in the river, the international boundary running just south of her island. To the south was the United States. To the north was Canada.

Suddenly, her cell rang.

Thanks to the magic of Caller ID, she could take the initiative when people called her. No more silly greeting exchanges ("Hello" "How are you this morning?" "I'm fine. How are you?" "I'm fine."). Instead, she simply asked, "You're up early, aren't you?"

"Probably not as early as you," said Jason Montclair. "How is Island World today?"

"Terrible. I was all settled in to enjoy a beautiful day, when this hot-rodder roars by in a speedboat, upsetting my spiritual balance."

"Maybe you should take a meditation break."

"Can't. I want to finish the portrait today."

"I'm looking forward to seeing it."

"How do you know that I'll show it to you?"

Jason laughed.

"I don't. I sincerely hope you will show it to me."

"Maybe I will."

"Or maybe you won't."

Katherine smiled, but she didn't laugh since she didn't want to give Jason the satisfaction of being right. "You might get lucky."

Jason could tell from her voice that she was smiling.

"Luck has nothing to do with it," he boasted.

"You have a high opinion of yourself, don't you?"

"Someone participating in this conversation has to."

Katherine sipped her coffee. She enjoyed sparring with Jason, but it wasn't like it was the highlight of her day. Sometimes she liked her coffee more than she liked him. After a long pause, she asked, "You buying dinner tonight?"

"I thought you were buying."

"Just testing you. How about seven?"

"See you then."

Katherine returned her designer cup to the rock and resumed painting. As she worked, a thin strand of tears trickled down her cheeks. Her mind rushed through tearful images, one after another, all painful remembrances from the past. She brushed the tears away with the back of her free hand as she continued to touch up her subject's hair.

Once she had it the way she liked it, she put her brush down and stared intently at the painting. After a long moment, she got up and went into the cottage and returned with a small mirror. She sat in front of the painting and held the mirror so that she could see her own reflection. She looked at the image in the mirror. Then she looked at the painting of the young girl. The two images were almost identical, except for the age difference.

Katherine sighed and lowered the mirror to her lap, her brow furrowing ever so slightly.

* * *

The sunlight coming in the window at Katherine's kitchen sink was always bright and cheery. Unless it was dark outside, she never had to turn on the overhead light. She was standing at the sink, washing dishes, when she saw the boat again, the boat she'd screamed at when it passed by earlier.

This time the boat was preceding very slowly, its engine barely chugging past a fast idle. She stared out the window for a full minute before she realized that the man piloting the boat was looking at her cottage. Actually, it was worse than that. He was staring at her window. She cringed when he waved.

She waved back, not sure what else to do.

Oh, no she thought as he slowed down and turned into the dock. To her surprise, he leaped out of the boat and secured it to the dock. Then he looked toward the kitchen and waved again and started toward the house, a broad grin on his face.

Katherine looked down at her blouse, which was splashed with water, and at her slacks, which had specks of paint on them, and she let out a muffled sigh. She didn't have time to change clothes.

He was almost to the house.

Oh, to hell with it she thought. *Who wants to impress him anyway?*

Katherine dried off her hands and went outside to greet her visitor on the deck, with Bessie running circles around her. Bessie barked when she saw the visitor. Katherine told her to hush and she did. Then she told her to sit—and she did.

The visitor smiled and waved again. Not until then, when he was close enough for her to see his face, did she recognize him. Taylor Prescott was the Member of Parliament from that area. She'd never met him, primarily because she wasn't all that much into the social scene, but she'd seen his photograph in the newspaper many times.

As she quickly learned, the photographs didn't do his blue eyes and blond hair justice. He had the poise of a professional athlete and good looks of a movie actor.

He stepped up onto the deck and extended his hand.

"Taylor Prescott," he said with confidence.

Katherine took his hand and shook it briefly.

"Katherine Summer," she said.

"The artist?"

"Yes."

"I've seen your work. As a matter of fact, I have one of your landscapes in my office."

"Really!"

"Really," he answered, though that wasn't really true. He made a mental note to ask his assistant to purchase one of her landscapes through a gallery in Ottawa.

There was an awkward pause, during which Taylor glanced at her blouse and her slacks. Just a fleeting look.

"I was washing dishes," she explained. "I get sort of wild and crazy when I get my hands in dishwater. Suds go everywhere."

She felt no need to explain the paint on her slacks. Surely, he was bright enough to figure that out for himself.

"So what brings you by?"

Taylor chuckled.

"When I passed by earlier, I couldn't help but notice that you were a little upset with me."

"Oh, that—."

"Whatever I did, I'd like to apologize. I'd certainly hate to lose your vote."

"Oh, you lost my vote when you ran as a Conservative. I support the Liberal Party."

"Really. Then I suppose I'll have to earn your support."

"Good luck with that."

"Out of curiosity, what did I do to piss you off?"

Katherine was shocked to hear a MP use such common language, but as she was soon to learn, he had more surprises in store.

"I was *angry* because you came by so fast and furious and made so much noise."

She hoped that he picked up on her choice of a better word. She said piss all the time, but she didn't want a man she didn't know using it in her presence.

"Thank you for the grammatical correction. I apologize for that—and for making such an ass of myself when I sped by." He paused for dramatic effect. "I'm sorry—did I use another inappropriate word?"

Katherine smiled.

"No, in that case, your word choice was entirely appropriate."

Taylor laughed. It was an indication to Katherine that he didn't take himself too seriously. An attractive trait in her eyes.

"Nice place," he said, looking around.

"Thanks."

Suddenly, his smile evaporated and he adopted a more serious expression on his face. "I read about what happened to your husband and daughter. I'm so sorry. Are you doing all right?"

Katherine nodded. She wondered if he was sincere.

"Is there anything you need?"

"No, there isn't. It's something I have to work through. But thank you for asking."

Taylor stuffed his hands into his front pockets and gazed out at the river.

"I've been coming here since I was a youngster. My family is from up near Smiths Falls, and every summer, while I was growing up, we used to come to the river to camp out and cook under the stars. Great memories—but it seems like every year there is an accident or two. You never think it will happen to you—or to anyone you know."

"We were always aware of the bad things that could happen on the river, but the good things always seemed to outweigh them. You can't go through life worrying about the things that might never happen."

"I agree. It's true that there is no present or future, only the past, but that doesn't mean we should choose to live there."

"I've never thought about it that way."

Taylor reached down to pet Bessie, but she turned away and looked at Katherine for guidance.

"It's okay," she said, prompting Bessie to walk toward him, tail wagging.

He reached down and scratched Bessie's ears.

"She's a fine looking dog," he said. "Have you had her since she was a puppy?"

"Yes—she's a great comfort to me. You might say she's my best friend."

"Sorry to hear that," he said, grinning foolishly. "A beautiful woman like you needs lots of human friends."

He regretted saying it the instant the words came out of his mouth. It was a stupid thing to say. Widows, at least those recently widowed, don't want to hear that they are beautiful, even if they are beautiful and know it. They want to think that they look like warmed-over crap because of the pain they feel inside.

Katherine's stricken face told him all he needed to know. He quickly added, "But I'm sure you're not ready for lots of friends."

"No . . . no," she said, absently rubbing her hands against her slacks. "I'm not ready for a normal social life."

"Of course. Of course. I don't know what I was thinking."

He pulled a business card from his shirt pocket and handed it to her.

"My home and office numbers are both there. Please call me if you ever need anything."

"Thank you—I will," she said, examining the card. Then she reached out with her hand. "I want to thank you for stopping by."

He shook her hand, holding it perhaps a little too long.

"No problem. I owed you an apology. I hope you won't hold it against me."

"Everything's fine."

"Glad to hear that." As he was leaving, he turned and asked, "Would you care to have lunch tomorrow?"

"I don't think so. But thanks for asking."

She watched him walk across the lawn to the dock and unfasten his boat. He waved one last time and then got into the boat and pulled away from the dock, careful not to idle his engine too loudly.

Katherine remained on the deck until he was out of sight. She had never understood men like that. *I bet he just has to be the center of attention. When he enters a room, don't you just know he expects all eyes to be on him. He's handsome . . . rich . . . powerful. I may be the first woman to ever have said no to him.*

A smile crept across her face. The encounter made her feel better about herself. As she walked back into the house, she did so with a new lightness in her step.

Feeling differently was Bessie, who turned and barked at a man who no longer was there.

* * *

When Katherine got out of the shower, she dried off and walked over to the picture window that dominated her upstairs bedroom. She gazed out at the river, wearing nothing but a diamond necklace that'd been a gift from her husband.

There was a sailboat about a hundred yards away.

A man and woman with two children.

Katherine shook her head with dismay when she realized that no one in the boat had on a life preserver.

Why is it that some people can dance around the rough edges of life and not stumble and fall to the other side? It's not fair. It's simply not fair!

Not until a ship's foghorn sounded did Katherine realize that her nude revelry at the bedroom picture window was being enjoyed by more than herself. She instinctively covered herself with her hands and hastily backed away from the window.

Bessie barked at her sudden move, reinforcing her embarrassment.

Katherine sat at her dresser to put on her makeup. She grimaced when she saw the ever-so-tiny crows' feet in the corners of her eyes. Were they there yesterday? She wasn't sure. Perhaps it was a reaction to something she ate.

She quickly dressed, putting on an emerald-green sweater and black slacks. It was her "casual dating" ensemble. She wondered why choosing clothes for a husband and choosing clothes for a date were such different undertakings.

Bessie waited until she finished dressing before she released her *take me outside right now* bark.

"OK, OK," said Katherine following Bessie out of the room and down the stairway to the back door. Bessie beat her to the door and waited with muscles coiled to spring outside as soon as the door opened. She was gone in a flash. Katherine walked out onto the deck and watched her run.

For the longest time, she'd worried about Bessie running free on the island. Afraid she would leap into the water in an effort to watch a bird.

42

Afraid she would stumble and suddenly find herself in one hundred feet of water. As Bessie grew from puppy to adult she realized that she was much too smart to simply fall into the water. Bessie was the smartest person she knew.

Yes, Katherine did attribute human characteristics to Bessie. She had a vocabulary of several hundred words. She understood *everything* that was said to her, even if it was spoken in ordinary conversation—and she could communicate with clarity using her ever-bright eyes, and an endearing face that had the capacity to grin from ear to ear, or stare with stony, dead-eyed disapproval.

Bessie was no ordinary dog. That may have been because Katherine spent so much time with her, and because she'd conversed with her from the time she was an awkward puppy that couldn't walk ten feet without falling over her own feet.

Katherine glanced at her watch.

"Time to go!" she shouted.

Bessie was sniffing at the base of a tree in the distance. She turned and looked at Katherine, giving her a startled "are you talking to me" look.

"You heard me—come on!"

Bessie whirled and headed to the cottage at a full run, her ears trailing behind her like flags fluttering in the wind. Nothing made her quite so happy as pleasing Katherine. Her fluffy paws padded across the grass in a straight line to her best friend.

Suddenly, a chill raced through Katherine's body. What if something terrible happened to Bessie? How would she ever cope with that loss? With her arms folded, she rubbed her forearms to loosen the chill, lowering her hands just in time to catch the airborne Bessie. Katherine giggled as Bessie nuzzled against her neck and licked her face.

"You're getting too big to play like this," she said, gently lowering Bessie to the deck. "I want you to be a good girl while I'm gone."

Bessie ignored the comment and ran into the house, tail wagging.

Katherine made sure that Bessie had plenty of water. Then she locked up the house and went down to the dock. After the accident, she resisted purchasing a new boat, but not for long, since it was the only way to get to her home. Friends ferried her back and forth for a reasonable length of time and then politely suggested that she should get transportation of her own. Said one friend, "If you're going to live on an island, you've got to get a boat. End of story."

She purchased a classic, twenty-two foot runabout. It was smaller than the one that Roger had picked out for them, but it had similar lines. Dark green hull, with white finishing lines. Piloting the boat was like driving a car. She turned on the ignition, adjusted the throttle, and pointed it in the direction she wanted to go.

She hated to leave Bessie alone on the island. There had been a rash of burglaries on the river and she worried about Bessie being hurt by an intruder. Bessie could be fearless if the occasion required it. She'd never bitten anyone, but Katherine had no doubt that she would attack any intruder who entered the home.

As she neared the dock, she saw Jason standing beside his car, waiting with his hands in his pockets. She waved. He took one hand out of his pocket and waved back. Then she lost sight of him as she idled down and crept into the boathouse.

Actually, it was more than a boathouse. It contained a garage, where she kept her car, and an upstairs apartment, where she sometimes stayed if river conditions were not favorable for travel to the island. The boathouse also contained a fire-engine-red iceboat that she used during January and February, when the river was frozen solid. By the time she'd moored the boat, Jason walked into the boathouse.

"Did you give Bessie her instructions?"

"I didn't have to," she laughed. "She has the routine down pat."

As they walked to the car, Jason asked, "Did you finish your painting?"

"I don't know . . . I'm not sure if it's possible to finish it."

"What do you think that means?"

Katherine looked at him, slightly annoyed.

"I'm really not in a mood to be analyzed right now. I'll know when the painting is finished. I'm the one who has to be happy with it."

Jason opened the car door for her. She slipped onto the leather passenger seat of his BMW convertible. He closed the door and walked around the car to the driver's side. By the time he got into the car, Katherine had on her don't-talk-to-me-until-I-talk-to-you face.

CHAPTER
7

They said very little on the drive to the restaurant, a downtown Italian eatery not far from the courthouse. The owner knew Katherine, but he didn't know Jason, so she introduced them, prompting the owner to eye Jason a bit suspiciously, perhaps wondering why she was out with a man so soon after her husband's death.

Katherine saw the perplexed look and instantly understood.

Am I doing the right thing? she thought. *I'm trying my best.*

They were seated at a corner table, which unknown to Katherine, Jason had requested since he knew there would be less traffic there and fewer interruptions. The restaurant had a romantic air about it and the occasional clink of wine glasses only added to that ambiance. Of course, the tablecloth was white and billowy, and the candles flickered with warm consistency, creating the perfect atmosphere for a tension-free evening.

As they ordered, Jason couldn't help but eye the waiter with suspicion. He hoped that this twenty-something waiter wouldn't turn out to be as stupidly compassionate as the previous one. The waiter took their orders without comment and turned to walk away, only to whirl back around with a question for Katherine.

Jason's heart almost stopped. He just knew the waiter would say, "I'm so sorry to hear about what happened to your husband and your daughter."

Instead, the waiter looked at Katherine and asked: "Do you want your salad dressing on the side—as usual?"

Katherine told the waiter yes and he nodded politely and left.

Jason took a deep breath.

"He's sweet, isn't he?" Katherine said, a motherly tone in her voice.

"Oh, sure," answered Jason, struggling to relax again. He was certain that Katherine had no idea what kinds of fantasies the "sweet" waiter was having about her. He had a pretty good idea because he'd waited tables for a while when he was in college. It was always the women in their late twenties or early thirties that drove him wild.

Katherine reached over and patted him on the hand.

"I'll try not to get upset this time," she said. "I feel like I ruined our lunch at the marina." Having said that she withdrew her hand and placed it in her lap.

"You didn't ruin anything," he lied. "It was just one of those things."

"You're so sweet," she said.

"As sweet as our waiter?"

"I hope not," she said, smiling. "He's gay."

"Really—really?"

Katherine nodded.

Jason felt his ego scrunch up about the size of a grape. Normally, it was about the size of a fully-loaded pizza. He made a mental note to think before he spoke next time. He had allowed his insecurity about the waiter to cloud his judgment. Women had that effect on him, especially beautiful women. Not in the office, but at a social level. He was always afraid that they might be a step or two ahead of him. Usually they were.

After a few minutes of dead air, Jason asked, "Are you angry at me?"

"About what?" she said, feigning surprise.

"About referring you to another psychologist."

Katherine thought a moment. "At first—then it sort of made sense to me."

"So you're not angry?"

"I don't know what that would accomplish."

The first evasion escaped his attention. Not the second time. She had a right to be angry at him, he knew that. For him to try to bully her into telling him that she wasn't angry, thereby putting his conscience at ease, was an emotionally needy thing to do. He dropped that line of thinking and moved on to something else.

Before he could ask another embarrassing question, she jumped in with one of your own.

"Are you seeing anyone now?"

He was surprised by the directness of her question.

"No," he answered, not wishing to elaborate.

"If you had been seeing someone do you think you would have referred me to another psychologist?"

It was a fair question. "Yes—I think so."

"Would you have told your girlfriend about it?"

"No, I would never talk to anyone about my patients, not even my girlfriend. That would be unethical."

"So it would be ethical to keep your feelings for someone else from your girlfriend?"

"I don't know if ethical is the right word. Sometimes when you're in a relationship you realize that you have feelings for someone else. If you don't act on those feelings, I don't think it'd be wise to share them with your significant other."

"Is that your opinion as a psychologist, or as a man?"

"Not as a psychologist, no."

"Have you dated many women since your divorce?"

"Oh, I don't know . . . maybe six or eight."

"How'd that work out for you?"

"What do you mean?"

"What did you get out of those six or eight relationships?"

"Nothing lasting."

"But something?"

"Sure—companionship, if nothing else."

As they talked, the waiter brought a bottle of wine and quietly filled their glasses. They acted as if he were not even there. He disappeared without saying a word. Like a cloud drifting across a midnight moon. That small gift was noted by Jason, but he didn't say anything about it. He would repay the consideration at the end of the evening, when time came to calculate the tip.

"Why did you tell me that you have feelings for me?"

Taken aback by her directness, he paused long enough to go down a mental checklist of do's and don'ts, and then he cast it aside and said, "Because I realized that I was seeing you more as a woman than as a patient."

"And that means what?"

"That I feel attracted to you."

"By that do you mean emotionally . . . sexually . . . or something else entirely different?"

Jason laughed. "I don't think you are deliberately trying to put words in my mouth but the effect is the same. Let's just say that there's something about you that I find attractive."

"Do you believe in love at first sight?"

"I don't like to use that phrase. It's so trite. I don't know that anyone knows what it means anymore. I do believe in attraction at first sight. Science says it's possible because of the hormones that men and women give off."

He paused a minute, waiting for her next question. When none was forthcoming, he asked a question of his own: "Do you believe in love at first sight?"

"Yes—very much. But I think men and women experience love quite differently."

"On those occasions when you've fallen in love, has it always been a 'love at first sight' situation?"

"Love and 'love at first sight' are different categories, aren't they?"

"I agree."

"I think love takes time to develop. There have to be shared experiences. Shared dreams . . . shared disappointments, even."

She noticed that he seemed to be squirming in his chair.

"Am I making you uncomfortable?"

"No . . . no," he said, probably speaking a little too fast.

"Because if I am . . ."

"Not at all. All I want to know is whether you'd be interested in going out on a date with me."

"A date?"

"Yes."

"That's easy—unless I'm mistaken, we are out on a date."

Jason leaned back in his chair, a broad smile on his face. "Really?"

"Really. But don't let it go to your head. It's more or less an accidental date. I'm not sure that I'm ready to date again."

"So it's not a date?"

"You figure it out!"

*   *   *

Taylor Prescott thought about Katherine all the way back to the marina. There was something in her sad eyes that resonated with him. Determination. Intelligence. Wit. He wasn't sure exactly, only that it set her apart from any other women he knew. The only thing missing from her eyes was sparkle, but under the circumstances its absence was totally understandable.

When he arrived at the marina, Todd Sauve, his assistant, was waiting for him on the dock, clipboard in hand. Taylor pulled into his private boat slip and tossed the securing line to Todd, who caught it, clumsily dropped it, and then retrieved it.

Taylor smiled as he watched Todd struggle to wrap the line twice around a mooring post and then tie one of the most extravagant knots he'd ever seen.

Taylor got out of his boat and examined the knot.

"Where'd you learn how to do that?" he asked.

Thinking it was a compliment, Todd said, "Oh, I just picked it up along the way."

Taylor shook his head. Todd was one of the best assistants he'd ever had, but manual dexterity was not his strongpoint. He could have said something critical, but he didn't, instead asking him what he had written on his clipboard.

"Oh," he said, a big smile exploding across his face. "There are several important calls you need to make—and you have a meeting at 4 o'clock."

He handed Taylor the call-back slips and watched with anticipation as he thumbed through them.

"The Prime Minister, eh?" Taylor said, looking at one of the call-back slips.

"Yes—his secretary called. She said it wasn't urgent, but he would like to talk to you before the day is over."

"Fine," he said, already reading the notations on the other slips.

Todd continued: "Your meeting is in Gananoque. But you've got plenty of time."

Taylor nodded and handed the call-back slips to Todd. "You thirsty?"

"Sure."

They got a table near the window. Todd ordered coffee. Taylor ordered a Moosehead beer. When their drinks arrived, Taylor looked at the longneck bottle and said, "I miss the old stubbies."

"What's that?"

"The old stubbies—the bottles that they used when I was a kid. I remember my father drinking from them."

Todd looked perplexed.

Taylor continued: "The bottles were shorter, thicker, and fatter. They changed them in the Eighties after a survey found that women didn't like stubbies."

He laughed, an indelicate thought creeping into his mind.

"I guess that settles that old argument."

"What argument is that?"

"About whether size matters."

Todd blushed.

"All that was way before my time."

"Before my time, too—but I've devoted my life to finding out what women want. You should be taking notes, Todd."

Todd tapped his forehead.

"I've got it all up here, sir."

Taylor could see that Todd was uncomfortable, so he backed off. His previous assistant had been a young woman just out of college. She only lasted eight weeks. She left in tears. He talked too much, and about things he shouldn't—he knew that—but sometimes it was difficult for him to reign in his mouth. Growing up, people always said that he was full of himself. Since he was an only child, his parents spoiled him terribly, providing him with everything he wanted. The concept of wanting something—and not getting it—was totally foreign to him.

Taylor's father, Colonel Edward Prescott, had made a name for himself in the Canadian Army, long before he made a fortune developing and then manufacturing a wildly successful patent medicine called Edward's Little Kidney Pills. He sent Taylor to the best private schools money could buy in Canada, and then he sent him to Yale, where he encouraged him to seek out membership in the Brotherhood of Death, better known as the Order of Skull and Bones. Unknown to Taylor, his father had greased the skids with a million dollar donation to the secret society. Taylor was not the best student at Yale, but he quickly rose in the ranks of the Bones, and that opened doors for him.

After he returned to Canada with a degree in business administration, Taylor was encouraged by his father to serve his country, namely by applying for assignment in the Canadian Intelligence Corps, the Canadian equivalent of the CIA. That was not difficult to do since Bones had a long association with the CIA and supplied the secret agency with agents and supervisors for a span of several decades.

Taylor was reluctant to join the Canadian Armed Forces, because, as he explained to his father, he felt that military services was for the lower classes and he certainly didn't include himself in that group. He complied with his father's wishes, only after his father promised to retire early and install him as CEO of Edward's Little Kidney Pills.

The old man kept his promise. When Taylor returned home from service in the Canadian Intelligence Corp, the old man quietly retired and handed his business over to his son. To his disappointment, Taylor tired of the business after only one year and decided to run for political office. He ran for the Leeds and Grenville County Parliament seat that had been held for more than a century by the Conservative Party.

With no serious opposition, he was handily elected. There were some people in the voting district that swore that Taylor's father had purchased the seat for him, but they were wrong. The old man wanted his son to stay at the business, at least as long as he still was alive. But after the election, Taylor hired someone to run the business and to supervise a trust that generated something in excess of two million dollars a year for his living expenses. The old man was so horrified that he resolved never again to speak to his son, a decision that didn't bother Taylor in the least.

"Family is greatly over rated," he explained to Todd. "We've all got one, but how many of us truly value family over friends?"

The comment came in response to a question from Todd about concerns he had about his family's displeasure over his decision to work for Taylor. They told him that he could do better than being a yes-man to a rich, playboy politician.

"I just don't understand their attitude," said Todd.

"Aren't they strong supporters of the New Democratic Party?"

"Yes—and for as long as I can remember."

"There you have it! It's all about politics. They care more about their politics than they do about you. It's pretty clear to me."

Todd nodded. His boss was the smartest man he'd ever known. He'd be a fool to ignore his advice. The way he saw it, Taylor Prescott was his ticket to the good life. To cash in that ticket all he had to do was play the game.

Taylor continued: "I'll be honest with you. I had a fantastic childhood. My mother and father gave me everything I wanted. They never spanked me or scolded me. They praised me for every little thing I did. It was wonderful. But my final year of secondary school, everything changed. They insisted that they knew what was good for me and they pretty much mapped out my life for me."

"Don't you miss your mother?"

"She died while I was a Yale—and, yes, I do miss her."

"But not your father?"

"I don't have a father," he said curtly.

As they were leaving the restaurant, Taylor spotted a waiter that he knew.

"Back in a minute," he told Todd, leaving him at the door while he walked across the dining area to speak to the waiter.

"You've got a good eye," he said to the waiter, palming him a hundred dollar bill. "She's much prettier in person than she is in her pictures. Thanks for the information."

"She's hot, all right," said the waiter, grinning. "And in need of a strong shoulder to cry on, if you know what I mean."

Taylor winked and said, "If there's anything I can ever do for you, just let me know."

Across the room, Todd smiled when he saw Taylor shake hands with the waiter.

Always politicking. What a guy!

*   *   *

On the drive back to the island, Katherine and Jason interacted like lifelong friends. Conversation came easy and the awkward moments that had begun the evening seemed a distant memory as they laughed at each other's jokes, even when they weren't especially funny. Normally, when Jason was out with a woman, he asked lots of questions, but because of their previous therapist-patient relationship, he was reluctant to be too inquisitive about her past.

Katherine felt no such sense of restraint. Watching her ask questions was a little like watching a child kick a can along the side of the road. First one direction, then another. She was flattered that he was interested in her, but she wasn't yet sure if she was interested in him. He was good looking. Interesting. Sensitive to her needs. But she didn't feel that initial spark that she'd felt with Roger. She decided to withhold judgment.

Besides, she wasn't anywhere close to being over Roger.

"How long does it take to get over the loss of someone you love?"

"You asking a therapist or a friend?"

"A friend."

"In some ways, probably never—in other ways, memories begin to fade after a year or so and it becomes easier to accept new opportunities for growth."

"I see." She paused a moment, obviously troubled by something. "Do you visit your parents often?"

"They still live in Altoona. I try to visit them once a month, but it usually ends up being every six weeks. It's so hard for me to get away."

"Do they visit you often?"

"Not all that often—mostly on holidays, birthdays, that sort of thing. They have lives of their own. Mom plays bridge and she hates to leave town because that usually means she has to miss card games. And Dad is into fishing in the summer, and he doesn't like to leave the house in the winter because he hates the cold. It's funny how older couples maintain their relationships by creating new ones unrelated to each other."

"Do you miss not having a brother or sister?"

"Sometimes—but it's hard to miss something you've never had. I suppose the idea of not having a brother or sister bothers me from time to time. But there's nothing I can do about that, is there?"

Katherine shook her head. "I never missed not having a brother or sister until I lost my parents. There are plenty of people out there like me—people who have no one but themselves. Relationships are supposed to take the place of family, but I don't think it works out that way very often."

Jason cautioned himself to be careful with his questions. Seeing the sadness in her eyes when she spoke about relationships, he asked, "Do you have many friends?"

Katherine smiled, though it wasn't a happy smile.

"If you mean girlfriends, I've never had many of those. I don't know why. I'm sure your analytical mind could dredge up a reason or two."

"I wouldn't dream of it," he interrupted.

"Most of my friends have been males. It always seemed like we had more in common."

"Do your male friendships usually start out as friendships and stay that way, or do they evolve from romantic relationships."

"Both. I'm friends with everyone I've ever been romantically involved with."

She paused, realizing that what she'd said was no longer true.

"No need to elaborate," Jason said, cutting her some slack.

"What about you? Are you friends with everyone you've ever dated?"

Jason was taken aback by her question. It was obviously something he hadn't given much thought to. He ran down a quick mental checklist.

"No . . . I don't think I'm friends with anyone I've ever dated."

"Really?" She seemed genuinely surprised. "Why do you think?"

"Lots of reasons. People move around these days. They change jobs. Move to different cities. They get married. Sometimes romantic relationships run their course without ever fostering a true friendship. We're all ships passing in the night."

Katherine smiled.

"So when you're done with a woman, you're done."

Jason cringed. He didn't want to think of himself in those rigid terms, but he hadn't left himself much wiggle room. "It sometimes works out that way, but I don't feel that way in my heart. Stuff happens. People move on."

Jason decided it was time to shift the conversation away from himself. "Were you and Roger friends before you got involved?"

"I was a struggling artist in Toronto, trying to make a living—without much luck, I might add . . . anyway, he was in Toronto to research a book on Pierre Trudeau, a biography I should say. I don't know if I told you, but he was born in the U.S.—in Buffalo—and he'd always had his eye on Canada. He thought Trudeau was one of the most interesting leaders he'd ever read about, so he got a contract to do the biography."

"Was he still living in Buffalo?"

"Yes. It'd probably be more accurate to say that he was based there. His work took him all over the world, so I doubt he ever spent more than three or four months a year in Buffalo. He liked the arts scene in Toronto and he made several trips a year. On the day we met, I was displaying my work in an artists' flea market, not far from Yonge Street. He walked by and saw this redheaded hippie in an outlandish peasant dress, hawking her paintings as if her life depended on it—and it did—and he stopped to talk. I didn't like him at first. That might have been because he looked just a little *too* American, if you know what I mean."

So you divide Americans into categories, according to how they look?

"Yeah, something like that."

"Am I under American, over American—or smack down the middle American?"

"You don't look American?"

"Is that so?"

"You look more . . . I'd say you look Australian."

"Are you serious?"

"No—not at all," she said, laughing.

He laughed, too. "Okay, we weren't talking about me, were we?"

"We were talking about Roger."

"So he saw you at a flea market . . ."

"I had my favorite landscape on display and he stopped to admire it. Okay, so that's probably creative editing on my part. He leaned over and looked at the painting, his nose almost touching the canvas, so I naturally assumed he was infatuated with it. After giving it the once over, he turned to me and said, 'You need more blue in the snowcaps.' That infuriated me! My painting was perfect the way it was. I was so mad I didn't even respond. Instead, I snatched the painting off the easel and tucked it away behind a table.

"Don't get mad,' he said. "I was just being honest.'"

"You obviously hated him at first sight."

"Absolutely."

"How did you ever bridge the gap?"

"Each time he tried to speak to me, I turned and started a conversation with someone else. After a few minutes of that, he left and I returned the painting to the easel. About thirty minutes later, I looked up from my chair and he was standing there, a big grin on his face. He dropped a package into my lap. I unwrapped the package and found three hundred dollars in Canadian bills. That was about one hundred dollars more than I was asking for the painting.

"I'd like to buy it," he said. "It's beautiful.'"

"That changed everything, of course," observed Jason.

"We had dinner that night and never spent a night apart until . . . until the accident."

It was good timing, or bad timing, depending on your perspective, but it was at that precise moment that Jason drove up to the boathouse and parked. They sat in silence for a long moment, Jason trying to figure out what to say next, and Katherine struggling to move her thoughts away from her romantic first meeting with Roger.

Finally, Katherine said, "I'd invite you in for coffee—but then how would you get back?"

That was a scenario that hadn't occurred to Jason. If Katherine asked him in for coffee, it would be an unmistakable invitation to spend the night.

Katherine continued, "I had a wonderful time, Jason. Dinner was excellent."

"I enjoyed it, too."

To Katherine's surprise, Jason leaned over and lightly kissed her on the lips. It wasn't so much a kiss as it was a flickering gesture, like waving away a fly.

Katherine hurriedly got out of the car, leaving Jason to beat up on himself over the bad timing of his kiss.

"Goodnight," Katherine said, turning to enter the boathouse.

"I won't leave until I see your boat pull out," he said.

She waved and disappeared into the boathouse.

Moments later he heard the sound of the motor and then saw the lights of the boat as it slowly exited the boathouse and then turned toward the island.

Why did I have to kiss her? he thought. *That was so not the thing to do. I hate it when I do dumb things.*

CHAPTER
8

When Katherine returned to the island, she secured the boat to the dock and let Bessie out of the house so that she could make her evening rounds. She sat on the deck and enjoyed the reflection of the moonlight on the river. The night air was pleasant, fragrant with scents that changed from minute to minute.

In the far distance she heard a foghorn, but there were no boats in sight on the river. Sounds carried on the water. Inside the house the telephone rang.

Thinking it might be important, she went inside.

"Hello."

"This is Jason."

"Hi Jason."

"I know I'm breaking one of the rules by calling, but I wanted to make sure that you made it safely back to the island."

"That was nice of you. I'm fine. Bessie is out exploring and all is well on the island."

"Don't you ever get spooked out there by yourself?"

"Only when the fog sets in and the foghorns go non-stop. If you go outside and stand on the dock, you can see these huge phantom-like ships drift in and out of the night. That can get pretty eerie."

"Do you remember those old Sherlock Holmes movies? The ones where people were always walking in and out of the fog? Is that what's it like?"

"I remember those movies. Yes—it is like that. Only picture yourself in a fog and a mountain is moving in your direction."

"You should paint something like that."

Katherine paused, thinking it over.

"You know, you're right. I might do something along those lines."

She laughed.

"I could title it Gothic River."

"That's a painting I'd like to own."

"So I guess I'll have to pay you a finder's fee for the idea."

"A cup of coffee will do."

"Deal."

There was a long pause, while Jason tried to think of a graceful exit. He shouldn't have called. He knew that. But there was something about her that beguiled him. He felt powerless around her. It was while he was dealing with his angst over the telephone call that Katherine asked him a question that caused him even more distress.

"Do you mind if I ask you a personal question?"

"No—no, not at all."

"That day in your office, when you told me that ethically you could no longer be my therapist. Exactly what did you mean by that?"

Jason was taken aback by the question. He had tried to forget the incident, so he naturally assumed she had tried to forget it as well.

"I meant that there is a code of ethics that governs psychologists in the United States and Canada. If a psychologist violates that code, and a complaint is lodged, the incident will be investigated and the psychologist could end up losing his license."

"Sounds serious."

"It is."

"Have you ever been investigated?"

"No, I haven't."

Where is she going with this? he thought. *Do I have reason to be concerned?*

"So explain this code to me. What does it say specifically?"

"It prohibits psychologists from treating anyone with whom they have an emotional or social relationship. If it happens unknowingly, the psychologist would be expected to ensure that there was nothing exploitative about the relationship."

"So it has nothing to do with sex?"

"I didn't mean to give that impression. Yes it does. Psychologists are prohibited from having sexual relations with a client. Actually, it goes further than that. A psychologist can't treat or counsel anyone they've ever had sex with. And they are prohibited from having sex with a former client—unless at least two years have gone by."

"Now I understand why you were so insistent about me seeing another therapist. Being friends with a patient is a definite no-no. Don't the rules take into account a man and woman falling love?"

"Apparently not."

"What I don't understand is why you asked me out to dinner."

"I didn't—you asked me. Remember?"

"I did, didn't I?" She laughed. "But for you to accept, you must have been pretty sure that nothing would ever develop from that dinner."

"Why do you say that?"

"From what you just told me, if we started dating—and became lovers—you could lose your license. Isn't that why you told me?"

Jason took a deep breath. "I did tell you that."

"So why are you so certain that we'd never get involved? Was our dinner date a pity date?"

"Oh, God no—nothing like that."

"If it wasn't, then it's clear you are willing to risk losing your license to see me."

Jason felt like a cornered animal, heart pounding.

"Jason—Jason, are you there?"

"Yes. Yes, I am. I was just thinking how I should respond."

"Don't think. Just be honest."

"If you put it that way, I guess I am willing to risk losing my license in order to see you."

"How incredibly romantic—or incredibly stupid."

"I agree on both counts."

"This puts me in a really weird position."

"I know it does. I didn't mean for that to happen."

"As a professional counselor, what do you recommend that I do?"

"I can't counsel you on what to do. I can only ask you to have dinner with me again tomorrow so that we can . . ." His voice faltered.

"So we can what?"

"So we can sort all this out."

"I'll have dinner with you on one condition."

"What's that?"

"That we just have fun and not try to sort it out."

"Agreed."

"Fine. I'll see you tomorrow. Try not to get in anymore trouble on your way home."

Jason laughed. "I'll do my best."

Katherine went back out onto the deck and saw Bessie still running from one side of the island to the other. She hadn't even missed her when she went inside.

"Bessie!" she called out.

Bessie stopped in her tracks and looked toward the house.

"Time to come in!"

Bessie forgot whatever was holding her fancy at the moment and made a mad dash for the house, her ears flopping with wild abandon.

Once Bessie was inside, Katherine closed the door and locked it. She turned off all the downstairs lights and went upstairs to her bedroom, Bessie still at her heels.

As she undressed and got ready for bed, she thought about Jason. There were a lot of things about him that she really liked, but she wasn't convinced that they were on the same page as far as a mutual attraction was concerned.

What if we dated—and it didn't work out—and what if he lost his license because of me? I would feel so guilty!

She hung her outer garments on a hanger. Then she slipped off her bra and panties and dropped them into a hamper, and put on the T-shirt and running pants that she used as pajamas. She set her alarm for 6:30 and got into bed and turned out the light on her nightstand.

Moments later, she felt a big thump as Bessie leaped on the bed and curled up next to her. Through her window she could see clouds slowly coasting past a silvery moon.

CHAPTER
9

On the way to Gananoque, Todd drove the rebuilt 1955 Mercedes-Benz 300S convertible along the scenic highway, with Taylor in the passenger's seat, his neck turned sharply to the left so that he could watch the river. It was a dazzling car, with an exquisite leather interior.

Driving it was a thrill for Todd, who often told his friends that being Taylor's chauffeur was the best part of his job.

Taylor said very little during the thirty minute drive. His eyes were glued on the river, hoping for a glimpse of Katherine's boat. The silence was fine with Todd, who didn't like to be distracted from the finer points of the Mercedes-Benz. He was fixated on the many dials, switches and knobs that helped make the car special. As they were entering Gananaque, or "Gan" as the locals like to call it, Taylor broke the silence with a request.

"Todd, when you get back to Ottawa I'd like for you to go by the galleries and pick up a couple of paintings by Katherine Summer. Something for the office, and something for my home."

"Do you have anything special in mind?"

"Not really. I'm not sure what she does. Maybe a nice landscape. Or, if she does abstracts, that would be fine. A self-portrait would be great."

"Or maybe a nude?" Todd asked, grinning.

"How would I know if it was her—or someone else?"

"If the face shows in the painting, you would know."

Todd was looking back and forth, talking to Taylor, losing sight of the road just long enough to veer off the road. He quickly jerked the car back onto the highway, but not before Taylor exclaimed, "Geez, what the hell are you doing!"

"Sorry."

"Keep your eye on the road. I'll do all the talking. You drive."

One minute they were in the country, traveling parallel to the river, the soothing textures of nature their only distraction, and the next minute they were on Main Street, dodging motorists on their way to the drug store or the supermarket.

Gananoque is a quaint village, with a population of five thousand and little new construction other than the Top Gan Charity Casino, built in riverboat style on water's edge. In Ontario, casinos are run by the province, which divides the proceeds up among the host cities, various charities, and the province. Gan's cut of the pie was only five percent, which was why Taylor was meeting with Mayor Gord Brooks. He wanted Taylor to use his political influence to obtain a better income distribution for the village.

"Where are we meeting the mayor?" asked Taylor.

"Town Hall."

"Not at his office?"

"Mayor Brook wants to meet you where you'll have access to other city officials."

"I see."

The Town Hall was a two-story, colonel-style brick structure located at the east end of King Street. As they approached the building, Taylor said, "Why don't you just park out on the street."

"Don't you want to park in the parking lot, where the Merdi— (that's the nickname he'd given the Mercedes-Benz)—won't be an open target for stray bumpers."By that time, they'd already passed the parking spaces on the street

"Whatever," Taylor said as Todd gently wheeled the Merdi into the parking lot.

After he parked and turned off the engine, Todd asked, "Would you like for me to go in with you?"

"Sure—so that you can take notes."

As they walked up the sidewalk, Mayor Brook flung open the door and rushed down the steps to give Taylor a hearty handshake. He gushed, "So glad you could come."

"Anytime I can help you, all you have to do is call." He glanced at Todd. "You know my assistant, don't you?"

"Yes indeed," the mayor said, pumping Todd's hand. "He's been a big help."

Mayor Brook led them into a conference room in the Town Hall. Already there were about a half dozen men and women, most of them city council members. Taylor made the rounds, shaking hands with each person, making a comment or two as he moved along. Once the greetings were over, the mayor seated him at the head of a large conference table. Todd sat in a chair next to the wall.

Mayor Brook started the meeting by saying, "I suppose you're wondering why we wanted to meet with you?"

"Todd said it had something to do with the casino."

"Yes—that's right."

"Of course, you know that is a provincial matter, not one under the jurisdiction of the federal government."

"Yes, of course. Our problem is that our MPP, Sam Tucker, is opposed to gambling. He's not interested in hearing anything about our casino."

"With good reason," said Taylor. "You well know that if the operation of the casino was left up to voters in Leeds and Grenville, there'd be no casino. You have the casino because the voters of Gananoque want it—and because it has the support of the province. If Tucker aligned himself with the casino, he probably wouldn't be re-elected."

"That's why we're hoping you can help us. You must know that Gan voters gave you your largest percentage of votes in Leeds-Grenville?"

"I'm well aware of that—and I genuinely appreciate it. Is there anything special you have in mind about how I can help you?"

"There is," said one of the councilmen. "We're hoping you will meet with Sam Tucker and use your considerable skills of persuasion to convince him of the rightness of our cause."

The mayor interrupted with, "You might want to remind him that Gananoque's success with the casino has made it possible not to raise county taxes."

"That's a good point," said Taylor. "But to be totally honest with you, I know Sam quite well and I can tell you that the casino is a moral issue with him. It's highly unlikely that I'll be able to change his mind about that."

"We understand," said a city councilwoman. "But we'd appreciate it if you would try. We desperately need to increase our proceeds from the casino. So much of our future depends on it."

"I will try," said Taylor. "I'll do my best. But in the event that fails, is there another tactic you think might be helpful."

Mayor Brook broken into an enormous smile.

"As a matter of fact," he said. "How would you feel about spearheading an effort in the House of Commons to federalize all the casinos in Canada?"

Taylor looked surprised. "What good would that do?"

"At the moment, we've got a provincial government that is run by the Liberal Party and a federal government that is run by the Conservative Party. The Conservative Party, as you know, takes a more businesslike approach to the casinos. If the Conservatives succeeded in making it a federal issue, it would be possible to allow American casinos into the country. I have reason to think that American casino operators would be willing to decrease the percentage given to charities and increase the percentage given to municipalities. That would certainly solve our problems here in Gananoque."

"What do you think?" asked the councilwoman.

Taylor thought a long moment, weighing the issues involved.

"Let me think this over," he said. "You've made some good points."

After the meeting, the mayor and the entire city council walked Taylor and Todd outside to the car, their faces bright with optimism. Politicians are never so happy as when they have planted the seeds of what they consider a fool-proof deal. That was the case here, though not in an especially negative sense. Politics is the art of getting what you want while concealing your goals from your opponents.

On the drive back to Brockville, Taylor said almost nothing, absorbed in thought.

Finally, after they'd been on the road for ten minutes or so, Todd turned to him, a snickering smile on his face, and asked, "Are you thinking what I think you're thinking?"

Taylor looked surprised at first, but then lowered his guard and smiled.

"I want you to do a little polling for me."

"All right."

"We've got a scenario here where the voters in my district are very much opposed to casinos on moral grounds—they're not interested in doing Gananoque any favors when it comes to the casino—but I think they could be persuaded to support the federalization of the casinos since they'd like the idea of the Conservative Party being in charge of the casinos nationwide. As it is, the Liberal Party controls the casinos in Ontario. My voters are against anything that will help the Liberal Party."

"Are you going to meet with Sam Tucker?"

"Not a chance. I don't want him to get wind of this. If I succeed in spearheading a federalization effort, my Conservative voters will thank me for taking the casinos away from the Liberals. I don't see a real downside. All my speeches in the counties will be anti-Liberal, not pro casino. Unless I'm misreading the people I've lived among for most of my life, they'll put their moral reservations aside long enough to sting the Liberals."

"You're a genius."

"I won't disagree with you, in a general sense; but in this particular case it's Mayor Brook who's the genius. He's devious in a good sort of way. I like the way he thinks. If I'm not careful, he'll be after my seat in a term or two. The man is always two or three steps ahead of everyone else."

Taylor laughed, but Todd didn't.

"You don't think he'd do that, do you?"

"Not a chance. He's built up a little fiefdom that suits him just fine."

"If you pull this off, it could land you in the Prime Minister's office."

"Let's not get ahead of ourselves."

"You're right. Sometimes I dream out loud."

"I'm curious. How do you feel about casinos?"

"Oh, I love casinos. I won eight thousand dollars at the one in Gan. I used the money to travel to Scotland. I had enough to pay my friend Bob's way. It was one of the best vacations I ever had."

When they arrived in Brockville, Todd parked the Merdie at Taylor's mansion, not surprisingly named Prescott Place, and got into his Honda and drove off into the sunset. Taylor went into the house and tossed his keys onto the countertop of a two-hundred-year-old English mahogany table and walked into the sitting room that he had converted into a den. Prescott Place was a magnificent, 18,000-square-foot stone home that'd been built in the style of the grand country homes of England.

During construction, marble was brought across the river on ice sleds from New York during the winter months. The Italian-style garden was designed by Frederick Olmsted, who also designed New York's Central Park. It featured three elaborate fountains, assorted statues, and a selection of evergreens chosen for their year-long beauty. Some people said it was one of the most beautiful gardens in Canada.

Situated on a bluff overlooking the river, Prescott Place was a favorite stop for the tour boats during the tourist season. Taylor allowed the tour operators to stop in the river outside his home, but they had strict orders never to dock. Look but don't touch.

As he walked through the house, he looked at each and every painting along the way. All had come with the house. They looked expensive and historic, but there was nothing exciting about any of them. He took down a portrait of a gentleman in typical English dress (the painting was probably one hundred years old) and he slid it behind one of the three sofas in the room.

That's where I want Katherine's work to shine he thought. He made a mental note to have Todd call an electrician to install a special light to illuminate that section of the wall. *If that doesn't impress her, I can't imagine what would.*

Taylor went into the kitchen and got a beer out of the fridge. Then he returned to the den and loosened his tie and sat on his favorite sofa. He sipped the beer, looking about the room, enjoying old memories. He adjusted one of the cushions on the sofa and discovered something behind the cushion that didn't belong there.

An earring.

He held it up in the light, examining it, trying to remember the ear to which it had been attached, but he drew a blank. He put it on the table, confident that its owner would return to retrieve it. *It looks expensive,* he thought. *That narrows the choices.*

CHAPTER
10

When Katherine awoke, the sun was shimmering into her bedroom, sheets of brilliant light that created random shadows all across the room. She heard something downstairs and sleepily, without any thought to it, called out: "Roger! Is that you?"

She'd been in a deep asleep. She felt disoriented when she opened her eyes and looked at the other side of the bed. The sheet corner was still folded down. No one had slept next to her. Gradually, as she rubbed her eyes, she remembered she was alone. A wave of sadness swept over her, causing her to release a long sigh.

Then she heard the sound again.

"Bessie—is that you?"

Moments later, she heard the cocker spaniel's feet padding up the staircase. Bessie burst into the room, a silly grin on her face and a napkin from the trash stuck to the top of her head.

"Bessie, you bad girl! Where have you been?"

Bessie ran over to the bed and pulled herself up, paws on sheets, to convince Katherine of her innocence. Katherine removed the napkin from her head and showed it to her. Shamefaced, Bessie backed away and sat on the far side of the room, avoiding eye contact with Katherine.

"Haven't you learned that there is no perfect crime?"

Bessie ignored her comment, prompting Katherine to get up out of bed and walk across the room to the bathroom. One of Katherine's morning rituals was to wash her face with cold water before looking at herself in the mirror. Once that was done, she patted her face dry with a towel and hesitantly looked at the image in the mirror.

There was sadness in her eyes that'd never existed before the accident. She conjured a broad smile, but it looked so insincere that it made her look weepy, like a sad-eyed clown with a painted smile. She turned on the faucets and got into the shower, turning her back to the cascading warm water that soothed her muscles.

When you have everything you ever wanted—and then lose it, how do you start over again? she thought. *I've got to try. Roger would want me to try.*

As she dried off, she looked into the mirror. Before the accident, she always checked herself out carefully after each shower or bath. She had a swimsuit model's figure—and she wanted to keep it. After the accident, she'd begun to think of herself as dowdy. She saw herself as more of a Whistler's Mother-type. Dismally bleak. This morning, in the fogged mirror, she saw herself for what she was—a very attractive woman in her prime of life.

After she returned to the bedroom, she looked through her closet, sliding one hanger after another, until she found exactly what she was looking for—a dark-green suit, for which she chose a pearl blouse, one she'd purchased on a trip to New York. She put the suit and blouse on the bed, neatly spread out.

Then she worked from the ground up.

Matching black panties and bra. Pearl half-slip. Diamond drop that she inherited from her grandmother. She put the blouse on and buttoned it. As she walked across the room to chose a pair of shoes—dark green that matched her suit—she couldn't help but think about Roger. He loved to stay in bed and watch her dress. His favorite part was when she put on a shirt or blouse and walked about the room wearing nothing else. Knowing how he felt about it, she always put a little something extra in her walk.

She finished dressing and looked at the finished product in a life-size oval mirror, an antique that'd been in Roger's family for a hundred years. She wondered if she should return it to his family. It occurred to her that she didn't know the proper etiquette for dealing with family heirlooms once a spouse has died. She straightened her collar and pulled at her jacket. She looked spectacular—and she knew it.

Was it too warm to wear a jacket? She suffered a brief moment of indecision, and then shrugged. It really didn't matter. Her car was air-conditioned. The gallery was air-conditioned. Anywhere she went would be air-conditioned.

She went downstairs and fed Bessie, topping her water dish. The sunroom was where she worked when the weather wasn't conducive to painting outside. The entire room was devoted to her art. There were a couple of wicker chairs and a wicker sofa, but much of the space was taken up by finished paintings that stood propped against the walls, stacked three and four deep.

She looked through her inventory, choosing a half-dozen paintings to take to the Ottawa gallery to sell on consignment. She priced her paintings from five thousand to ten thousand dollars, the price depending on the size and content. Usually, there was a waiting list to view her most recent work. It was rare for the gallery to display one of her paintings for longer than a month because they sold so quickly.

It only took a few minutes to load the paintings into the boat, but she returned to the house and said goodbye to Bessie before leaving the island. It was a beautiful day. Blue sky. White Clouds. The sunlight hitting her arms felt warm and inviting.

By the time she reached the boathouse and unloaded her paintings into the car and set out for Ottawa, she was feeling good about the day. She wondered if maybe she spent too much time alone on the island. Solitude breeds solitude. She understood that and she resolved to manufacture more outings off the island.

Perhaps Jason was right. Perhaps she should make an effort to move on.

The drive to Ottawa could best be described as unassuming. Once she left the scenic highway and turned north, there was not much to distract her from the trees that lined the road. Thirty miles out of Ottawa, she stopped for gas at Kemptville, a town within the greater town of North Grenville, one town inside the other, like those decorative Russian eggs. Despite new construction, the town had retained the quaintness that had made it her favorite stopover on the way to Ottawa.

From the time she hit the suburbs of Ottawa, it seemed to take forever to get downtown, where the Macmillan Gallery was located. There was nothing artsy looking about the building. With its colorless, high- rising concrete walls it resembled a metropolitan museum more than it did a modern art gallery. Incredibly, she found a parking space directly in front of the building. Inside the gallery it was very cool, the product of an overly ambitious air-conditioner.

She no sooner walked through the door than she was greeted by Elizabeth Spencer, the gallery owner.

"So glad to see you!" Elizabeth gushed as she hurried across the room to give Katherine perfunctory pecks on both cheeks, followed by a gentle hug. "I hope you brought us lots of new work."

Katherine liked Elizabeth well enough, but she didn't really care for all the hugging and kissing that usually accompanied her visits to the gallery.

"I have six new pieces in the car. Should I bring them in?"

"Just try to stop me from seeing them!"

Elizabeth linked her arm around Katherine's elbow and escorted her back to the door, chatting about everything and anything, saying nothing in particular. At the car, Elizabeth examined each painting as Katherine lifted them, one at a time, and gently leaned them against a light post.

"Oh, this is marvelous!" explained Elizabeth, eyeing a river landscape.

Then she picked up a moonlight scene. "Breathtaking."

Amazingly, Elizabeth found four additional adjectives to express her reactions to the paintings. The six paintings represented commissions totaling nearly ten thousand dollars. Elizabeth figured they'd sell within a week.

Katherine and Elizabeth each took three paintings into the gallery. They went into the back office and put the paintings on the floor, gently leaning them against the wall.

"I already know where I want to display them," said Elizabeth. "There are twenty-four people on the waiting list. I'll put them on the wall and then start making calls."

"I appreciate all the support you've given me over the years."

"Are you kidding? There's nothing to thank me for. People love your work. Representing you has more to do with controlling traffic than it does sales. If you brought me ten paintings a day, I would sell each of them and still have a waiting list."

Elizabeth wrote Katherine a receipt for the paintings and handed it to her. She used that moment as an opportunity to hold Katherine's hand between the two of her hands. "Are you all right, dear?" she asked. There was a look of pity on her face.

"I'm doing much better," said Katherine. "I'll get through it. Everyone does."

"Well, not everyone. I had a first cousin who committed suicide after her husband of ten years passed away."

Katherine winced.

Elizabeth paused, thinking that perhaps she shouldn't have said that. She tried to rebound by saying, "Of course, she had mental problems that went back to childhood, when she lost her parents. That probably had more to do with it than losing her husband."

"It's difficult under any circumstances."

Katherine gently slipped her hand from the woman's grasp and turned to the door.

"I really must go. I have a couple of meetings to go to. You know how it is."

"Oh, do I ever!"

Elizabeth hugged her again and released her with a slight shove, as if she were releasing a wounded bird and was eager to avert her eyes. Misty-eyed, she said, "I'll update you on the sales!"

"Thank you," said Katherine, hurrying for the door.

Once she got into her car, she leaned back into the seat and sighed. She enjoyed painting and she enjoyed receiving payment for her painting. What she didn't particularly enjoy were the interim social interactions that were required for the completion of that enjoyment. She took three deep breaths. Then after a moment's hesitation, he reached into her purse and retrieved her cell and a business card. She looked at the card and punched in a telephone number.

On the third ring a male voice answered with, "Mr. Taylor Prescott's office."

Katherine sat up a little straighter in the car seat.

"This is Katherine Summer from Brockville. Could I please speak to Mr. Prescott?"

There was a pause during which Todd clamped his palm over the telephone mouthpiece and whispered, "It's her! Katherine Summer!"

Taylor hesitated. Then he whispered back, "Tell her that I'm on the other line. Take her number and tell her I will call her right back."

Todd did as he was told, adding, "I'm sure he will return your call within the next few minutes."

After Todd hung up, Taylor said, "I bet she's in town. I can't invite her to the office since I don't have one of her paintings yet."

"Why don't you call her back and invite her to lunch. Meanwhile, I can try to locate one of her paintings. I'll call you on your cell if I do."

"That sounds like a plan. Just make sure the paintings aren't recent."

Katherine had about decided to leave town when her cell rang.

"Hello."

"Katherine, this is Taylor. Todd told me that you called. Are you in town?"

"Yes, I dropped some paintings off at the Macmillan Gallery."

"Really—the Macmillan Gallery," he said, winking at Todd. "I imagine they were delighted to get them."

"They're happy to get anything that will earn them a commission."

"I've always heard that the owner—what's her name, Elizabeth Spencer—is devoted to the arts."

"I'm sure she is. I shouldn't be so cynical."

"I don't think you're cynical. Just realistic. So do you have time to meet me for lunch?"

"Sure. Where would you like to meet?"

"Have you ever been to Big Daddy's Crab Shack and Oyster Bar?"

"Over on Elgin? Sure. What time should we meet?"

"It's a quarter to twelve now. If you're free, I can be there in fifteen minutes."

"It's a date," she said, then added, "I don't really mean a date date."

"A luncheon date?"

"Yes, that's it."

"See you there."

As she maneuvered out of the parking space and headed to the restaurant, she thought *When did I become so spastic? I don't even like the guy. I can't stand him! Why would I regress to being a teenager when I talk to him?* She shook her head with dismay.

She found the restaurant without difficulty and parked in a hourly-rate lot down the street. By the time she got there, Taylor was waiting at the front door, a big grin on his face. He started talking to her while she was still half a block away, practically shouting at her, speaking loud enough that people leaving the restaurant turned to see whom he was addressing. Not sure how he would greet her, she stuck out her hand when she walked up to him and gave him a firm handshake.

"I'm so glad you called," he said, escorting her into the building. "You look well. I hope you aren't having problems of any kind."

"Oh, no," she said. "I'm not here to ask you for any favors."

"I didn't mean to imply . . ."

She interrupted with, "Isn't that why constituents usually call you—to ask for favors?"

Taylor smiled knowingly. "You're right. It's never ending. But you know what? I enjoy doing things for people. That's why I ran for office."

"You'd definitely have to be a people person to do your job."

The hostess, a sweet looking college girl who looked radiant even without makeup, asked them if they wanted to eat inside in the dining room or outside on the patio. Before Katherine could suggest indoors, Taylor answered, "The patio, of course."

By the time they were seated, Katherine was already contemplating removing her jacket. Their table was beneath an umbrella, but the reflected sunlight was quite warm.

Taylor ordered the crab Alfredo and Katherine chose blackened yellowfin tuna, the restaurant's specialty. Katherine found herself staring at Taylor. He was actually quite handsome, more so than she realized at their first meeting.

"Do you come here often?" she asked.

"Quite a bit. It's close to my office."

"Ah, the office . . ." she intoned. "Where my work hangs in perpetual homage."

Taylor laughed. "Something like that."

"I thought about dropping in on you at your office, but I'm glad we met for lunch."

"I am, too."

An older man in wire-rim glasses approached the table. He shook hands with Taylor and apologized to Katherine for interrupting their conversation.

"He's not trying to sell you a bill of goods, is he?" the man joked, pointing a finger at Taylor.

Katherine answered, "Not yet—but we just got here."

The man laughed. "I can see that I'm in the way here. Taylor, I just wanted to let you know that we've finished with that polling you requested."

"Excellent," said Taylor. "Would you please have your people shoot the data over to my assistant, Todd?"

"Certainly will."

"Outstanding," said Taylor.

As the man walked away, Taylor, said, "I'm sorry about that. When you work for the public, it's sometimes difficult to have private moments when you're in a public place."

"No problem. I understand. In some ways, it's exciting, I guess."

"The first year it's exciting. Not so much after that. Surely, you must run into the same thing in your work. Don't you have to go to social occasions to promote your paintings? Don't you have to be polite and talk to people you wouldn't ordinarily be associated with?"

"Well, to be honest . . . that is a part of it. "

"See—we're more alike than you thought."

Katherine dismissed the thought and changed the subject.

"What's on your agenda for the upcoming session?"

"I'm working on a few things I think will be of interest. Once I have things worked out, I'll run my ideas past you to see what you think."

"I'm flattered, but I know very little about politics."

"You know more than you think. Besides, as someone once said, nothing is politically right which is morally wrong."

"Who said that?"

"I forget. Doesn't matter who said it. Politics is all about deciding right and wrong. Taking a stand for the common good."

"I didn't realize you have such an evangelical approach to your work."

Taylor laughed. "This conversation is getting way out of hand."

"Like a runaway horse?"

"Let's change the subject."

"What would you like to talk about?"

"You."

"Okay, give it your best shot."

Taylor lowered his voice and broadcast his most sincere facial expression. "Do you mind if I ask you a personal question?"

"I'm not sure—how personal?"

"Are you seeing anyone?"

Katherine paused before answering.

Was she seeing Jason? Was she technically dating him? It was questions like this, when she was married, that always made her glad that she was married.

It was a delicate question to answer.

"I'm going out with someone, but I don't think anyone would call it dating."

"Is it anyone I know?"

"His name is Jason Montclair. He's a psychologist in Ogdensburg."

"A shrink, eh?"

"Something like that."

"Is it a serious relationship?"

"I wouldn't call it that. No."

"Then you're not exclusive."

"It's never even come up—and I doubt it will."

"Why's that?"

"I probably shouldn't be telling you this, but we have this . . . *thing* . . . between us. It's very complicated."

"You're not making much sense."

"Okay, I'll just tell you outright—you promise to keep it confidential?"

"Of course."

"I went to Jason for counseling after I lost Roger and Dedi."

"He was your shrink?"

"Yes. But a year into it he referred me to another psychologist."

"Why would he do something like that?"

"That's where the problem comes in. He told me that he was attracted to me and he explained that psychologists have a code of ethics that prevents them from ever having a romantic relationship with one of their clients, past or present."

"So he dumped you as a client and started dating you?"

"That's about it."

Taylor shook his head, a frown on his face.

"He could lose his license for that. Did he tell you that?"

"Sure. But I would never report him to the ethics board."

"Still . . . he's taking a big chance."

"You're sworn to secrecy—remember?"

"Of course."

Taylor's cell rang, shutting down their conversation. It was Todd. He explained that he was standing outside the Macmillan Gallery with two original Katherine Summer paintings in his hand.

"I'll take them to the office, but if I were you I wouldn't invite her to stop by since it'll take a while to find the right place for them."

"Thanks for the update," Taylor said and flipped off his cell.

He paused a moment, collecting his thoughts.

"Where were we?" Before she could answer, he continued, "I think we agreed that since you are not exclusive to this fellow Jason, it'd be all right for you to have dinner with me at my home on Friday."

Katherine seemed powerless to stop a smile from creeping across her lips.

CHAPTER
11

On her way back to Brockville from Ottawa, Katherine called Jason and suggested that they grill-out on the island instead of going to dinner as they had planned. That was fine with Jason since he'd never seen the island or her home.

"I'm just in the mood for a homey meal," she explained, not mentioning that she felt stuffed from her lunch at Big Daddy's Crab Shack and Oyster Bar. By eating at home, she could have a salad and grill him whatever he wanted.

She thought about Taylor all the way home. He was the kind of man she usually wouldn't give a second glance. She knew that he had a reputation as a ladies' man, and after spending the lunch hour with him she understood why. Apart from his obvious physical good looks, there was something attractive about the way he treated her. He didn't talk down to her. He didn't look at other women in the restaurant. He tried to make her feel good about herself—gestures that emotionally resonated with her.

I can tell he likes me she thought. *He'll call. I know he will. Should I go out with him—or should I explore my relationship with Jason more deeply?*

The road home took her directly past Prescott Place. She'd wanted to paint it for years, but the opportunity to discuss it with Taylor never arose. She couldn't imagine that a man as warm and intelligent as Taylor would be happy living alone in a house that large. To be happy there, she decided, he'd have to have an ego the size of a barn.

When she arrived at the boathouse, she parked beneath a maple tree and paused to look at the foliage along the river. The dark green colors that had dominated all summer were beginning to lighten, and the flowers along the bank were thinning. Fall would arrive soon and everything would be covered with a blanket of snow. There were only two seasons in that part of Canada—winter and summer. Fall and the spring were little more than week-long events. Gone in the blink of an eye.

Katherine locked her car and went into the boathouse. The first sound she heard as she entered the building was water lapping against her boat. Normally the boathouse was quiet as a church. She knew that meant there had been a lot of traffic on the river that day.

She untied the boat and hiked her skirt to get inside. She couldn't wait to get back to the house. She didn't like leaving Bessie alone, though she was certain that she enjoyed having exclusive use of the house. The ride out to the island was one of her favorite things to do. It allowed her to view her island as an outsider. She wondered what she would think of the island if she had never been there. Would it have an air of mystery about it? Would it invite questions about the person who lives there?

As soon as she docked and turned off the motor she heard Bessie barking inside the house. She couldn't imagine Bessie waiting at the window all day. She was much too curious about things to be that passive.

No, the only explanation for Bessie being at the window was because she had an instinct that Katherine was on her way to the dock. Perhaps it was a physic connection. Or perhaps the boat motor has a distinctive pitch that Bessie recognized. Whatever the reason, it never failed to make Katherine smile.

As soon as Katherine opened the door, Bessie was all over her, twisting and turning, barking her distinctive greeting.

"Did you miss me?" asked Katherine.

Bessie barked twice. Two barks meant yes. Three barks meant no.

"Good girl," she said, petting her.

Katherine checked her voicemails and then went upstairs, undressing as she ascended the staircase. By the time she reached the bath off her bedroom, her skin was water friendly and she wasted no time getting into the shower. She thought about Jason as the hot water soothed her back muscles, sore because of the drive from Ottawa. She enjoyed Jason's company, but she feared he was moving at a different speed. Would there be a problem if they kept seeing each other? Why was getting to know someone so complicated?

After she dried off, she discarded the towel and started downstairs, with Bessie nipping at her heels. Bessie had a highly developed sense of order. Anytime Katherine violated that order—such as going downstairs naked—it set off alarms bells inside Bessie's head. Bessie had a delicate sense of right and wrong.

"It's all right, sweetie," Katherine said, trying to reassure her.

She went into the sunroom and quickly surveyed it for the best light source.

Then she gathered up a quilt from the sofa and spread it across on the floor. When she had it arranged just so, with the corners neatly folded out and pressed down, she put two mirrors on either side of the quilt and adjusted them so that she could sit on the quilt and look into one mirror and see her reflection in the second mirror. She tossed a sketchbook and piece of charcoal onto the quilt. Then she got into position, a little awkwardly at first, not sure how to arrange her legs.

Never had she painted herself nude. Today was as good a day as any to start.

Bessie continued to scold her for doing something different, nervously darting on and off the quilt. Katherine instructed her to sit quietly in the corner, which she did without protest though Katherine heard her sigh before she put her head down.

Katherine posed so that she could see her back in the mirror facing her. She stretched her legs out, one on top of the other, and she propped up on her left hand. That left her right hand free to sketch. What she had in mind was a rearview nude that did not show her face. The mirrors were arranged so that she could see both sides of her figure. She was surprised that her abs looked so flat in that position. Her stomach was not rock-hard, like an athlete's, but rather flat and smooth, without the small bulge so common in women her age who have had children.

Katherine drew her lines as she saw them in the mirror, crafting a feminine form that brought a smile to her face as she corrected minor flaws in her figure, making her hips somewhat smaller than they were in real life and her back somewhat more appealing than it was in actuality. She had no intention of advertising the finished painting as a self-portrait; her artistic vision was to create a feminine form that radiated accessibility, not sexuality, as if the model had been captured in a private moment.

She made several sketches, a process that lasted almost two hours. When she finished the final sketch, she rolled over on her stomach, like a child watching television, and she examined the sketches, moving them from left to right, up and down, until she found the one that she liked best. She yawned, the result of a tiring day. Ever since Roger's death, social interactions had left her exhausted.

She knew that she had to get ready for her date with Jason, but she didn't want to think about that just now. Instead, she put her head down to rest for just a minute or two before going upstairs to dress.

An hour later, she awakened to a knocking sound, and to Bessie's barks as she lunged back and forth to the window. She raised her head to listen. Someone was rapping on glass.

Who could be knocking on my door?

She rolled over and looked at the windows that opened to her deck.

Standing there, his knuckles gentle rapping against the glass, was Jason! When she looked his way, he waved and smiled.

"Jason!" she called out, covering herself with her drawings.

"What are you doing here?"

He answered, but she couldn't hear him. He motioned for her to go to the back door. Instead, she raced up the staircase, Bessie at her heels, and put on jeans and a T-shirt. She looked at herself in the mirror, fussing with her hair a moment. Then she hurried back downstairs and opened the back door.

Bessie stood to the side and growled in a low voice.

The first words out of Jason's mouth were, "I'm so sorry—I saw you on the floor—I thought you were unconscious, or even worse. I'm so glad you're all right."

Her hand still on the doorknob, Katherine stared at him a moment, speechless.

"May I come in?" he asked.

Katherine was thinking *this man has seen me naked.*

"Sure," she said, stepping aside.

But she could not stop thinking *this man has seen me naked.*

As he walked into the room, he reached out to pet Bessie. At first she backed away, but when Katherine told her that it was all right, she inched toward Jason and allowed him to pet her, but just briefly.

Katherine pulled up a chair to the kitchen table and sat down. Jason started to sit in the chair across from her, but then changed his mind.

"I can't believe this happened," he said, pacing. "You didn't come to the door, so I looked in the windows. I saw you on the floor and I thought something bad had happened to you."

"You already said that," she said. "What are you doing here?"

This time it was he who looked shocked.

"It's a little after seven. We had a date for six, remember?"

Katherine glanced at the clock on the stove and her hand shot to her mouth.

"We did! I must have dozed off."

She looked at him, perplexed. "But how did you get to the house?

"I waited at your boathouse for thirty or forty minutes. I called you several times, but you never answered."

"My cell was upstairs."

"I was really concerned about you, so I flagged down a passing boat and they brought me over to the island."

Finally, he sat at the table, his head hung in shame.

"I didn't mean to see you that way. Surely, you can understand why I reacted the way I did?"

Katherine nodded. "It's not your fault. I was sketching a nude of myself and when I finished I put my head down for just a second."

She glanced at the clock again.

"I can't believe it's so late. I must have slept for an hour. I apologize."

"I'm the one who should apologize."

"No, you had a right to be concerned. Living alone, I've spoiled myself. I do what I want, when I want to do it, without considering anyone else's feelings."

There was a long pause as they stared across the table at each other, the initial shock of the event now passed.

Katherine smiled. "You'll have to marry me now."

"What do you mean?"

"You saw me naked. You have to marry me to make an honest woman of me."

Jason laughed. "People have gotten married for a lot less."

Katherine got to her feet. "Before we start the dinner thing, would you like to see the rest of the house?"

"I'd love to."

Katherine took him upstairs and showed him the master bedroom and bath and the two spare bedrooms. Then, back downstairs, she showed him the living room and den, and finally the sunroom she used as a studio.

"Can I see what you're working on?"

Katherine hurried across the room and gathered up the drawings and held them behind her back as if she'd been caught doing something bad.

"Everything but these," she said. "The world is not ready for these."

"Do you have any other nudes?" he asked.

"No."

"Do you mind if I look at your work?"

"No, knock yourself out."

Jason slowly looked through the paintings, pausing to comment on the ones he really liked. He handled them as if they were fragile, a gesture that did not go unnoticed by Katherine, who appreciated the care he took when lifting and lowering each painting.

Sometimes she showed her paintings to people who burrowed through them like they were digging in a dumpster, tossing canvases from side to side as if they were indestructible. Jason's way with her paintings reminded her of Roger, who always worried about damaging her paintings when he had to lift or move them. Her thoughts drifted. Roger was the perfect husband. The perfect lover. The perfect friend.

"These paintings are outstanding," Jason said, interrupting her thoughts. "Why do you have so many here at home? Why don't you put them on the market?"

"I took a few to Ottawa today. I don't want to flood the market, so I pace my releases. Besides, I've found that if I put my work aside and then look at it again later, maybe a week or so later, I will have a new perspective. If I think a work doesn't measure up to my standards, I'll start all over again and paint over it."

"I'd hate to see you discard anything."

"You have to do that sometimes. Not everything works out the way we want it to. Sometimes it's out with the old and in with the new."

"I don't have that luxury in my work."

"What do you mean?"

"I seem to see the same patients, year after year. Old patients die. New patients come in as young children. It's to the point now where I can predict which children will be with me for many years. There aren't many mental illnesses that can be cured overnight. Believe me—there are patients I would like to paint over so that they could start over fresh. Just doesn't work out that way."

The more they talked, the more Katherine realized that she had many things in common with him. He was the sort of man who had to grow on a woman. Even at this early stage of their relationship, Katherine understood that. Her concern about dating him was that he would get too far ahead of her in his expectations.

As a teenager, the best advice Katherine ever got from her mother was that bad timing destroyed many a relationship.

"Go slow, dear," her mother told her. "Speeding around curves is not always the best way to make time on a trip—and that's all a relationship is, two people on a trip."

By the time Jason finished looked at her paintings, the tension between them had evaporated. Katherine practically forgot about the episode of her being naked on the floor, and she assumed that he did, too, though that wasn't true.

Actually, he couldn't get the sight of her out of his mind—he kept telling himself that it was one of the most beautiful things he'd ever seen in his life—but he did a magnificent job of making her believe that he had forgotten all about it and he figured that counted for something.

When they went back out onto the deck to grill dinner, he saw why she was so devoted to the island. The view of the water was magnificent. Someone who has never been on an island in the middle of a river, with water flowing on all sides, would be hard-pressed to understand the emotional appeal. Simply sitting there was a religious experience, partly because of the emotional surrender that level of passivity required, but also because the stark, raw power of the river served as an ever present reminder of human frailty.

"Do you think you'll ever leave the island?" he asked.

"I can't imagine ever living anyplace else."

Jason put his arms around her.

They hugged and exchanged a cursory kiss.

Katherine lingered in his arms.

"How did you ever get to be such a nice guy?"

"Keep saying that. The more you say it, the more you'll believe it."

Jason kissed her again. In no time at all they were kissing like teenagers on a first date. They made out for more than an hour in the dark, but before it went any further, Katherine gently pushed him away.

"I think it's time to call it a night," she whispered.

"I can see that you're tired."

Katherine got to her feet. "Bessie," she called out. "To the boat!"

Bessie scurried from beneath a nearby chair and ran to the dock.

"Can I have one of those drawings for a souvenir?" Jason sheepishly asked. "I'll happily pay the asking price."

"Not a chance," she said smiling. "They're not for sale."

"If you ever change your mind, let me know."

Jason reached for her hand and held it as they walked to the dock.

"I enjoyed my dinner," he said. "I'm sorry you didn't want anything from the grill. It was excellent."

"For some reason, I wasn't hungry."

Bessie jumped into the boat first and sought out her favorite seat.

Jason and Katherine said very little on the ride to the boathouse, other than noting the slight chill that was in the air. Summer was on its way out.

CHAPTER
12

When Todd got to the office, he hurriedly removed the two photographs on either side of the door going into Taylor's office—one was a photograph of Prime Minister Paul Martin and the other was a photograph of the Ottawa skyline—and he stashed them in a closet. He studied the two paintings he purchased at the gallery, trying to decide if one was a "left" picture and the other a "right" picture.

One painting was of more than a dozen seagulls and cormorants gathered on a small rocky island that had only one tree, barren and stark, in which perched a solitary cormorant. It was dated '09. The second painting was a river sunset, the fiery, yellow-orange sun reflecting a shaft of light that stretched all the way from the horizon to the foreground. It was dated '10.

Perfect, he thought.

Todd put the seagulls and cormorants on the left because the focal point of the painting was to the left, and he put the sunset on the right. Temporary locations, to be sure, but prominent enough so that if Taylor walked in the door with Katherine she'd feel the work was well placed. At least he hoped that'd be the case.

When Taylor walked into the office alone, Todd was disappointed.

"I didn't want to risk bringing her back here—in case, you didn't make it back in time."

Todd nodded and pointed to the paintings. "What do you think?"

Taylor walked over close to the paintings, looking at first one, then the other, without comment. Finally, he said, "Good choices, Todd—my, she is a talented lady. Which one should I take home?"

"I'd take the sunset. It's more romantic."

"I think you're right. I have the perfect place for it. They aren't the ones she dropped off, are they?"

"I don't think so," he said, a sinking feeling in his stomach.

Taylor looked at the paintings a moment longer and then went into his inner office, with Todd right behind him. They were going over responses to several constituent requests when they heard the door open. Todd got up to see who had come into the office. It was a courier with a large brown envelope. Todd thanked him and took the envelope into Taylor's office and opened it.

"It's the survey results," said Todd.

"Excellent—what are the highlights?"

"Let's see . . ." Todd skimmed the document, his facial expression providing no indication of its contents. Finally, he said, "When voters in Leeds-Grenville were asked if casino gambling was a moral issue, 67 percent said yes. When they were asked if they favored allowing casinos into the united counties, 58 percent said no. When they were asked if they favored federalizing casinos so that individual provinces could not license or regulate them, 72 percent said yes. When they were asked if they favored allowing American casinos into Canada, 55 percent said yes."

Todd put the papers on the desk in front of Taylor so that he could read them for himself. "Looks like you were right about the potential of that issue."

"I know my neighbors fairly well."

"How would you like to proceed with this?"

"Civic organizations are always asking me to speak at their luncheons. Look through our requests and pick out several that you think would be good fits. Contact each of them and set it up. Let them know that I'll be willing to speak about fifteen minutes or so. Once you get that out of the way, I'd like for you to draft me a speech that talks about the evils of gambling and harps on wrongheaded leadership of the Liberal Party. Have me say something to the effect that the only way to control gambling in Ontario is to put the regulation of casinos in federal hands, where the Conservative Party has a majority vote."

"This is certainly ironic."

"What do you mean?"

"The voters here despise the casinos—and they despise federalization. But they despise the Liberal Party most of all, so they'll go along with the casinos and federalization in order to knock the Liberal Party down a peg or two."

"That's the way the numbers seem to work out."

"You could end up prime minister once the smoke clears."

"Let's not get ahead of ourselves."

Todd got up from his chair. "I'll get right on this."

Once he left the office, Taylor read the survey results in detail, calculating the strength of the issue on a neighborhood by neighborhood basis. In the neighborhoods where the issue was weak, he'd make certain to downplay it. His goal was to build support for his plan without creating opposition to it, a delicate balance with a big payoff.

Todd was correct. There was nothing in life that Taylor wanted more than becoming prime minister, though he'd die before he'd ever let Todd know that for certain. Before leaving the office, Taylor asked Todd to load the sunset painting into his car, adding, "I'm going home tonight."

"You mean to Brockville?"

"Yes—I'll work from my home tomorrow."

"So you'll need me in Brockville?"

"No, no. I want you to stay here at the office."

Todd's body language indicated that he was a little miffed at what he perceived to be a slight, but he took down the painting without comment and carried it out to the garage and dutifully put it into the passenger side of the Merdie as Taylor put his briefcase in the trunk. Taylor gave Todd some final instructions and left, leaving Todd in the shadows, waving not at his boss but at the beloved Merdie.

Once he left the city, Taylor called Katherine on his cell.

"Shouldn't you be working?" she asked, the telephone squeezed between her ear and her shoulder so that her hands could be free to apply paint to her pallet.

"How do you know I'm not?"

"Because you're talking to me."

"Have you never heard of coffee breaks?"

"Yes—but hardly ever at four in the afternoon. I could be wrong, but judging by that roar I hear in the background, I'd say that you're in your car."

"You're right—I'm on my way back to Brockville. I just wanted to check in with you to make certain that we're still good for dinner tomorrow night."

"As far as I'm concerned."

"Excellent. I'll pick you up at seven."

Katherine paused, thinking about the awkward moment she had with Jason over not inviting him to the island after their first date.

"Thank you, but I think I'd rather just meet you at your house, if that's okay with you."

"That's fine. I'll see you at seven."

*　*　*

Katherine put down her cell and continued to dab paint onto her palette from various tubes. For her self-portrait, she decided to use an impasto consistency of acrylic paint, which she felt provided a more realistic skin tone. She mixed two colors on her palette to get the shade she wanted for the outline of her body.

She liked the odor of fresh paint. It made her smile because it reminded her of better times. If the labels didn't specifically prohibit it, with dire warnings about the effect on her liver and other organs, she gladly would smear it all over her body.

Usually, she cleared her head of all competing thoughts when she worked, but she had a difficult time doing that today. She'd never had trouble with men. The dating she did before she met Roger was always casual and short-term. Throughout their marriage, they had few problems that required soul-searching conversations. Well, practically none to speak of. If they had a problem, they talked it out—and that was that.

For some reason, she couldn't get Jason and Taylor out of her mind. She sensed trouble with both of them, but she couldn't put her finger on anything specific. She'd been dealing with men her entire life. Why, all of a sudden, was she feeling hassled by these two men in particular?

An inner voice warned her to go slowly.

Why? she asked herself. *Why can't I be friends with two men? I'm not sleeping with either one of them. What's the problem?*

With one of the sketches she'd made yesterday propped up in a chair, she faithfully followed the lines in the sketch. Soon she forgot that she was reproducing her own body. It was all about lines and shades and textures. The image taking shape on the canvas was her, but then again it wasn't her.

What was it exactly that Jason and Taylor wanted from her? Was it merely sex? With Jason, she sensed that it was more, raising the question, when is more too much? With Taylor, she was pretty sure it was a sexual attraction, at least on his part. Was that a bad thing as a starting point for discovery? She wondered.

When she first met Roger, it was everything all at once—the fireworks of mutual attraction, the soothing comfort of deep emotion, the laughter of soul mates on a spiritual mission. Doesn't every type of male-female interaction have its own value? Who made up the rules, anyway?

She wished she could have a few bad thoughts about Roger. That would give her hope for the future. Roger was *too* perfect. Maybe that kind of love only happens once in a lifetime. Maybe she'd had her place in the sun. Maybe God was done with her, satisfied that one perfect romance was enough for one lifetime.

She immersed herself in her painting, stroking, dabbing, fine-tuning, making something of nothing. Even as she painted, she debated whether anyone other than herself and Bessie would ever see it. Was it something she'd ever feel comfortable selling to a stranger? She had no answers for those questions, only an obsession for perfection.

CHAPTER
13

By the time Taylor awoke on Friday, his kitchen staff of two was already on the job. None of his home personnel—two cooks, a housekeeper and a groundskeeper—slept at the mansion. All began work at 7 o'clock each morning.

Taylor had an official bedroom, where he kept his clothes and his personal items, but he seldom slept in that room. After an incident with a psychotic mechanic who went crazy after Taylor wouldn't allow him to work on his car, the Royal Canadian Mounted Police suggested that one way to increase security would be for him to sleep in a different bedroom each night. He was reluctant at first, but then he tried it and liked it. He had ten bedrooms in his house, each decorated in an entirely different style.

Since he dated several women, at the same time, separate bedrooms made sleep-over arrangements more manageable. Each time a particular women spent the night with him, he slept with her in her designated bedroom. That way it prevented one woman from stumbling across another woman's left-behind items, like the earring left beneath the pillows on the downstairs sofa. He gave that earring to his housekeeper, Emma, and instructed her to look through the things in the bedrooms upstairs to see if she could find the matching earring. She found it in the Seven Seas room, where he slept with Judy.

Taylor slipped on jeans and a T-shirt and went downstairs, lured by the scent of fresh-brewed coffee. He preferred African beans, and he liked it ruggedly stout. He took a few sips and went outside and called for Robert, the groundskeeper.

He took in a deep breath. It was another beautiful day, with blue skies and a cool breeze that twisted its way through the garden. Robert appeared in less than a minute.

"Robert," he said, as the groundskeeper came into view. "I need you to help me hang a picture in the den."

"Yes sir. I'll go get some fasteners and my tools."

Taylor went inside and removed the painting from the closet. He took it into the den and held it up in the vicinity of where it would hang. It was the perfect size for that wall. When Robert arrived, hammer in hand, he commented on the beauty of the painting, saying it reminded him of a sunset that he remembered with fondness from childhood.

"Funny how you remember things like that," Robert said.

"Maybe you remember it because you associate it with something special in your childhood."

"Could be. I think that I was out fishing with my father."

Robert attached two fasteners to the wall and lifted the painting into place.

"How does that look?"

Taylor stepped back and turned his head from side to side.

"I think it's tilted a little to the right."

Robert made an adjustment.

"Perfect," said Taylor. "Looks like it's been there for years."

After Robert left, Taylor sat in different chairs around the room, sizing up the painting from different angles. Certainly the painting was in good company. Directly across the room was a Picasso, a painting from that period of his life when he flirted with cubism. Also in the room were paintings by Marc Chagall and Salvador Dali.

"Impressive," he said aloud. "This will get her attention."

Most of the women he dated had no idea that his paintings were so valuable.

One woman, upon recognizing Picasso's style, commented that she, too, had Picasso prints in her apartment. Taylor didn't bother telling her that his was not a print. Why bother? She was already impressed enough by his house to ask what they would be having for breakfast. He never had to put out much effort to get women into bed. He knew that he was handsome—he'd always been told that—but he never knew if his success with women was due to his good looks or his wealth, or perhaps a mix of the two.

After breakfast, he checked in with Todd and wrote down the telephone calls he needed to return. There were fifteen in all. Then he went to his downstairs office and made a list of things he wanted to accomplish that day. The view from his office was spectacular. Sometimes it was difficult to work there for that very reason.

Todd was moving quickly on his casino project. Taylor liked that about him. His previous assistant had been a daydreamer. Todd was one of those people who felt compelled to work. It wasn't so much that he wanted to impress Taylor, though that was certainly a factor, but there was something inside him that made him run at full throttle. It was a comfort to know that whatever the assignment, Todd would get the job done.

Taylor spent almost two hours on the telephone. One constituent wanted help with his application for a pension. Taylor called the Director of the National Pension Fund, with whom he often played tennis, and the problem was cleared up by the end of the day. Another constituent had been turned down to adopt a child. That one was not so easy. There was absolutely nothing Taylor could do to help. Yet another caller wanted help with a stalled visa application. He let Todd handle that one.

Being a lawmaker was not nearly as glamorous as people imagined. The House of Commons was usually an exciting place to be, even when MPs were boring each other with esoteric speeches. Unfortunately, Taylor spent only a small percentage of his work day in the House. Mostly he dealt with constituent complaints and business executives who wanted his help landing lucrative government contracts. It was yeoman's work, not the sort of thing he'd want to turn into a lifetime career. However, as a stepping stone to the prime minister's residence, it was the price one paid for political immortality.

As it turned out, Taylor spent all morning on the telephone.

"Yes, I'll take care of it no problem"

"Wish I could help, but it's out of my hands."

"Someone will call you back from the Department of Revenue."

And so it went for most of the morning.

After lunch he sat out on the deck for a while, watching the river traffic. He couldn't get Katherine out of his mind. Her face. Her voice. Her figure. It was the perfect package. He wanted her. The way he saw it, the only thing standing in his way was her relationship with the American.

Taylor picked up his cell and called Todd.

"I've got a favor to ask of you."

"Sure—whatever you need," said Todd cheerfully.

"I want you to call the New York Psychology Board and make an ethics complaint about Dr. Jason Montclair of Ogdensburg."

There was silence at the other end.

"I don't understand . . . how do I do that?"

"Look up the telephone number on the Internet. Call and say you want to report that Dr. Montclair is having an affair with one of his patients named Katherine Summer. Explain that Katherine is Canadian and give them her address. When they ask for your name, say that you prefer to remain anonymous."

"That's all I have to say?"

"That should do it."

"I'll get right on it."

"Thank you, Todd."

Taylor gave instructions to the cooks for dinner and then went into his private workout room. His plan was to take the rest of the day off so that he could work on his biceps at the weight bench and then take a nap. He wanted to be rested for his date with Katherine. He slipped off his shirt and stood in front of the mirror.

Women told him that he had a big chest. He wasn't sure what a big chest was, but if women liked big chests, he was glad he had one. Whatever made them happy made him happy. He flexed his right bicep.

Not bad he thought. *But I can make it much firmer.*

CHAPTER
14

Jason lived in a ranch-style home in one of the better neighborhoods in Ogdensburg, but it wasn't the sort of house that a real estate agent would feature on the cover of a sales brochure. Most of the best property in the city was on the southern shore of the St. Lawrence River, where the waterfront property was highly developed, much as it was across the river in Brockville.

When Jason awoke, something hit him for the first time as he looked about his bedroom. His walls were completely bare. Not a single photograph or painting. Actually, there were no photographs or paintings on any of the walls in his house. It was one of those things on his bucket list that he never got around to taking care of.

"If I don't do it now, I never will," he mumbled as he got out of bed.

He went into his den, yawning the entire way, and turned on his computer. After a few searches he found a respectable looking website that sold prints. For $49.95, he could order ten prints from a series called The World's Greatest Artists. He looked over the list of artists featured in the collection. Most of them he'd never heard of, but there were a couple of names that he remembered from high school. Picasso. Dega. It looked like a solid package to him, so he ordered it, using a credit card.

Once the prints arrived, he planned to take them to a local business and have all ten mounted and framed. He didn't know if Katherine would ever visit his home, but if she did he didn't want her to think that he was a total putz when it came to art.

By the time I'm done, this place will look like a museum.

In the bathroom, he tossed into a wicker hamper his briefs and T-shirt, his usual sleep gear. Then he checked himself out in the mirror. He still had the athletic build, though he could no longer imagine fending off tacklers to throw a pass to a wide receiver.

Not bad for a man his age, he knew that, but he also knew that he could stand to lose a little weight.

He ran cold tap water into a glass and opened a paper sack that bore the emblem of a local drugstore. He removed the contents, examining each bottle before opening it and putting it down on the sink. Multivitamins. Vitamin E. Vitamin B-complex. He took a pill from each bottle and gulped them down with a swig of water.

Katherine was his reason for taking the vitamins. When the time came for their relationship to get physical—and after seeing her naked, he sincerely hoped it would be soon, for she literally took his breath away—he wanted to have his energy at a high level.

Later, on the way to the office, he thought about Katherine. Two or three times he had nightmares about that day in the office when he told her she needed to see another therapist. In the nightmares, the door always burst open to reveal police officers in riot gear, shouting at him, ordering him to put his hands in the air or else. In each dream, he was cuffed and taken away, leaving Katherine alone in the office.

Silly dreams he told himself as he entered his office building. *Freudians would say that I have consciousness of guilt—and they'd probably be right. But what difference does it make? I did the right thing by terminating the sessions.*

When he entered his office, he saw that his 9 o'clock appointment was already there. He wished he had a private entrance to his office. He hated to parade himself through the waiting room each time he arrived or departed. He nodded at the couple waiting to see him and he stopped to pick up his telephone messages from his secretary.

"I'll be with you in a minute," he said to the couple, quickly disappearing into his inner office.

The couple nodded, each of them nervously thumbing through a magazine without reading the contents or even looking at the pictures.

Jason hurriedly went through his telephone messages. Nothing there from Katherine. There was no reason for her to call him. He'd just hoped that she would. He put the messages aside and picked up the telephone and punched in Katherine's number.

"Hello."

"Hi, it's Jason."

"Good morning. I was just thinking about you."

"Really?"

"Yes, I was thinking that I'm glad you didn't have a heart attack when you saw me zoned out on the floor."

Jason laughed. "It was a close call. In case that happens again, have you been certified to resuscitate?"

"Just what I've seen on television. Any resuscitation I performed would strictly be experimental."

"But greatly appreciated."

"Let's not let it happen again, okay?"

There was a slight edge to her voice, so he knew he should back away.

"I do apologize for storming your island. It won't happen again. I promise."

"Thanks."

"Speaking of the island—are the natives restless today?"

"Bessie has been pawing at the door to get outside."

"And you?"

"I'm sitting here with a giant mug of coffee, looking out the window at the river. I'm pretty content I must say."

"That's too bad. I was hoping you'd be a little on the restless side so that I could take you to dinner tonight."

"Thanks for the invitation, but I'm doing something with a friend tonight."

"Oh," he said, his voice trailing off.

There was an awkward pause before Katherine said, "But if you're free Saturday night, I'd love to do something with you."

"Oh, sure—that would be great. Why don't we get together late in the afternoon and have a picnic dinner somewhere out on the river?"

"I think that would be just wonderful."

"Is 4 o'clock too early?"

"No, that will be fine—see you then."

She started to hang up, but then caught herself, half-laughing, "I'll meet you at the boathouse."

"See you then."

Jason hung up the telephone, his heart racing. Katherine excited him more than any woman he'd ever known. Was that a good thing? Or was that a bad thing? He wasn't sure. In every relationship, one partner cares more than the other, even if only by a fraction. In his previous relationships, he was always more comfortable when it was the woman who cared the most. That wasn't the case with Katherine, and he knew it.

Jason called his secretary on the intercom. "Send them in, please."

He opened their file and glanced through it as they entered the office and sat in chairs directly across from his desk. Man on the left. Woman on the right.

Bob and Judy Wright were all wrong for each other. Sometimes two wrongs make a right, but not in this instance. Judy was much more intelligent than Bob, and that in itself wasn't an issue, though it contributed to what was at issue—Bob's extreme jealousy. Since Judy was more intelligent, she had more varied interests than Bob, which led her to form a wide variety of friendships, all related to her interests.

Jason addressed Judy first. "How are you and Bob doing today?"

"Not worth a damn," said Bob, his voice tinged with anger.

"Bob, I was speaking to Judy."

Bob grimaced but held his tongue.

"Not worth a damn," Judy said.

"See!" exclaimed Bob. "That's exactly what I said."

Jason ignored Bob. "Why do you say that, Judy?"

"Because he makes me sick! Yesterday I had coffee with a friend from work. A male friend. When we walked out of the restaurant, Bob was in the parking lot, waiting for us. He caused a big scene and threatened my friend."

"I did not threaten him!"

"You did, too! You shook your fist at him and said you were going to teach him a lesson."

"That's not a threat."

"Yes, it is—and I'm getting sick of this."

"Bob, I have to agree with Judy. That was a threat. Why did you follow them to the restaurant?"

"If your wife went out with another man, wouldn't you follow them?"

Jason ignored the question. "Judy, are you having an affair with your friend?"

"God, no!" she said, her eyes welling with tears. "I love Bob. This is just a guy that I work with. We had coffee together. That's all."

"Did you hear that, Bob? She says she loves you. What makes you think that she's cheating on you?"

"Because she had coffee with that son-of-a-bitch."

"So you think men and women can't have coffee without having sex?"

"If I was having coffee with a woman, it'd be because I was banging her."

Judy seemed incredulous.

"We were having coffee, Bob. C-o-f-f-e-e. We weren't having sex in the restaurant. We didn't have sex before going to the restaurant. And we made no plans to have sex after leaving the restaurant."

Bob grew sullen. "To my way of thinking, if a woman goes out with a man, for any reason, there's sex on somebody's mind."

Jason leaned back in his chair, and put his hands together, fingertips touching. He leveled an intense gaze at Bob, hoping to connect with him at some emotional level.

"Bob, your wife says she loves you. Do you love her?"

"If I didn't I wouldn't have married her."

"But do you love her?"

"She's got eyes. I work hard, bring home a solid paycheck. I buy her everything she wants. What more is there?"

"I think she wants to know if you love her."

Bob avoided looking at Judy. Instead, he engaged Jason in a stare-down. "Why do you keep asking me that? You trying to make me say something stupid?"

"It's a simple question, Bob. Do you love your wife?"

"I was willing to fight for her. Doesn't that say it all?"

Then something happened that made Jason remember why he hated doing couples therapy. Judy reached over and put her hand on top of Bob's hand.

"You do love me, don't you?" she said, smiling.

"Hell, what do you think?"

Judy leaned over and put her arms around Bob's neck, prompting Bob to wink at Jason, a manipulative gesture that celebrated his victory over the therapist. Bob shook his head in dismay. Therapists dislike couples therapy because all too often one of the partners subverts the process by giving in to the other partner. Judy was the perfect victim, and Bob understood that all too well. Despite Jason's best effort, their life would remain chaotic until Bob either killed Judy or decided to leave her for another woman.

The phrase, "but I love him," was one that made him cringe with disgust. Some women are so much in love with love, and so riddled with self-doubt about their capacity to be loved, that they can't distinguish potentially dangerous behavior from loving behavior. In Judy's mind, if Bob was abusive to her, it was her fault, not his.

Judy said, "Dr. Montclair, I'm not sure we need therapy anymore."

"Yes," chimed in Bob. "You usually bring up all the issues we try to forget, and we end up fighting on the way home. I think you do us more harm than good."

"Perhaps we should review your treatment plan and talk about our goals."

"Sure," said Judy, getting up from her chair. "We'll be in touch."

She reached out to shake hands with him. He took her hand, not certain what to say. "You are a wonderful therapist," she said. "We never would have worked this out without you."

"Call me if you need me," he said, thinking *I'll never see these two again.*

Bob leered at him, but said nothing as they walked out the door.

With forty-five minutes to kill before his next appointment, Jason removed his coat and loosened his tie and dropped to the floor to do push-ups. He wanted to firm up before his date with Katherine. He tried to focus his thoughts on her, but that was impossible since all he could think about was Bob and Judy and all the couples like them.

Very seldom did couples therapy ever result in everyone living happily ever after. Sometimes the goal was to engineer a civil parting for the couple. Other times the goal was keep them focused on their children.

Up and down he went.

Five . . . ten . . . fifteen . . .

Huffing and puffing. The grit in the carpet pressed against his flattened palms.

Twenty . . . twenty-five . . .

No one knew better than he the pain that came with relationships. Sometimes the pain was greater for the therapist than it was for the couples seeking help.

Thirty . . . thirty-five . . .

CHAPTER
14

Katherine took her time getting ready, beginning with a long, steaming bath that soothed her muscles and relaxed her from head to foot. She liked everything about a bath—the ripple of the water when she dragged her fingers across the surface, the embracing warmth that held her when she slid far down into the tub, even the occasional drip drip drip of the faucet that challenged the dexterity of her big toe.

She wasn't sure where the phrase "think tank" came from, but it seemed appropriate for her experiences in the tub, since that was where she did most of her serious thinking, often with Bessie curled up on the bathmat.

Some artists paint from instinct alone. Not Katherine. She saw her paintings in her mind's eye in their totality, long before she touched brush to canvas. Many of her paintings were visualized while she was in the tub. She wasn't sure if the people who purchased her paintings and found places of honor for them on their walls were interested in where she obtained the inspiration to do the paintings, or whether it mattered to them that she was naked in a tub of water when the creative energy was released, but it was the truth and that amused her, if no one else.

She was looking forward to visiting Prescott Place. She'd seen photographs of the mansion in the local newspaper, and she'd admired it from the river, but she'd never been inside the building, so she had no idea what to expect. She hoped he wouldn't think her too forward if she asked to sketch the mansion.

When she stepped out of the tub and reached for a towel, Bessie trudged out of the room. For some reason, she didn't like it when Katherine dried off with a towel, nor did she enjoy watching Katherine walk around with no clothes. Apparently, even dogs have their limits when it comes to human behavior.

After she dried off she went into the bedroom and opened her closet. *What does one wear to a mansion?*

She scooted one hanger after another along the rack, looking for something to catch her eye. After much screeching of hangers, a pair of medium-green leather pants caught her eye. She matched the pants with a sleeveless wool shell that was a shade or two lighter than the pants. Then she went to her dresser and took out her favorite nude-colored bra and panties—and she was all set.

After she was dressed, she brushed her hair, adding extra strokes long past the point where they were needed. Thoughts raced through her head like a laser show.

You're nervous—admit it she told herself, though she couldn't figure out whether it was the house or the man, or both. Taylor Prescott wasn't really her type. There was something about him, something vague and mysterious, that grated against her artist sensibilities. She struggled with it, concluding that her problem with him was his obvious—and, yet, legendary—resistance to domestication.

I don't think men who aren't domesticated are bad she argued with herself. *I just think they're not domesticated. Basically, I like them. I think. Maybe not. Who knows?*

Before leaving the house, she put out an extra bowl of water for Bessie in case she tipped one over. She couldn't bear the thought of Bessie being thirsty.

As she left the island, the wind blew through her hair, destroying the work she'd done with the brush, but she didn't care. Hair perfection wasn't something she really aspired to have. She'd brush it again in the car and be done with it.

The boat hit a rough patch and jolted her. She glanced back over her shoulder at her house and felt a fleeting chill, as if she were leaving something important behind.

* * *

The trappings of wealth were undeniable. She turned into a circular driveway and pulled her black Jeep SUV up behind Taylor's Mercedes-Benz, with its top still down. Parked in view at the side of the house were a vintage Mercedes-Benz limo and a silver Maserati GT, a beautifully designed car with a 450 horsepower, V-8 engine.

She got out of her Jeep and walked toward the door, surprised to see it open while she was still twenty feet away. Framed in the doorway was Taylor, wearing a white silk shirt and cream wool pants. He looked like he has just stepped off the cover of GQ magazine's country-squire edition. He glanced at his watch and smiled broadly.

"I see that you're fashionably late by one minute. I'm impressed. How on earth did you manage that?"

She didn't tell him that she'd arrived in town early and spent the last ten minutes parked on a side street, glancing at her watch every minute or two. Instead, she said, "Precision planning—I had to calculate the river currents, air speed and traffic probabilities. I'm glad you're impressed."

As she walked past him into the foyer, he noted the way her leather pants fit and he remarked, "That shade green really makes your hair look terrific."

Misdirection. The key to seduction.

"Thank you," she said, smiling, knowing full well that it was the pants that got his attention. "But I'm afraid my hair got blasted on the boat ride over."

"If that's the case, blasted is my new favorite hair style for women."

Taylor led her into the den and motioned toward her painting, adding, "It's my favorite of all the paintings in the house."

She walked over and looked at the painting, an incredulous look on her face.

"This is the painting you told me about that you've had for several years?"

"The one and only."

All guys lie she thought. *At least this one lied in a supportive way. She could forgive him for that.*

Taylor said, "I've never seen a more beautiful sunset."

"It was difficult to turn it loose."

Katherine turned and looked about the room, her jaw dropping when she spotted the Picasso. She hurried over to the painting so that she could get a better look.

"Is this for real?" she asked.

"You tell me. You're the expert."

Katherine couldn't believe her eyes.

"This has got to be the best-kept secret in town. Who knows that this painting is here?"

"My friends."

"Amazing. It's simply beautiful" Another painting caught her eye and she gravitated to yet another wall. This time it was a Salvador Dali original, a fish in a red bowl. She moved over a few feet and spotted a Marc Chagall painting of a violin.

"This is unbelievable," she said. "You have a fortune in artwork, just in this room. "Did you acquire all of them yourself?"

"I bought the Picasso. The Dali is a gift from my father. The Chagall came with the house."

"Aren't you afraid someone might steal them?"

"Not really. There's always someone at the house. I've never had any problems."

Katherine stepped out into the center of the room and whirled around like a young child, her arms outstretched. "I feel like I'm in Heaven."

"I'm glad they make you happy."

Taylor wasn't all that much of an art fan. He viewed his paintings more as investments than priceless works of art. He'd never tell Katherine that, of course. He was pretty sure now that he'd found the way to her heart, a potential use of the paintings that never occurred to him when he acquired them. That was what he most liked about having wealth—the way it continuously generated pleasant surprises.

They sat of the sofa and attempted to maintain a conversation, but Katherine had a difficult time taking her eyes away from the paintings. Taylor felt the same way about her, so the long pauses during which she looked longingly at the paintings and he looked longingly at her were not all that awkward.

"Do you go to Ottawa often?" he asked.

"Not really," she said. "I mainly go to do business with the galleries. Or to attend the theatre or the odd symphony concert."

"Next time you go, give me a call and I'll show you some places I bet you've never seen."

"Like what?"

"I'd rather it be a surprise."

"I like surprises."

Taylor looked at her moist, parted lips, which wore only a hint of pink lipstick, the sparkle in her eyes, and there was nothing he wanted more than to take her in his arms, but he kept his distance. His philosophy was that men should wait until the woman makes a move, however subtle.

"Have you done any self-portraits?"

"I'm working on one now."

"I would love to see it when it's finished."

"It may go straight into the closet."

"Why do you say that?"

"Indians don't like to have their photographs taken because they feel that it captures their soul. I'm sort of the same way about my work. I put myself into my paintings, too much so sometimes. If I have a sentimental attachment to a painting, it's difficult sometimes to turn loose of it. That sunset is a good example. I painted it after a very emotional day and to me it represents more than simply a setting sun."

"So what does your self-portrait represent?"

Katherine laughed.

"You might say it is the essential me, with everything of dubious value stripped away."

"Sounds intriguing."

Katherine flushed somewhat. "Now I wish I hadn't brought it up."

"Will you promise that if you decide to sell it, you'll give me first crack at it?"

"I'll think about it."

Their line of thought was interrupted by one of the cooks who politely stepped into the den to announce that dinner was ready.

Taylor escorted her into the dinner room, an enormous space that had the high-ceiled ambiance of a medieval castle. Tapestries punctuated the walls and in the center of the room was a twenty-foot mahogany dining table, polished to a high gloss. Taylor seated her to the right of the head of the table, a position he took for himself.

For Katherine this was becoming something like an out-of-body experience. She was a sophisticated woman, who had dined at some of the best restaurants in the world, but lately she had not wanted to leave the island.

Basically, when she was at home, she was a barbecue and chips kind of woman. Nothing fancy. The idea of driving her Jeep to a private home in her hometown to dine in a house as magnificent as Prescott Place had never occurred to her as a possibility. It all had a dream-like quality to it, as if she were a child playing dress-up.

They began dinner with caviar and champagne, the bubbles tickling her nose, and then quickly moved on to a clear, wild-mushroom soup. The main course was a spit roast, served with potato gratin, a butternut squash puree, and Belgian endive with beets and apple, served with a walnut and sherry vinaigrette.

"This is delicious," said Katherine. "Where did you get the recipes?"

"From a restaurant in Washington, D.C. owned by Chef Nora Pools. I had this meal at the restaurant a year or so ago, and when I asked Nora for the recipes for each dish, she didn't hesitate at all. My cooks are wonderful. I bring home new recipes for them all the time."

For dessert, they shared a slice of chocolate almond cake with a hot chocolate glaze. They dug into the cake, miniature chunks of chocolate speared on their forks and then twirled in the glaze, heads leaned over the dish, almost touching, the sweet scent of her making his heart race, the nearness of him intimidating and yet welcome at the same instant, more laughter than conversation, so that by the time they finished dessert and returned to the den, she was in his arms and they were kissing with a passion that she had not felt in a very long time.

At one point, seeking air, she gently pushed him away, saying "I'm not ready for this, I don't think."

CHAPTER
15

This time, when she looked at her self portrait, it somehow looked different. She worked on the shoulders and upper arms of the person she saw coming to life on canvas. Was it possible to paint a self-portrait and have it evolve into someone else?

She wasn't certain if the image was a reflection of her or a reflection of a woman she didn't really know. Was it her imagination? Did the woman in the image hold herself differently? Was her body leaner, more athletic? Are we ever who we think we are? Not hardly, she concluded. *That's the source of my difficulty*, she thought. *I am who my lover thinks I am . . . but my lover no longer exists.*

There is magic in an artist's strokes. The moving hand sometimes has a mind of its own, bolstering the argument that there is randomness to truth. Katherine always knew that when she made a design mistake that should be corrected, especially proportional miscalculations, but she seldom recognized the deeper truth in her work, other than when the finished product made her feel good about herself.

Canvaswoman had a mind of her own. She sat quietly as Katherine toned her arms and squared her shoulders, but when the brush moved to her buttocks, the extra-fine brush bristles tickling her skin, she flinched, eliciting a frustrated "damn" from Katherine as she worked to correct the mistake.

She heard a scratch on the window pane.

Oh, no, she thought. *Not again!*

She turned and saw a sparrow, its tiny feet gripping the wood, its head cocked in her direction, its eye round and reflective of light from some unknown source. The bird watched her with one eye and then it flicked its head and watched her with the other eye.

Was the bird trying to communicate with her? If so, what was its message? Even from the distance, she could see the bird's throat throbbing with a pulse beat ten times faster than her own.

She looked about the room, verifying that she was alone, and then she spoke to the bird, saying, "What? What is it that you want?"

She and the bird swapped gazes, the bird's eye without emotion, unlike her own. There was an odd sensation on her cheek. She wiped it with her hand and found a falling tear. At the precise instant that she looked back at the bird, it fluttered and was gone.

Katherine put her brush on the easel, gently. Then she turned loose of whatever emotional ledge she clung to and she had herself a really good cry. She felt like a butterfly emerging from the safety of a cocoon, only to find a topsy-turvy world she didn't recognize or completely understand.

She cried and cried and cried.

Ever since the day she'd met Roger, she felt safe. Now, without him—the only knight in shining armor she'd ever known—and without Dedi, one of the most perfect children who ever lived, she felt threatened, but from what she wasn't entirely certain. The threats against her wellbeing seemed vague, unrealistic, nothing she could put her finger on, just a slow-burning sense of something not being exactly right.

Bessie ambled into the room and sat on her hind haunches, looking at Katherine, her facial expression providing no clue about what she saw.

"Hey, girl—you come to keep me company?"

Bessie wagged her tail and stretched out on the floor, where the cool tiles always felt good against her belly.

Suddenly, the telephone rang. The caller ID said "unavailable."

She answered anyway. "Hello."

"It's me, Taylor."

"Good to hear from you." Katherine's voice sounded upbeat. "I was just thinking about you."

"Really—dare I ask in what capacity?"

"Nothing in particular."

She couldn't tell him the truth, that she was crying because of him . . . *or was it because of her? She wasn't certain.*

"Just wondering if you saw how blue the river is today?"

"As a matter of fact, that's why I called. I did notice. And I wondered if you might want to go out in my boat with me to scout some locations to paint."

"Ordinarily, I'd love to. But I've got a friend coming over."

"That's too bad. I'm sure there will be other blue-water days."

"I'll write a note and post it on my fridge—'call Taylor when the water turns blue again.'"

Taylor laughed. "I bet you will."

Katherine felt sort of offended. She was serious. "I will—I promise."

Katherine's telephone beeped, the signal that she had an incoming call.

"I've got another call," she explained. "Let me grab it and take a number."

"Okay."

Katherine double-clicked.

"Hello."

Jason seemed to start in mid-sentence. Right to the point.

"I'm here," he said, "with enough food to feed a pair of river rats."

"Oh, hi Jason. I'll pick you up in just a minute."

"Can't wait."

Katherine flipped back to Taylor.

"I'm sorry, but my friend is here. I need to go."

"Oh," there was genuine disappointment in his voice. "Well, how about if I pick you up for brunch tomorrow. Sunday brunch at the Hampton is always good."

"That sounds great."

"I'll pick you up at noon."

"Great—I'll see you then."

Katherine clicked off her phone and hurried upstairs where she undressed, tossing her clothing every which way. Bessie was right behind her, thinking that an adventure was in the making. If Katherine moved quickly like that, it usually was a good omen for Bessie. Road trip.

Katherine put on a clean pair of jeans, a white T-shirt, and white tennis shoes without socks. She was good to go. She went into the bathroom and brushed her teeth. Then she hurriedly brushed her hair, all without looking into the mirror to see if she got it right. She was on automatic pilot.

Then it was downstairs, with Bessie at her heels, locking up the house and running, her long legs stretching out like those of a long-distance runner, all the way to the dock, where she leaped into the boat and caught Bessie in mid-air, when it looked as if she might miss the boat and fall into the water.

On the way to the boathouse, the air flowing through her hair, Katherine wondered if she ever again would have time to paint. The only good thing about it was that it left her very little time to feel sorry for herself, except for feeling guilty over not getting her work done.

Men are nice she thought *except when you wake up and they are gone. My work awaits me every morning, the perfect companion in an uncertain world.*

As she entered the inlet where the boathouse was located, the wind suddenly blew off, leaving behind a sudden stillness, the boat's motor her only distraction. She throttled down and coasted into the dock.

Jason was nowhere to be seen. The silhouette of a cat moved into the shadows, prompting Bessie to protest with her anti-cat bark, leaping from the boat onto the dock, closely followed by Katherine's command, "Bessie, no—come back!"

Bessie didn't come back. She ran out the door and into the bright sunlight. Without bothering to tie off the boat, Katherine jumped up onto the dock in hot pursuit. When she burst into the sunlight the cat was nowhere to be seen, but Bessie was there, playfully jumping up on Jason. Katherine was shocked. Roger was the only man she'd ever taken to. Now here she was behaving as if Jason was her best friend.

"Bessie, don't *ever* do that again!" she scolded.

Bessie ignored her, so happy was she to see Jason.

"Don't be too hard on her," said Jason, smiling. Then he spoke baby-talk to her, "You're a good girl, aren't you?" Unseen by Katherine, he slipped Bessie a liver treat, a gesture that caused her to grin ear to ear.

With the dog crisis averted, Jason and Katherine hugged, not passionately, more like second cousins, something that was not lost on Jason, who was becoming more and more tormented over the possibility that Katherine did not share his feelings.

"You ready for a fun-packed outing?" he asked.

"Very ready," she answered cheerfully. "But I'm not sure how long I'll be able to last."

"Why's that?"

'I was up late last night and didn't get much sleep."

"Working on that painting?"

"No, I took a trip to Tahiti."

Is it possible to be cruel to a man if he doesn't know that you are being cruel to him? *Why did I say that? s*he thought, overcome by a sick feeling in the pit of her stomach. *Am I feeling some unrecognized hostility toward him? God, I hope not.*

"So you were dreaming. Good for you."

"Yeah, good for me."

Her voice was without sarcasm, but her thoughts were laced with that type of sarcasm that accompanies self-loathing. If she were Catholic, she'd want to delay the picnic long enough for her to go to confession.

Jason went to his car and retrieved a picnic basket and an ice cooler that he'd filled with beer. Bessie watched his every move, ever hopeful of another treat.

"What's for dinner?" asked Katherine.

When he answered, his voice was hardly filled with self-confidence.

"I wasn't sure what would be appropriate, so I picked up a couple of deli sandwiches, some grapes and cheese, a roasted chicken and a couple of bags of chips."

"And what's in the cooler?"

"Beer."

"Lots of it—and I brought a bottle of wine in case you didn't want beer."

"Looks like you've thought of everything."

Jason knew better than that. He was overeager. He just didn't know what else to do. His greatest fear was that, socially, he never progressed past college, at least where women were concerned.

They loaded the picnic basket and the cooler into the boat, along with Bessie, and slowly backed out of the boathouse. Katherine reached down beneath the console and pulled out a dog's life preserver. She tossed it to Jason.

"Would you mind putting that on Bessie?"

Jason looked surprised. "Are you serious?"

"Yes, of course I'm serious."

"I've never seen a dog on the river with a life preserver, but I'm game." He paused, looking up at Katherine. "Wait a minute—does Bessie want a life preserver?"

"Probably not. Don't worry. She won't bite you."

Jason reluctantly fitted the life preserve onto Bessie, who obediently complied, her head hung with resignation. Nonetheless she glared at the two of them with daggers in her eyes, daring them to even attempt an additional indignity.

The river was remarkably calm. The boat skimmed across the water, occasionally bobbing in the wake of other boaters.

"Where do you want to go?" shouted Katherine, above the roar of the boat's motor.

Jason leaned forward, almost touching her face, shouting back into the wind, "Rock Island Lighthouse!"

Katherine smiled. "Good choice . . . would you like to pilot the boat?"

Jason nodded and took over the wheel.

Katherine moved to the back of the boat, where she sat with Bessie and gazed out at the river, seeing sights she'd never before seen, though she had passed this spot hundreds of times. The river was like that.

Always changing.

Always providing a new perspective.

She watched Jason, his eyes scanning the river, his head moving left to right and then back again. Jason was the protective type and she found that very endearing. She whispered into Bessie's ear, "See—Jason is being very careful. He won't let anything happen to us."

When they arrived at Rock Island, the sun was still an hour or so from setting. The original name was Bush Island, when it was sold to the United States government in 1847. The lighthouse was built that year to help control traffic on the river.

After they tied off at the small dock, Jason said, "You're an illegal, you know."

"You plan on turning me in?"

"Technically, it is illegal for you to step foot on the island without a temporary visa from the immigration department."

"So your plan is what—to get me locked up in New York, so that you can get a government contract to provide me with therapy?"

"Never thought of that. That's an excellent idea."

Katherine unfastened Bessie's life preserver and she jumped onto the dock and disappeared into the shrubbery surrounding the lighthouse.

Jason lifted the picnic basket and the cooler onto the dock. He looked over to the side of the lighthouse.

"There's a picnic table over there. Does that look like a good place to you?"

"I've got a better idea," said Katherine. She rummaged through a storage cabinet and withdrew a blanket. "Let's eat on the grass, over there on the hill."

"That looks perfect."

They spread the blanket out across the grass, after which Jason opened the cooler and looked inside.

"Still plenty of ice in there. What will it be? An ice-cold beer—or a glass of merlot?"

"Let's go with the wine."

Jason closed the lid on the cooler, the disappointment barely showing on his face. He pulled a bottle and a corkscrew from the basket and opened the wine. Then he unwrapped two wine glasses from a neatly rolled towel and poured the wine.

"What should we toast?" he asked, his glass poised in midair.

Katherine thought a moment and then answered, "To the wonders of psychology."

That wasn't what Jason wanted her to say, but it was better than nothing.

"Cheers," he said, and clinked his glass against hers.

After they finished off the deli sandwiches and nibbled on the chips, Katherine plucked a grape and pressed it to his lips, surprising him so that it took a moment for him to realize that he was supposed to open his mouth.

"You're supposed to eat it, not kiss it," Katherine kidded.

"Oh," he said, taken aback.

They stretched out on the blanket, propped on their elbows so that they could watch the river traffic. No one said a word for at least fifteen minutes. There was no need to speak—the moment was good, even without conversation. That was one thing that Katherine really liked about Jason. She felt no need to constantly entertain him. If she didn't say anything, he didn't seem to feel a need to fill the void.

Bessie curled up on the blanket between them and put her head down.

A piece of driftwood, about the size of a 1955 Buick, floated toward the island. The driftwood had branches on it, with leaves that fluttered in the wind. Seeing it sent a chill up Katherine's arms. It was large enough to sink a good-sized boat. Large enough to ruin lives. The driftwood veered to the left and for a while she thought it would glide past the lighthouse and into a heavily traveled channel, but at the last minute it jutted back to the right and lodged on the rocks that encircled the lighthouse.

Katherine settled back into a more comfortable revelry. Finally, she turned and looked around and said, "It's odd that I've never painted this lighthouse."

"I think you should."

"I could include Bessie."

"Would I be in the picture?"

He said it quickly, using a tone of voice that in ordinary circumstances would have been recognized by her at once; in ordinary circumstances she might even have comprehended the meaning of it. But not now—these weren't ordinary circumstances and she didn't have the presence of mind to hear the self-mocking implication of his question, so her thoughts took another direction.

"I could put you in the lighthouse," she teased.

"You mean at the very top where my light could shine on thousands?"

"No . . . I was thinking more about placing you inside the lighthouse."

"Oh. I see."

"You know, there but unseen. Like the Wizard of Oz."

For no reason that he could think of, then or any day since, he reached over and took her in his arms, kissing her gently on the lips. She fell into a more passionate kiss, losing herself in the strength of his arms, the warmness of his touch, slipping away into something comfortable until she realized what was happening. She withdrew from him, gently pushing against his chest. Her touch was light as a feather, but to him it had the oppressiveness of a ton of bricks.

"Now is not a good time for this," she said, speaking with tenderness. "I'm just not ready. You understand, don't you?"

"I understand," he said, but he didn't really.

CHAPTER
16

Katherine sat on a bench near the boathouse. She and Roger had made a children's park out of a stretch of land that extended from the boathouse to the road. Two benches with dark-green wooden slats. A playground with a swing and slide. Dedi loved to play there, and the benches made a convenient waiting area.

Just sitting in the park brought back memories of Dedi. Tiny grasping hands. Boney knees. Scrapped shins. Bare feet running in circles. Laughter, lots of laughter. Cries of "Mommie, look at this!" Better days played inside her head, sometimes rewinding and playing again and again.

The park and boathouse were on a valuable piece of land, and she'd received several impressive offers after word got out about Roger's death, but she needed the boathouse for as long as she lived on the island, and that would probably be for the rest of her life. She couldn't imagine ever leaving.

For brunch with Taylor, she wore her favorite dress—a rust matte-jersey halter dress, with matching sandals, an outfit that emphasized her elegant, toned arms and shoulders. She leaned over and touched the smoothness of her bare legs and smiled. She was most comfortable when she was in her studio in jeans and T-shirt, but dressing up and looking good brought out both the little girl and the mature woman in her.

If men understood that concept, a woman's complicated need to be both woman and child, relationships would not always be so precarious, or so she thought.

She was holding up her feet, checking out her toenails, when her solitude was broken by the sound of a 450 horsepower Maserati GT. She looked up to see Taylor shifting down to navigate the steep incline down to her parking lot. Through the windshield she could see his smiling face.

Katherine got to her feet, a broad smile on her face.

Taylor stopped the Maserati and got out of the car. He had on an off-gray one-button, single-breasted jacket with peaked lapels and besom pockets, with matching pants, and an ivory dress shirt opened at the collar. Katherine liked his casual way of being dressy. It seemed to reflect a deeper level of thought.

"Good morning," he said cheerfully, walking toward her.

"Technically it's afternoon." She glanced at her watch. "We left the morning sphere three minutes ago."

"Oh, so you're going to be like that, are you?"

He put his arms around her and kissed her lightly on the lips.

"I am what I am," she said.

"Yes, indeed," he said, admiring her dress. "You look like you're ready to walk down the red carpet. I think you've missed your calling."

"I'm afraid the closest I ever came to the red carpet was when I was ten and a boy named Oscar pulled my hair in class."

"The fiend!"

"Things worked out. I once did a painting that required a little boy with a bully's face. I used my recollection of Oscar."

"Ouch—you take no prisoners."

"Don't ever forget that," she laughed.

Taylor opened the passenger door for her and she slid onto the plush leather seat. "Nice," she said running her fingers across the soft leather. "Very comfortable."

After he turned around and drove back up the hill to the road, he apologized for being late. "Actually, I was about ten minutes early, but I came upon an accident and stopped to help out."

"Oh, that's terrible—was anyone hurt?"

Taylor frowned. "I'm afraid so. The driver of one of the cars involved, a man in his mid-twenties, was killed."

Katherine pondered that grim scenario for a moment. Then she broke into a broad smile. "You had me there for a minute."

"What do you mean?"

"I mean, I believed you."

Taylor looked sincerely surprised.

"You believed me a minute ago. And now you don't?"

"Let's just say that it's one of the best excuses I've ever heard."

"If I'm ever on trial for something I didn't do, I surely wouldn't want you on the jury." He thought about defending his statements—he was not a man who easily tolerated having his integrity impugned, not even by a beautiful woman—but then he decided to let it go since it'd be more trouble than it was worth. There were other things to talk about.

The Hampton was one of the oldest, most tasteful restaurants in the region. Housed in a nineteenth century, two-storey stone house, it was furnished with turn-of-the-century cherry furniture that was understated in its presence but not in its impact. Crystal light fixtures, silver tableware and goblets, and luxurious curtains befitting royalty, all helped to generate a dining experience that appealed to all the senses.

Taylor and Katherine were escorted to a small private dining room on the second floor, where they had a private window overlooking the river. "It's beautiful," said Katherine as she was being seated. "I've never eaten here, but I've always wanted to."

The waiter, who was extremely polite and solicitous, took their orders with a minimum of dialog, encouraged perhaps by Taylor's stern unwillingness to hear the waiter's dramatic rendition of the "special of the day."

The waiter had only been gone for a few minutes, when a boisterous man in khaki pants and shirt sleeves burst into the room, obviously out of breath. He wore a hat that was peppered with dust.

"I'm sorry to bother you, sir," he said, panting. "But I wanted to get a statement from you about the accident."

Taylor looked at Katherine.

"Have you met Ed Bradley from the *Brockville News.*"

"I don't think I have," she said, extending her hand to him.

The reporter took off his hat and shook her hand, speaking rapidly, "I'll be out of here in a second. I just need to get a comment from you before deadline. Your assistant, Todd, told me that I could find you here."

"There was a photographer at the accident. I spoke to her and I thought . . ."

"Oh, she was just getting information for the caption. She's not authorized to interview you about the accident."

"Very well."

"Just so I have it straight. You came along right after the accident. You didn't witness it, did you?"

"That's correct."

"You pulled the man out of the car and saw that he was dead . . ."

"Yes."

"Then you pulled the woman out onto the road, and you saw that she wasn't breathing . . ."

"Yes."

"And you administered artificial resuscitation?"

"Yes, I did."

"How did it make you feel when she started breathing again?"

"I think you can imagine how I felt."

"Everyone I interviewed at the scene called you a hero."

"How do you feel about that?"

"I did what anyone else would have done."

The reporter stuffed his notepad in his back pocket. "Thanks for the interview. I apologize for interrupting your lunch."

"No problem," said Taylor.

Then the reporter was gone.

Katherine looked at Taylor in amazement.

"I feel like a fool." She touched his hand. "Will you forgive me, please?"

Taylor grinned with smug satisfaction. It couldn't possibly have worked out better for him. If relationships were poker, he just laid down a straight flush.

"There's nothing to forgive. My story did sound outlandish, didn't it?"

They both had a good laugh over it and quickly put it out of mind.

*   *   *

They were having coffee when Taylor asked her the question that he'd held back all through brunch. "I know this is short notice, but I have a really big favor to ask of you."

"What's that?" she asked.

"The Governor General is having a luncheon tomorrow for Prince Harry and his lovely wife Meghan. I would be so flattered if you would be kind enough to be my date."

"What? What did you just say?"

"I'm asking you to go to lunch with me at the Governor General's residence in Ottawa. Would that pose a problem for you?"

"Are you serious? That's nearly a two-hour drive . . . I have nothing to wear."

"I've taken care of everything. I have a dress in the car that will be perfect for you. I had Todd ask the owner of LePaul's to open her shop yesterday. I described you to her and she made several suggestions and I chose the gown that best captures your elegance. Todd brought it to me yesterday."

Katherine wasn't quite sure what to say. Stunned, certainly. Angry at the short notice, no doubt about it. But mostly she was flattered and dazzled by Taylor's grand vision of her as a woman. She leaned across the table and kissed him on the cheek.

"I'd love to go to the luncheon with you. It sounds like it will be a wonderful experience."

"Phew!" he said, making a faux wiping gesture across his brow. "I was afraid I had overstepped. I'd glad you want to go."

Katherine looked at him with what Taylor recognized as an adoring gaze.

"What I don't understand is why you have never stumbled into marriage."

Taylor laughed. "Oh, I came close a couple of times. But, in the end, there was always something about the relationship that wasn't right for me. When I get married, I want it to be forever. I don't believe in starter marriages."

"Your sincerity is very appealing."

"As a servant of the people, I have nothing if I don't have sincerity."

"So true."

They looked out the window at a bright-red British tanker headed west. It was larger than some of the islands in the river. Katherine drifted away in her thoughts for a moment; returning, she said, "I have a question to ask you and I'm not sure if it's proper for me to ask it or not, but I'm going to do it anyway."

"I'd expect nothing less than that from you."

"Are you dating anyone now . . . ?"

Taylor reached for her hand and held it with both of his hands. He could have told her the truth—that he was seeing an Asian actress in Toronto, and a blonde lawyer in Montreal—but to what end? He didn't know how he felt about those women. He wasn't even sure about how he felt about Katherine. She excited him more than any other woman. He wanted to tell her that in the hopes that she would understand that is all anyone can ask from a relationship, but the simple fact that she asked the question was indication enough that she didn't want to know the truth.

Instead, he looked her squarely in the eyes and said, "I don't have a lot of time for dating . . . but, to answer your question, no—I have eyes only for you."

* * *

As soon as they pulled into the parking lot at the boathouse, Katherine turned and looked into the abbreviated backseat of the Maserati GT and—seeing nothing—said, "Okay, where is it?"

"Where is what?"

"The dress, silly."

"Oh, the dress."

Taylor laughed and got out, with Katherine practically leaping from the passenger seat to join him at the rear of the car. He opened the trunk and lifted out a gift box and handed it to her. "Hope you like it."

Katherine put the box on the rear of the car and opened it. She tried not to gasp when she pulled the tissue paper aside and looked inside, but she made one of those involuntary sounds that occasionally slip out during moments of sudden happiness.

"Unbelievable," she said, lifting a silvery gown from the box.

The gown was made of a form-fitting clingy fabric and had a hemline that she knew would fall an inch or so below her knees. It had thin straps that highlighted a moderately cut bodice. She looked at the label. Gucci!

"Oh, you shouldn't have done this!" she said.

She peered over into the box and saw a pair of black shoes with two-inch heels. Again, Gucci.

"This is too much! You must have paid a fortune for this!"

"I wanted you to look nice for the Prince."

"But how did you know my sizes?"

"Todd is a genius at figuring out those things."

She put the dress back into the box and hung her arms around his neck, kissing him on the mouth, lingering, but then gently biting him on the lip as she withdrew.

"I'm glad you like the dress . . ."

"Believe me, 'like' is an understatement."

" . . . be that as it may, I have something to ask of you."

"What's that?"

"I'd like to see your new painting—the self-portrait."

"Right now?"

"Right now."

Katherine hadn't planned on him going to the island with her. And she certainly hadn't planned on showing him the portrait. Ever. Under the best of circumstances, she was reluctant to show her work before it was finished. Sometimes, even after it was finished, she held it for years before she allowed anyone to see it.

What was she to do? He'd given her the most fabulous dress she'd ever seen. He'd be terribly offended if she didn't allow him to see her work. She had to show him. There was no other choice.

When they arrived at the house and opened the door, Bessie was beside herself with happiness over seeing Katherine. She jumped up on her and made this half-squeal, half-bark sound that Katherine had never heard come from any other dog.

But when Bessie spotted Taylor, who by then was reaching out to pet her, she backed away, not barking at him, but not especially glad to see him, either.

Seeing the way Bessie reacted to Taylor, Katherine said, "Don't you be grumpy to our guest. Give Taylor a proper greeting."

Bessie reluctantly approached him and sat on her back haunches and lifted her paw for him to shake. He did—and then he petted her on top of the head, a gesture that Bessie wiggled away from, slowly backing away until she was on the other side of the room. Said Taylor: "She loves me—she just doesn't know it yet."

With obvious hesitancy, Katherine led Taylor into her studio. The first thing he saw after entering the room was an easel shrouded with a piece of fabric.

"That it?" he asked.

"Yes," she said, walking ahead of him so that she would get to the painting first. "But there's something I need to explain."

"Okay."

"It's not a traditional self portrait."

"What is it—one of those cubist, modern renderings."

"No, it's not like that at all."

Taylor waited for her to uncover the painting.

Instead, she stood staring at him, as if she expected him to do something first.

"Am I missing something here?" he asked.

"No—I'm just building up nerve to show you."

"Please show it to me. What's the worst thing that can happen?"

"The worst thing is that you will want it."

"What?"

Finally, she reached out and snatched the cloth from the painting.

Taylor's eyes said it all. He walked closer to the painting, obviously totally in love with it. "I certainly don't have to ask who that is."

"It's unfinished."

"I can see that. But I also can see your exquisite features. You're right about one thing."

"What's that."

"I've got to have that painting."

"I was afraid of that."

"That's a good thing, isn't it? I mean, that I want it."

"It's a very good thing. But I don't know if I will want to part with it. I've never painted a nude of myself."

"You should do nothing else but—so how much do you want for it?"

"It's not for sale. If you ever see the painting finished, it will because I want you to see it. Let me think about it. I would never sell it to you. But I'll consider giving it to you."

She paused, a mischievous smile in place.

"Unless, of course, Prince Harry wants it. Then it's every man for himself."

"I accept that challenge."

Katherine put the cover back on the painting and invited him to have a drink out on the deck. There was a hint of fall in the air. They kissed. And then they kissed again. In between kisses, he said, "I would love to see the rest of your house."

*　　*　　*

When Katherine awoke she felt that she was someplace that wasn't familiar to her. She looked next to her and saw Taylor, face down, the sheet covering half his body. He was still asleep. She wondered why Bessie wasn't on the floor next to her, but then she remembered. Taylor wasn't comfortable making love with Bessie in the room, so she was banished and the door was closed.

She lay perfectly still, thinking. The room was filled with light. She looked at the digital clock on her nightstand. It read 3:34. It was mid-afternoon on a Sunday, and she'd make love to a man she barely knew.

I'll go to hell for this, for sure.

She turned and watched Taylor as he slept. In some ways, it seemed being next to him was the natural thing to do; in other ways, she felt she'd betrayed the memory of her husband, Roger. She looked at the closed bedroom door, behind which she was certain lay Bessie. Never once during her marriage to Roger did they ever close their bedroom door. It was always open in case Dedi ever cried out to them during the night.

Never once did Dedi ever come into the bedroom while they made love. Never once did she leave her bedroom at night. Never once did they feel the need to isolate themselves from the people—or animals—

120

they loved.   Katherine's head swirled with questions. How do you prepare yourself to move on with your life? Is being with a man a betrayal of the man you were with before him? In her thoughts, she pleaded with Roger for help in understanding her new life.

Send me a message! Please!

She got out of bed and went into the bathroom to get a drink of water. When she returned to the bed, Taylor was stirring. She sat on the edge of the bed and was about to lift her legs onto the sheets when she felt something on her back. She turned and saw Taylor's smiling face, his arm outstretched touching her back. She leaned over and kissed him. Then she asked, "Have you had enough sleep yet?"

"No, I haven't had enough."

"I don't think you're talking about sleep."

They embraced and kissed. Then she rolled over into his arms. For a long while they lay in silence, enjoying the peacefulness of the room and the unceasing sounds of the river outside the windows. Suddenly, he spoke, his voice low and unobtrusive: "Is that your husband?"

The words startled her at first, but then she look at him and followed his gaze to the dresser across the room, where there was a framed photograph of Roger with his arms affectionately folded around her waist.

"Why . . . yes," she said.

"He was a good looking man."

"I think so."

"What was he like?"

"What do you mean?"

"How would you describe him to a stranger?"

Katherine wasn't prepared to discuss her late husband with Taylor, at least not emotionally. Her thoughts stalled. Her stomach tightened.

What would possess him to bring up Roger?

After an awkward pause, she said, "Loving . . . totally honest . . . wonderful father . . . generous."

"I can't even imagine the pain you must have felt."

"Feel, not felt. I've read all the books by the experts and I still don't understand what I've been through. I still hurt. Every day I hurt in some new and unexpected way."

"But you say being in therapy helped."

"Yes, but I really don't want to talk about that."

"I understand."

CHAPTER
17

When he awakened, he was wrapped in a blanket in a dimly lit room. He lifted the blanket and saw that he was naked.

"Hey there!" he called out. "Where is everyone?"

The silence that greeted him had a metallic resonance to it. His bed trembled ever so slightly. He felt as if he was moving, not fast, but moving nonetheless.

"I said, where the hell is everyone?"

He sat on the edge of the bed, the blanket wrapped around him. He felt somewhat dizzy, as if he had been spinning around and around. He touched his fingertips to his forehead and looked at his hand. Specked with blood.

Just then the door opened.

"How you feeling mate?" asked a man dressed in white.

"Where are my clothes?"

"Not to worry. I had them washed and pressed. They should be ready by now."

"And what's the deal with this?" he asked, holding up his bloodied fingertips.

"Oh, that. Our medic looked at your cut and said it was superficial. Nothing to worry about. Now that you're awake there are some questions we'd like to ask you."

"Questions?"

"Yes—there was no identification in your clothing. We need your name and country of origin."

"I have some questions of my own."

"Yes."

"Who the hell are you?"

"Sir, I am Junior Officer Muller."

"I see. Am I in the navy?"

"No sir, I don't think so." He paused a moment, noting the confusion on his face. "Now that you know my name, I need to know your name."

"Name?"

"Yes, if you don't mind."

He looked at the man in white, a hundred disconnected thoughts racing through his mind.

"I don't . . . know . . . I honestly don't know."

"Nothing? You remember nothing?"

"Why am I here?"

"We pulled you out of the river."

"What was I doing in the river?"

"Sir, I really wouldn't know."

"What is the nationality of this ship?"

"South African, sir."

"What is your port of entry?"

"Toronto. Are you American or Canadian?"

"I wish I knew."

"Sir, right now, I would say that you are a man without a country."

CHAPTER
18

Jason really loved his office. He loved it more than he loved his home, which is why he spent more time at his office than he did at his home. His office was located on the ground floor of one of the oldest office buildings in Ogdensburg.

When he first looked at the office space, he was shocked at the barrenness of the rooms. The real estate agent told him that it had been used by a lawyer who went to jail for shoplifting, a doctor who performed illegal abortions, a psychic who helped solve serial murders, and by a televangelist who made so much money that he bought a building of his own on the other side of town.

People told him he was crazy to put so much effort into leased office space, but Jason went all out to create an office that fit his image of what a psychologist's office should look like. No plastic chairs. No decades old magazines on coffee tables. No pictures on the walls of cats with yarn, cartoon ducks or galloping horses.

To make the space his own, he had the hardwood floors refinished and polished to a high gloss. He bought Persian rugs for each office. Then he had the inner and outer offices paneled with polished mahogany. The leather sofas and chairs he chose for the outer office were just a shade darker than beige. He bought several paintings by local artists and very soon after he stopped counseling Katherine Summer, he drove to Ottawa and purchased one of her river scenes, which he hung in the inner office, directly across from his desk. She'd probably never see the painting, but that was okay with him. He bought it for himself, not to please her.

On this day he got to the office a few minutes early. He wasn't there long when the telephone rang. At first, he was hesitant to answer the telephone, afraid it might be a client. It's not that he wouldn't want to talk to one of his clients. It's just that he didn't like to talk to them when he wasn't prepared to answer their questions.

As it turned out, it wasn't a client. It was an old college friend who was on the staff of the New York Psychology Board.

"Jason, is that you?"

"Yes—who is this?"

"Chester Venable—what's the matter? You can't afford a secretary?"

"Oh, Chester. Good to hear from you. You're right, I can't afford a secretary, but I've got one anyway . . . no, I'm in early today. My secretary is not here yet. What can I do for you?"

"I'm calling you off the record to give you a heads up . . . we had a lot of good times together in college, didn't we? Anyway . . . I didn't want you to get blindsided."

"What on earth are you talking about, Chester?"

"A letter went out to you today that you'll probably receive tomorrow or the day after."

"What's it about?"

"There's been a complaint filed against you and the board sent you a letter to inform you of the complaint and to provide you with an outline for the investigation."

"Complaint . . . investigation! I don't understand. What kind of complaint are you talking about?"

"It's an ethics complaint."

"Can you be more specific because I have no idea what you are talking about?"

"Sure, Jason. I understand."

He paused and Jason heard the rustle of paper in the background.

"Here it is . . . it is alleged you had a relationship with one of your clients."

Jason's heart sank. "Do you have a name?"

"Sure. The woman's name is Katherine Summer."

"Did she file the complaint?"

"It doesn't say. Complaints against psychologists are usually confidential."

"I don't know what to say, Chester. I had a patient by that name, but for the life of me I can't imagine her filing a complaint about me. Just doesn't make sense. I went on a picnic with her Saturday—and she didn't say anything about this."

"What kind of picnic?"

"Just the two of us . . . Chester, you aren't writing this down are you?"

"No . . . no . . . but if I were you, when you talk to the investigator, I wouldn't say anything about a picnic."

"No. I won't . . . so what happens next?"

"You will get a letter notifying you of the complaint."

"Then what happens?"

"Someone will visit to interview you and the woman named in the complaint. If the facts of the complaint are confirmed, there will be a hearing."

"And the punishment?"

"Of course, you could lose your license. I told the board chairman that this was ridiculous, but you know how it is—rules are rules. I wouldn't worry about it if I were you. I know you're innocent. Just ride out the storm and you'll be fine."

"Chester, I really appreciate you letting me know about this."

"It's like I said. We were pretty tight in college."

"Thanks, again. I'm sure I'll be in touch."

When Jason put down the telephone, he jumped to his feet, pacing from one end of the room to the other. Why would Katherine betray him? It didn't make sense. The only people who had firsthand knowledge were Katherine, himself, and his secretary, who transcribed his notes for Katherine's file. He didn't tell a soul. Why would he? That left Katherine or his secretary.

As he paced, walking from window to window, pausing to peer outside, seeing nothing of interest, he heard his secretary come into the outer office.

This could ruin me! I could lose my license!

He listened as his secretary went through her morning ritual—putting her purse in the bottom drawer of her desk—putting on a pot of coffee—checking her email. She spoke to him when he came into the room, but he didn't acknowledge her greeting, which seemed strange to her because he always was very good about that.

After a couple of morning pleasantries, he got right to the point.

"Before you came in, I received a call notifying me that the New York Psychology Board had me under investigation for unethical behavior involving a former client, Mrs. Katherine Summer."

The secretary's eyes widened, but she said nothing.

"Do you have any idea who would file a complaint against me?"

"No, I don't. This is the first I've heard about it."

"The complaint should arrive in the mail in a day or so. It apparently alleges that I have a personal relationships with a former client."

"I recall typing the notes for her file in your dictation, you said that you recommended that she see a psychology in Canada. Is that right?"

"Yes, I did."

"I don't see anything wrong with that, do you? I mean, for there to be a complaint, wouldn't there have to be some hanky-panky?"

"I don't know many of the details of the complaint and I'm certainly not an expert on the board's ethical rules and regulations."

"It must be a mistake of some kind."

"That woman was upset when she left, I remember that, but I can testify that she hasn't been back to the office since then."

"That's right."

"And she hasn't been to your house, has she?"

He was somewhat taken aback by her question.

"No, she doesn't even know where I live."

"Then they've got nothing to go on, do they?"

Jason paused, searching for the right words. Finally, he said, "I need to ask you something—and I hope it doesn't hurt your feelings."

"Why?"

"The way I see it only three people even know I counseled Mrs. Summer—you, Mrs. Summer, and of course, myself. Forgive me for asking you this, but did you file the complaint?"

"Why, Dr. Montclair, I'm surprised you would ask me that."

"I'm sorry. But I know I didn't file the complaint. I can't imagine she would file it. That leaves only you."

"I can see why you would feel a need to ask me that, but I assure you that I was not the person who filed the complaint. Have you spoken to Mrs. Summer?"

"Not yet."

"Perhaps you should talk to her. She was pretty upset when she left that day."

"I will. I'll give her a call."

He returned to his office and closed the door. His secretary was right. It had to be Katherine. There was no reason for his secretary to report him, and her responses to his questions were totally in order. But why would Katherine do such a thing?

He reached for the telephone, but then he pulled back. Should he call her or should he drive across the river and talk to her in person?

That's no good he thought. *I'd still have to call her when I got there.*

CHAPTER
19

The first thing that Katherine did when she awoke on Monday was to go straight to the closet to look at her beautiful gown. In the morning light the fabric looked even more spectacular. She hoped the lighting at the party would be equally flattering.

With the dress still on a hanger, she held it up against her and walked over to the full-length mirror on the bathroom door. There was no doubt about it. It was one of the most beautiful gowns she'd ever seen. She returned to the closet, almost walking on tip-toes, and hung the gown on a door hook, backing away from it, still looking at it, backing all the way across the room until she reached the bathroom.

You're so silly! It's just a dress!

As soon as she came out of the bathroom, she looked at the clock. It was half-past nine. Her ride was supposed to be at the boathouse at ten. That left her only forty-five minutes to get ready for the party of a lifetime.

Thirty-five minutes later she was running along the dock in high heels, the *pop pop pop* sounds resembling gunfire. She stopped to remove her shoes, after which she ran the rest of the way to the boat in her bare feet. Surely, on that day, she was the best dressed boater on the river.

On the ride to the boathouse, the wind rippled though her hair, but she didn't worry about it. She'd just brush it out when she got there.

As she neared the boathouse, she looked in the parking lot for a car, but didn't see one. She took a deep breath and slipped the boat into the dock and hurried over to a mirror she had installed on the wall for exactly this type of emergency. As she brushed her hair, she heard a car pull into the parking lot.

The Mercedes-Benz, with Todd behind the wheel, was still rolling when she emerged from the boathouse door, looking cucumber cool.

"Don't you look dazzling," shouted Todd from the car.

Katherine smiled and took her time getting to the car. Before she got there, Todd hurried around to the passenger side to open the door for her.

"Thank you, Todd," she said matter-of-factly.

As he maneuvered the car out of the parking lot, he asked, "Do you like the dress?"

"Yes—it's quite nice," she said, stifling her excitement about the dress. "I understand you had something to do with its purchase?"

Todd smiled broadly. "Yes—it's one of my many duties."

"I don't know what Taylor pays you, but you deserve a raise."

I'm going to like this woman Todd thought. But he said, "My salary is quite generous. I have no complaints."

Once they got on the road, Todd seemed more interested in driving the car than in engaging her in conversation, which came as a great relief to her. Once she agreed to make the trip, the only nagging reservation she had about it was making conversation with Todd all the way to Ottawa and back. He seemed nice enough, but she didn't want to feel like she was in a situation where she'd have to entertain him.

Thankfully, Todd seemed to understand. During the first ten minutes of the drive, he asked sporadic questions—"Do you go to Ottawa often?" "Have you ever been to the Governor General's residence?"—but once he went through a perfunctory list of casual niceties, he stifled whatever urge he had to be friendly and concentrated on the road.

Right away she noticed the way he caressed the steering wheel with both hands, sliding his fingers back and forth over the soft leather. It reminded her of the way she interacted with Bessie, repeated caresses that seemed to occur without conscious effort.

They'd already made it through Brockville and were halfway to Prescott, when Katherine's cell rang. She recognized the number on caller ID. She paused a moment to consider whether to answer, glancing over at Todd; but then her curiosity got the best of her and she took the call.

"Hello."

"Hi Katherine—it's Jason."

"Good morning." She started to ask where he was, but then she realized she'd have to respond in kind. "Business must be slow for you to call this time of day."

There was an awkward pause that Katherine picked up on.

"Not really. My waiting room is full."

Katherine felt extremely uncomfortable talking to him in Todd's presence, but she couldn't very well say that she was busy and ask him to call back later. Before she could think of something smart to say, he said, "There's a roaring sound in the background. Where are you?"

"I'm in a car on my way to Ottawa."

"Oh, do you have a showing or something?"

"Not really. . ."

Another long pause, at the end of which Katherine continued, "What are you up to?" She already felt uncomfortable, but his odd, jerky telephone behavior made her discomfort even worse.

"There's something I need to talk to you about."

"Okay."

"I received a call today from a friend on the psychology board . . ."

Katherine's heart raced, though she had no idea why.

"It appears that someone has filed an ethics complaint against me."

"That's terrible, Jason!"

It was the first indication Todd had of the caller's identity. When he heard the name he perked up, his eyes darting from Katherine to the road and back again.

"I'm supposed to get official notification in a day or so."

"Who would do such a thing?"

"I was hoping that you could help me answer that question."

"Me? Why me?"

Katherine was extremely self- conscious over not revealing too much about the caller. It wasn't that she wanted to keep her friendship with Jason a secret. It had more to do with her inability to define their friendship—and by implication, her feelings for him.

"Because the complaint was over my relationship with you."

"Me! Are you kidding?"

"No, my friend read the particulars of the complaint and it is about my decision to refer you to another psychologist."

"How would they even know about that?"

"That's a good question."

There was an edge to his voice now. Not hostile, but not especially friendly, either. There was a long pause. Then he asked, "Did you file the complaint?"

"Are you serious?"

"Who else could it be?"

"I don't know—but it certainly wasn't me."

"Did you tell anyone?"

The question hit her between the eyes like a hammer.

"I wish you wouldn't use that tone of voice."

"I could lose my license over this."

"I understand that."

"So did you tell anyone?"

"I don't think so . . ."

She couldn't believe that she was lying to Jason.

What choice did she have? He should know better than to have a conversation like this on the telephone.

"You don't think so? Wouldn't you know if you did?"

"I told you I'm on the road. I really can't discuss this now."

"When will you get back from Ottawa?"

"I'm not sure. Probably around dark."

"Why don't I meet you at your place at seven? This has really got me spinning. My whole life is on the line."

"I understand . . . let's not set a time since I'm not sure when I'll get back. It's a short drive from your place to mine. Why don't I call you when I get back?"

"That's fine . . . I'm sorry if I sounded accusatory. I really am."

"I understand. I really do."

"Okay. Just give me a call later."

"I will . . . bye."

Katherine turned off her cell and put it back into her purse. She looked at Todd and saw that he was glancing at her.

I wonder if he understood who I was talking to . . . or what I was discussing. I don't think I said anything that would give him a clue.

They drove on in silence.

After a while, Todd turned to her and said, "Personal problem?"

"No . . . well, yes."

"I'm sure everything will work out."

"Thank you, Todd. But it's not a serious problem. At least I don't think it is."

"Don't you hate it when people call you when you're on the road—and try to fight with you?"

"Oh, it wasn't a fight."

"I didn't mean to be out of line."

"That's quite all right, Todd. And, yes—I do hate it when people call me when I'm traveling."

Katherine and Todd had one thing in common.

A little bit of conversation went a long way. They managed to drive the rest of the way to Ottawa without exploring new conversational ground, an unspoken social truce that suited them both.Todd drove her directly to the office, parking in the temporary loading area clearly marked at the front of the building. He escorted her up to Taylor's office and then returned to the car so that he could move it to the parking area.

Taylor was waiting in the outer office when Katherine walked in the door. When he saw her, his eyes went from dim to bright, like the headlights of a car.

"Katherine, you look positively elegant," he said, taking her hands in his, as if he were weighing each of them, and then releasing them so that he could put his arms around her.

"Thank you, Taylor," she said. "I think this is the most beautiful dress I've ever worn."

"No one—and I mean no one—could do more for that dress than you."

"You look pretty nice yourself."

She backed away slightly to admire his new suit.

"We'll certainly be the best dressed couple there."

"As it should be."

He took her into his inner office, which was pretty much what she expected—an oversized desk, expensive furnishings, walls filled with photographs of him shaking hands with celebrities and diplomats. It was while she was looking at the walls that she spotted her painting.

"Oh," she said walking over to what she called her "bird art."

"What can I say—I'm a fan."

She looked up at the river scene, refreshing her memory about the date.

"So you've had this one for a long time, too."

"Oh, yes, it was love at first sight."

It was the second lie he'd told her that she knew about. It bothered her that he would lie about something it was not necessary to lie about, but she took into consideration his motivation, which was to please her and she had a difficult time finding fault with that.

No one is perfect she thought. *If someone is going to lie to me, I want it to be because they don't want to hurt me.*

Taylor clapped his hands together. "Well, are you ready to meet a prince?"

"Sure," she said, smiling. "Will that unattractive woman be with him?"

For the first time since she met him, she saw Taylor's face morph into a horror mask. "No, no . . . you mustn't say that. Her name is Camilla and she should be addressed as the Duchess of Cornwall."

"I was just kidding."
"Really?"
"Really."

CHAPTER
20

Rideau Hall, the official residence of the Governor General of Canada, is a magnificent stone structure that was built in 1838 for a prominent stone mason and contractor. The architecture, an amalgam of Victorian and Edwardian styles, is an appropriately visual reminder of Canada's ties to England in view of the Governor General's title as the Queen's official representative to that country. It is the Governor General, not the prime minister, who stands as Canada's de facto Head of State.

As Taylor and Katherine neared the residence in the backseat of his Mercedes limo, with Todd in the driver's seat, Taylor asked, "Have you ever visited Rideau Hall?"

"No, I've never had reason to."

"It's a beautiful building, isn't it?"

"I can't wait to see what it looks like inside."

"It only gets better."

"I am intrigued."

Todd pulled the limo up in front of the building at One Sussex Drive, where several of the Queen's Guards, dressed in ceremonial red tunics and oversized bearskin hats, stood at attention. Once the car stopped, a man in a dark suit rushed out to the car and opened the passenger door. As they got out of the limo, Katherine asked, "I probably should know this, but are these guards brought over from England?"

"They are all homegrown Royal Canadian Mounted Police officers, but the uniforms are authentic—shipped from the Old Country."

Taylor was greeted by several men in dark suits, who nodded politely and addressed him by name. They were taken by a gentleman with a back as straight as a rail into the ballroom, where several hundred people gathered to greet Prince Harry and his wife Meghan in a receiving line. Behind them was a large painting of the Queen and Duke of Edinburgh. In the center of the room was a dominating Waterford chandelier that was presented to Canada by the British government more than half a century ago.

Katherine's eyes widened when she saw the prince, but they widened even more when she saw the painting.

"That's by Lemieux, isn't it?" she asked.

"You know, I think so, but I'm not sure."

"I see she is here with him."

"The Duchess, you mean?"

Katherine nodded. "Maybe you should brief me on the etiquette?"

"Sure," he said smiling. "I don't come to many of these things. Perhaps because of that the Governor General's secretary once advised me on what is expected at these events. The way he explained it to me, you refer to Prince Harry as Your Royal Highness. And you refer to Camilla as Duchess. That's first reference. If you speak to them later, you use 'sir" or 'ma'am.' "

"Am I supposed to curtsy?"

"Yes—definitely. And when we go to dinner, you must wait for the prince to eat before you lift a hand."

"I didn't realize there were so many rules."

"The British are very good at rules."

As they stood in line, Katherine noticed that passersby took note of her gown, sometimes smiling when they made eye contact with her. Every few minutes someone stopped to shake hands with Taylor and make comments about the affair.

Taylor was more popular than she ever imagined. Some of the people there treated him as if he were a rock star. Everyone, it seemed, wanted to shake his hand.

Impressive.

Katherine spotted Prime Minister Martin across the room and nudged Taylor. "What do you think of him?"

"He's led the Conservative Party for a long time. He's got many friends."

"Will you support him if he runs for the leadership position again?"

"That depends on who he's running against."

"He's in his seventies, isn't he?"

"Yes—but he's still very active."

Katherine made eye contact with the Prime Minister and he smiled. To her surprise, he started across the room toward them. It reminded her of all those high school dances at which she had to be careful not to look at any of the boys because the slightest eye contact usually meant an offer to dance. She averted her eyes, but he kept coming.

The Prime Minister walked up to Taylor and extended his hand.

"Taylor, you didn't tell me that you'd be in the company of such a lovely woman."

Taylor shook hands with him, smiling broadly.

"Some things a man just doesn't want to share."

"Well, aren't you going to introduce us?"

"I'm sorry . . .Katherine Summer, this is our Prime Minister Paul Martin."

Katherine smiled prettily and offered her hand. The Prime Minister held it a little too long, she thought, but she attributed it to his age. Older men hold the hands of young women so seldom they are sometimes reluctant to turn loose when they do have the opportunity.

Taylor continued: "She's an artist—and a damned fine one, too."

"Oh, really," said the Prime Minister. "What do you paint?"

"Landscapes mostly. Some portraits."

"I'd love to see your work sometime."

"I have some pieces at the Macmillan Gallery."

"I'll be sure to stop by. Do you live here in Ottawa?"

Before she could answer, Taylor stepped. "She's a constituent of mine. She lives on one of the islands."

"The Prime Minister's eyes widened and he smiled.

"I love the islands. I spend weekends there every chance I get. I imagine it's a wonderful place to work."

"It is everything I've ever dreamed about," she said. "I can't imagine living anyplace else."

The Prime Minister glanced over at the royal couple. "So you're waiting to meet the guests of honor, are you?"

"I've never met a member of the royal family," said Katherine.

The Prime Minister looked at Taylor with a knowing nod.

"You know the prince rather well, don't you?"

"I wouldn't say that I know him well. I once spent a weekend fishing with him in Scotland."

"That was when he was still with Di, wasn't it?"

"Yes . . . yes . . . she went on the expedition with us, but fly fishing wasn't really to her liking."

Katherine looked at Taylor in astonishment.

"Are you serious?"

The Prime Minister chimed in.

"Oh, he's serious all right. Quite the asset to the Conservative Party."

"Thank you Mr. Prime Minister."

"I hear you have something in the works on the casino issue."

"I do. But I'm not at a point yet where I can speak intelligently about it."

"I look forward to hearing your ideas."

The Prime Minister glanced at a crowd of restless people off to the side.

"Well, I suppose I have to glad-hand my way out of the room."

He started away, but then he turned back long enough to say to Katherine in a breathy whisper, "When I met the Duchess I didn't know whether to bow or feed her a carrot." Then he was gone, chuckling to himself as he crossed the room.

"See, I'm not the only person . . ."

Taylor shook his head.

"He does have a devilish sense of humor."

"Maybe I should be dating him," she quipped.

"Don't think you won't be asked."

"Are you serious? Isn't he married?"

"He's a widower—and, from what I hear, entering the randy phase of his life."

"Oweeeee!"

People continued to approach Taylor as they made their way to the Prince and Duchess. By the time they arrived, they had shaken a couple dozen hands, not as many as the royal couple, but enough to give Katherine a slight cramp in her right hand.

Katherine saw the recognition in Prince Harry's eyes as Taylor stepped up to greet him. Taylor bowed slightly and took the prince's hand when it was offered. The prince's normal stern demeanor dissolved into a broad grin.

"I was hoping I'd see you today. I've got something to tell you. I was in our old fishing hole a few months back and landed a splendid salmon with a Black Boar."

"Really," said Taylor. "I haven't been salmon fishing since our trip."

"He put up a fight, let me tell you—all ten pounds of him—but the Black Boar held, like I knew it would, and I landed him after about five minutes. Harry was with me. He wasn't a Black Boar man before that day."

The prince laughed and smiled at the Duchess.

"But I understand that he wears a Black Boar under the lapel of his dress tunic now for good luck."

"Good for him," said Taylor.

"Oh, I'm sorry," said the prince, looking momentarily embarrassed. "I don't think you've met Camilla have you?"

Taylor turned toward her and bowed, intoning, "Duchess."

"I've heard so much about you," she said.

"Thank you. I hope we haven't bored you with our fishing tales."

"Not at all—I'm quite used to it."

"And where are my manners?" Taylor said, introducing Katherine to the prince and the duchess. Katherine curtsied and first took the hand of the duchesses, holding it for a few seconds, and then the hand of the prince. She said, "I hope you will be able to do some fishing while you are in Canada."

"Only that I could. I'm afraid from here we go directly to Tokyo."

Taylor and Katherine exchanged another comment or two and then moved on. As they walked away, Katherine whispered, "You mean we waited in line for an hour for that."

"Weren't you happy to meet the prince?"

"I must admit it was pretty exciting."

"When he gets a fly rod in his hands, he's like any other Joe."

"I got that impression."

"We've got time before lunch to look around the residence, if you'd like."

"I'd love to."

The left the ballroom and wandered about the residence, first passing by the Royal Window, where a stained glass piece commemorated the fortieth anniversary of Elizabeth's accession to the throne. There were more paintings than there are in many museums. Katherine wandered from painting to painting, hardly aware that Taylor was at her side. They resembled two holiday tourists, inching along the wall, their eyes glued to the paintings, some donated by the royal family, others purchased by the Canadian Arts Council to highlight the work of Canadian artists.

"I can't believe that I didn't know this existed," said Katherine, speaking softly so as not to bother the couple standing next to them.

"They offer tours every day," said Taylor, "but I'm afraid it's not advertised outside the city the way it should be."

They turned a corner and walked down a short hallway that opened into a room that contained paintings done by contemporary Canadian artists. Katherine looked at each painting carefully, sometimes pausing for several minutes to absorb the imagery.

Suddenly, she came upon a painting that left her speechless. It was a beautiful river landscape that bore her name.

"Taylor!" she exclaimed, reaching out for his arm without removing her eyes from the painting. "Look at this!"

"What's that?" he said standing next to her.

"That's my painting!" she said, unable to contain her enthusiasm. "How did it get here?"

Taylor leaned over and read her name on the painting.

"Congratulations," he said. "I had no idea."

"You didn't know it was here?"

"I come here often, but I haven't been in this wing for five or six years."

"How did it get here?"

"I imagine that someone from the Arts Council saw it in a gallery and purchased it to display here. It's quite an honor."

"Yes, it is—I really don't know what to say. An artist does a painting because she loves what she sees, but she sells it to make a living—and to share it with others. It's rare that I ever know who—or why—someone has purchased one of my paintings."

"Now you know."

Seeing her painting just made her more excited about seeing the other paintings. She moved from frame to frame, like a child looking at candy in a store window. She spent several minutes studying the surreal fairy-tale paintings of a Toronto artist named Shary Boyle. She never met Shary, but she frequently saw her work in the local galleries while she was hawking her own work on the street. Then it was on to Marcel Dzama, who was best-known for his pen and ink drawings. And then there was Annie Pootoogook, who's engaging drawings depict ordinary life in the far north.

Taylor glanced at his watch. "The luncheon will begin soon, so we need to be on our way."

"Oh, sure," she said, putting her arm around his waist. It felt like such a natural thing to do she wasn't even aware of it.

She turned to go back the way they'd come, but he gently pulled her the other direction.

"That's not the way we came."

"I know—there's something else I want to show you."

He led her into the Monck Wing, a nearly 150-year-old part of the residence that contained a suite of bedrooms and drawing rooms, all decorated in the Edwardian style. He took her hand and took her into the large drawing room, which had appointments elegant enough for the royal family. He closed the door behind them, a smug look on his face. Then he took her in his arms.

"What are you doing?" she said, more surprised than offended.

"I'd just like a few moments alone with you."

"This is not safe."

"I don't like safe."

They kissed more passionately than ever before. When the kiss began, Katherine shut her eyes tightly, but then as the kiss lingered she opened her eyes and glanced at the door. Finally, she gently pushed herself away from him, only to have him move in closer.

"Taylor, are you out of your mind? Someone could come in the door."

"I like danger, don't you?"

"Well . . . Not really."

Taylor reached out and put his hands on either side of her hips. Then he gathered up her dress and began lifting it . . . past her knees, and then past her thighs.

"Taylor!" she protested, her eyes riveted to the door. She was so concerned about the door that she didn't notice the way that he was admiring her bare legs.

"Just give me one more minute," he pleaded.

He cupped both hands against her hips.

"But this is so wrong. The prince and the duchess are in the building."

"I know," he grinned. "I've always been attracted to danger."

"What would they think if they walked in the door and saw us this way?"

"I pretty sure we aren't doing anything they haven't already done."

Katherine attempted to push her dress back down, but he held tightly to the fabric.

Suddenly, they heard the knob turning on the door, the sound reaching them at the same instant, so that he quickly released her gown and she even more quickly smoothed it down, shaking her hips twice to help it along its way—and when the door opened, revealing the Prime Minister and a young lady, they both were facing the door smiling.

Seeing the two of them, the Prime Minister blurted out, "Oh, I'm sorry. Come along dear—this is not the room I wanted to show you."

He nodded a friendly greeting and backed out of the room, practically dragging the young lady by the hand.

Katherine let out a long sigh of relief.

"We came so close," she said. "You must have a political death wish."

"Okay, that was wrong of me, and I admit it—and I apologize, I really do—but you've got to admit it was exciting."

"It was that all right," she said, not bothering to conceal her smile. She walked quickly to the door, with him right behind her.

When they reached the dining hall, a magnificent, high-ceilinged space called the Tent Room, most of the seats at the table were filled. They were seated about half a dozen chairs away from the head of the table, close enough to feel included in everything that happened, but not close enough to participate in the conversation.

Katherine was thrilled to be dining so close to the prince and the duchess. She was even more thrilled by the artwork evident in the grand room. Behind the prince and the duchess was a large portrait of Queen Victoria, depicted making a grand gesture while standing amid regal trappings. But that was just the centerpiece. Assorted English paintings, all donated by the crown, decorated the walls along the full length of the room. When she saw the sterling silverware, Katherine couldn't help but wonder how many of the guests would pocket a fork or two to keep as a souvenir. She watched the other guests all during the dinner. Once or twice she looked at Prince Harry and saw him watching her survey the table. She smiled. He smiled back.

Surely, after all he's been through, he understands how ridiculous all this is she thought. She accepted his smile as confirmation of that shared realization.

All through lunch she kept glancing at Taylor, who was glancing at her, back and forth like balls in a tennis tournament. She wanted to talk to him about what happened in the drawing room, but this wasn't the place, so she said nothing.

She could tell that he liked having secrets. Perhaps she did, too. She wasn't sure. All she knew for certain was that Taylor had introduced her to new sights, sounds and, yes, feelings that she'd never before experienced. There was something to be said for that. She was experiencing new emotions, feelings that offered the key to her heart.

"You seem to be having a good time," said the man next to her.

"Why do you say that?"

"Because you've been smiling ever since you were seated."

"Maybe it's a tic or something," she laughed.

The man laughed. "I never considered that possibility. By the way, let me introduce myself . . . we met in the receiving line, but I doubt that you remember me."

The man was right. She didn't remember him.

The man continued: "My name is Donald Kelly. I'm the attorney general of Canada."

"I apologize," she said, looking truly embarrassed. "I've met so many new people today that . . ."

"No need to explain. I understand."

"I see you on television all the time. I just never put two and two together."

The Attorney General leaned far back in his chair so that he could introduce Katherine to his wife Rose. The two women smiled and nodded at each other.

"Rose and I are familiar with your landscapes. We think you're one of the best."

"Thank you."

"Do you ever do portraits?"

"Yes, I've done a few."

"Would you be kind enough to consider doing a portrait of Rose?"

Katherine was taken a bit off guard, because no one had ever asked her to do that. The portraits she'd done were all of people she knew and cared about. She looked at Rose, noting her high cheekbones and symmetrical face. She was very attractive, probably in her early thirties.

"I'd want to know more about what you wanted in the way of a portrait, but, yes, I'd love to discuss it further with you. She fished her business card out of her purse and gave it to him.

"Thanks," he said. "I'll give you a call in a few days."

Suddenly, there was a high-pitched clinking sound as someone struck a table knife against a crystal glass.

"Ladies and gentlemen," boomed an authoritative male voice from nowhere in particular. "We invite you to dance to the music of the Canadian Armed Forces Band."

A curtain was drawn at the other end of the room, displaying a six-piece band, the members of which were all donned in their dress uniforms. The music that began was not what anyone would have expected. It was high energy rock music with a flirty rhythm and blues edge. Katherine looked at Taylor, a bemused look on her face.

Preston look at her, a shocked expression on his face.

Finally, he said, "No one is dancing."

"Well?" she asked.

He seemed disinclined to budge.

Katherine came to her feet and grabbed his hand, leading him out onto the dance floor. Applause erupted, most of the attendees convinced that Taylor would be the next prime minister.

Katherine and Taylor danced like there was no one else in the room, she circling him with moves he had never seen her do. It was as if she was competing in a television dance contest. She led, he followed. When the song ended they were still alone on the dance floor.

A murmur went through the room.

Appearing seemingly from nowhere, Prince Harry and Meghan glided onto the dance floor, encouraged by a burst of enthusiastic applause. Prince Harry saluted Taylor and grinned, and then began dancing. Soon the dance floor was filled with men and women who proceeded to dance with wild abandonment, many of them imitating Katherine's unique dance style.

* * *.

After the dance party concluded, Taylor and Katherine made their way through the crowd to the front of the building, where they saw Todd in the distance, standing next to the limo. Taylor waved and Todd waved back and got into the car and wheeled around in a u-turn to pick them up. He got out and opened the door for them.

Once he got back in the driver's seat he asked, "Did you have a good time?"

"We had an excellent time," said Katherine.

Taylor leaned forward and teasingly asked, "Todd, does the partition that seals off our section of the car still work?"

"Yes, sir—it does."

"Todd!" Katherine said, sounding a little too anxious. "Don't you dare. And please keep your eyes on the road!"

CHAPTER
21

When they returned to Taylor's office, Katherine went into the bathroom to freshen up for her ride back to the island. Once she was out of the room, Todd leaned over and whispered to Taylor, "There's something you need to know about."

"What's that?"

"Katherine got a call while we were driving in."

"And?"

"It was from that psychologist, Jason what's-his-name. From the tone of the conversation, he's probably been served with papers or something."

"I think it's too early for him to be served. Someone may have tipped him off."

"She was very careful not to say anything in front of me. But I could tell that she was upset by what he said. She told him that she was on her way to Ottawa and couldn't talk about it she returned home. Apparently, he's going to talk to her later today."

"You know not to . . ."

"Don't worry. I won't say a word and if . . ."

Suddenly, Katherine entered the room and saw Taylor and Todd standing close together, talking in lowered voices.

"If you're talking about me, I want to listen in."

The two men stepped apart, looking like children that have been caught doing something wrong.

Taylor smiled and said, "We were discussing how great you look in that dress."

"I can see why you'd do that," she joked.

As soon as Taylor starting talking, Todd faded away, quietly slipping into the outer office, where the secretary pulled him aside, desperate to know about Katherine.

Taylor put his arms around Katherine and gave her a wonderful kiss.

"I wish you would spend the night," he said. "You've never seen my condo."

"Maybe next time. I have some things I have to do at home."

They kissed again, harder than before, and then Taylor walked her into the outer office, where Todd was waiting. As they walked past the secretary's desk, Taylor paused.

"Katherine, I'd like for you to meet my secretary, Miss Sweeny."

Katherine exchanged pleasantries with Miss Sweeny, a neatly dressed woman in her late fifties. She wore oversized eyeglasses and resembled the stereotypical school teacher.

To Todd, Taylor said, "She's all yours—drive safely."

"I will," said Todd.

As they walked out the door, Katherine heard Miss Sweeny's solicitous voice: "She's very beautiful. I like her much better than the others."

Katherine glanced at Todd, who also heard the comment.

"What does she mean by the others?"

"Of course, he dated other women before he met you."

"Oh."

When they reached the street, Katherine saw the Merdie. Todd had obviously left the office and pulled it around to the front of the building. She couldn't help but notice that Todd looked at Merdie the same way Taylor looked at her. It was her first experience with someone who had car lust.

"I'm curious about something," she said.

"Okay," he answered.

"You left the office while Taylor and I were talking and well . . ."

"Yes."

". . . and you brought the car around . . ."

"Yes."

"You don't know your boss very well, do you? He asked me to stay."

"I knew he planned to do that. I didn't think you would accept."

"Oh."

"Why is that?"

"Just a hunch."

"You are beginning to scare me," she laughed.

As they drove out of Ottawa, Katherine's head swirled with thoughts of Taylor and the experience at the Governor General's resident, and with thoughts of Jason and his problem, a sweet-and-sour maelstrom that made her long for the simplicity of Bessie's love. She wanted to talk to Taylor about Jason while they were at the Governor

General's residence and then later at the office, but the time was never right and she pushed it out of her mind and now it was nagging at her and she dreaded dealing with it.

The road ran into trees not far out of Ottawa. Long stretches where farm houses and isolated residences stayed momentarily in view and then disappeared as the car zipped past. They went for long periods without seeing any sign of life, a desolate landscape with a concrete stripe lumbering across its sun-bleached back. Katherine saw beauty even in that, her artist's eye already shaping ghostly images for future use.

Whatever curiosity Todd initially had about Katherine had been assuaged at this point, for he seemed content to sit in silence, both hands on the wheel, occasionally reaching to adjust a knob or redirect a vent.

That was fine with Katherine, whose only curiosity about Todd was limited to whether he'd made any sense of her telephone conversation with Jason.

Katherine leaned back in the seat, eyes closed. The dress that had seemed so very much a part of her earlier in the day now seemed obtrusive. She was sorry she hadn't brought jeans and T-shirt to change into for the drive back home. The dress felt like extra skin. Sort of itchy and bulky. She desperately wanted to shed it the way a snake sheds its extra skin so that she could slip, slide, and wiggle her way into comfort.

She had drifted off into a dream-like state when suddenly there was a loud noise and a popping sound. She looked at Todd, who looked concerned as he struggled to control the car and direct it off the highway onto a narrow strip of grass. They both got out of the car to see what'd happened.

Katherine saw it first because it was on her side of the car. Blow out. The right front tire was flat. She leaned over and saw a small hole in the side of the tire.

"Look at this," she said, pointing to the tire.

Todd rounded the front of the car, his face terror stricken.

"This is terrible," he said.

"It's just a flat tire."

Todd looked at the tire for a long time, hands on hips.

"You have a spare, don't you?" Katherine asked.

"A spare?"

"Yes, a spare. They're usually in the trunk."

"Can you believe it? For as long as I've been driving, I've never had to change a tire. When I started working for Mr. Prescott I had to take a course on how to take evasive action in the event the vehicle came under gunfire, but no one said anything about what to do in the event of a flat tire."

He reached into the car, feeling his way under the dash until he found the latch that unlocked the trunk. Then he walked around to the back and opened it.

"I don't see anything resembling a tire," he said.

"Lift up the carpet and look beneath it."

"Okay," he said. He did as she suggested and he found the spare. He fumbled to unscrew the bolt holding it down and lifted the tire out of the trunk. He carried it in both arms to the front of the car and dropped it to the ground. He knelt and closely examined the wheel. He reached out and touched the lug nuts that held the tire in place.

Katherine could see that he didn't have a clue.

"The lug wrench is probably in the boot, beneath where the spare was."

"Oh, yes," he said, his quavering voice reflecting his uncertainty.

He walked around to the back of the car and rummaged in the trunk until he found the lug wrench. He stared at it as he made his way back to the front of the car, trying to figure out what to do with it. When Katherine realized that the situation was hopeless, she said, "Do you have any of those spring clips that people use to hold papers together?"

"I think I have some in my brief case. Why?"

"Would you get me a few clips, please?"

"Sure," he said.

He leaned over into the car and pulled his briefcase from the backseat. He removed the clips from three documents and handed them to Katherine. Then he put the briefcase back into the car.

"If this offends you, I'm sorry," she said.

Todd looked perplexed.

She raised her skirt up past her knees, about midway up her thighs, and then she used the clips to hold the fabric into place.

"My God, Katherine—that's a Gucci!"

"I know—I'm not going to hurt it."

Then she stepped out of her shoes and handed them to Todd.

"Would you hold these for a minute, please."

Todd held the shoes at arm's length, not sure what to do with them.

Katherine picked up the lug wrench and examined the threads. Then she leaned over and peered at the chrome-plated lugs on the wheel.

"Do you have a handkerchief?" she asked.

"Yes," he said, pulling a patch of cloth from the front pocket of his sports jacket.

Katherine examined it. "This is silk, isn't it?"

"Yes—and very expensive."

"I sort of need it to change this tire. But it will probably wreck the handkerchief. Do you have a problem with that?"

Todd sighed. "No. Do what you have to do."

Katherine walked around to the rear of the car in her bare feet. She looked incredible with her skirt hiked up her legs. She reached in and yanked out the jack and started back around the car.

"What's that?" asked Todd.

"It's the jack. We'll need this to change the tire."

When she made it back to the front of the car, she tossed the jack onto the ground and picked up the lug wrench. She covered one of the lug nuts with Todd's handkerchief and then she fitted the open end of the lug wrench over it and twisted it until she had the lug nut loosened. She did that for each lug nut, much to Todd's horror, because each time it left a dark ring on the handkerchief.

Once she had the lug nuts loosened, she put the jack in place and raised the car. She pulled off the tire and rolled it over to Todd.

"Would you mind putting it in the trunk?" she asked sweetly.

Todd didn't answer, but he picked up the tire, again holding it in both hands, and carried it to the rear of the car and dropped it into the trunk. As he made his way back around the car, Katherine already had the spare fitted over the lug bolts.

He thought it very odd to see a beautiful woman in an expensive gown, down on her knees in the dirt, twisting and turning the tire into place, her long legs looking spectacular despite the dirty job that she was doing.

He watched as she tightened the lug nuts, again using his handkerchief, and then lowered the jack and pulled it from beneath the car.

"Would you mind putting that in the trunk?"

Todd obediently picked up the jack and took it to the rear of the car.

When he returned, Katherine was slipping back into her shoes. She unfastened the clips and shook her hips so that the dress fell into place. She handed him the clips and did a modeling turn for him.

"See, no harm done."

"That's amazing," he said. "Your dress doesn't have a wrinkle in it."

"It's all in how you fold it."

"And how did you learn to change a tire like that?"

"My dad taught me when I was a little girl. I've had to change a few over the years. It's no big deal. I hope you took notes."

"I'll never forget it."

Todd noticed a grease smug on her nose, but he said nothing because his handkerchief was wrecked and he had nothing he could use to wipe it. He figured she could do that when she got home.

The rest of the drive to Brockville was uneventful. For most of the way, Todd had flashbacks—the image of her in a Gucci gown, down on her knees in the dirt, barefoot, changing a tire, was something he would not soon forget.

She's way too good for Taylor he thought. When they pulled off the road to her boathouse, there was a car waiting, with a man leaning against the front fender.

Todd thought he had a pretty good idea who the man was. He pulled the Merdie over close to the other car and stopped.

Katherine hurried out of the car and leaned over inside.

"Thanks for the ride," she said, loud enough for Jason to hear. "Have a safe trip back."

She stood and waved, waiting for him to back out so that she could join Jason.

Todd stalled so that he could see how she greeted the other man, but she waited him out, waving, a big smile on her face. Finally, he backed up and started up the lane to the road. In his rearview mirror, he saw Katherine rush over to Jason and hug him.

Katherine glanced at the car as it pulled onto the road and she said, "Hope you haven't been waiting for a long time."

"I've just been here a few minutes. Who's your ride? That's a pretty expensive car."

"Oh, that's Todd. He's Taylor Prescott's assistant. I was invited to a luncheon at the Governor General's residence to greet Prince Harry and Meghan . . ."

"Really," Jason said, eyes widened.

". . . and did you know that one of my paintings is on exhibit at the residence?"

"You're kidding—that's quite an honor isn't it?"

"It's a huge honor. I never realized that the residence was such a showplace for Canadian artists."

"Congratulations. How did you happen to hear about the luncheon?"

"Taylor's my MP—and he had his assistant come for me."

Jason paused, looking askance at her. "What's that?" he asked.

"What?"

He took a handkerchief from his pocket and reached out and rubbed the oil smug from her nose. He looked at the handkerchief and then showed it to her.

He said, "It looks like oil."

Katherine smiled. "It is—we had a flat and I helped change the tire."

Jason heard her say it, but he didn't respond because he was already interested in something else. "And look at you in that dress," he said.

He stepped back to get a better look.

"That looks like something that a movie star would wear. You look fantastic."

"Thanks, Jason. But enough about me. Tell me about this complaint."

Jason led her over to one of the benches and they sat next to each other.

"It's like I said on the telephone. A friend tipped me off that someone made an ethics complaint about me."

"I don't understand."

"The psychology board is going to investigate me, the end result being that I could lose my license. I don't understand how they could receive a complaint . . . not when you and I are the only people that know about what happened between us."

"Could your secretary have done it?"

"I spoke to her about it. And I'm convinced she did not."

"Well, that only leaves you and me."

"I believe you when you say you didn't file a complaint, but are you certain you didn't talk to someone about our situation? A friend, maybe?"

Katherine paused, blood pounding in her ears.

"I've been thinking about this all day . . . A while back, Taylor Prescott asked me how I've been doing since the accident . . . whether I needed any government assistance or anything . . . and I think I told him that I saw a therapist . . . and that we started going out as friends. Talking about it seemed harmless at the time."

"You don't think he would file a complaint against me, do you?"
"I don't know why he would. If you want me to, I'll ask him."
"Please, if you don't mind."
"So what happens next?"
"I will be interviewed . . . and I feel certain they will send someone to interview you."
"Me? Why me?"
"Because you were named in the complaint."
"Isn't that a violation of my privacy rights or something?"
"Apparently not."
"Should I talk to them? What should I say?"
"I don't think you will have any choice. As far as what you say to them, I strongly suggest that you tell the truth."
"Even if it costs you your license?"
"I'm the one who made a mistake, not you?"
"But I could never live with myself if I did something to hurt you."
Jason reached over and hugged her. She put her arms around him, pressing her hands into his back, holding him close against him. She whispered, "Please tell me this is not happening. It's a nightmare."

CHAPTER
22

Through the window, she saw it: against the backdrop of a cloudless sky, a solitary seagull hung in midair, its wings fixed in place like a stopped clock. She watched it for an extended moment that was beyond human measurement, mesmerized by the bird's ability to exist in stopped time, held in place by an unceasing gust of wind. Then she blinked, shredding time, and the bird lost its pose and swooped upward, carried by the winds to another place.

In a painting, the bird would look magical. Even though she was alone in the house, except for Bessie, she couldn't help but smile. Today she was painting herself. Someday soon she would paint the bird. That was the *real* job of the artist. To stop time dead in its tracks. It is why science is such an unrelenting adversary of art. Despite the best efforts of science, only art can stop, reverse or advance time. In the artist's eye, science is an ineffectual, though greedily ambitious, stepsister.

As she followed the lines of her own figure on the canvas, she thought about how her body had changed over the years. How different it had become as it transitioned from the fading baby fat of adolescence to the more muscular twenties, and then on to her thirties, the mirror reflecting yet more changes, however subtle.

She'd never seen women in their fifties, sixties, and seventies without clothes, but she speculated on the potential for even more change and she pondered the possibility of doing a series of figure studies depicting women, beautiful and wise and experienced, in various stages of their lives. *Would anyone be interested?*

She smiled, thinking about the clamor that would accompany such a project.

Why not? Older women are beautiful, too. Why in the hell not?

Suddenly, there was a knock on her back door. The sound startled her because it was so immediate. Then she was startled a second time when she remembered that she was on an island where door knocking was not a common occurrence.

She walked over to the window of her studio and peered outside. There was a man at her door. Tall man. Dark suit. Briefcase in hand. The sight of him was enough to make her heart pound. She would not have been made more anxious if he were holding an ax in his hand. Boaters sometimes stopped at her house when they ran out of gas or needed to use the telephone in an emergency. Never once were any of them dressed in anything other than jeans or shorts, usually with bare feet or scandals or ragged tennis shoes.

The man knocked again, his knuckles rapping with rude determination.

This can't possibly be good she thought as she walked through the house.

She opened the door and was confronted by a man, probably in his forties, who had the oval, beaming face of a twenty-year-old.

"Mrs. Summer?" he asked.

"Yes."

"My name is Buddie Loggins—and I'm with the New York Psychology Board."

He handed her a business card.

"I'd very much like to talk to you about a therapist named Dr. Jason Montclair. I understand you are a former client of his."

"How did you get on my island?"

"I hired a boat out of Brockville. The boat is waiting for me at the dock. May I come in please?"

Katherine stood in the doorway and showed no inclination to move.

"I'm busy right now. What is it that you want?"

The man cleared his throat.

"That's what I'd like to talk to you about. It's difficult to discuss such things standing in a doorway."

"Discuss what things?"

"Mrs. Summer, I detect a hint of hostility in your voice. I really mean you no harm. I simply want to ask you some routine questions about Dr. Montclair."

"I don't know you . . . and I wouldn't feel comfortable discussing Dr. Montclair with someone I don't know."

"If you'd like to call the telephone number on my card and ask for my supervisor, she will verify who I am."

"I know who you are. You are an American in Canada who knocked on my door without an appointment and asked me to discuss a very private matter. You do realize that you are in Canada?"

"Oh, yes . . . I would never . . . well, could we set a time when it would be more convenient for you to talk to me?"

"I don't think my private experiences with Dr. Montclair are any of your business. Don't you think that you might be violating confidentiality by even telling me that you know that I was a client of Dr. Montclair?"

"Oh, no ma'am. A complaint was made against Dr. Montclair. We have to investigate the complaint so that it can be determined whether it will be necessary to take disciplinary action against him."

"I have no complaints to make about the treatment I received from Dr. Montclair. I am perfectly happy with the counseling I received from him. I'd recommend him to anyone who's having problems of any kind."

"With all due respect, Mrs. Summer, your opinion of Dr. Montclair is not an issue in this investigation. Fact, not opinion, will determine the disposition of the case."

"You must think it is pretty cut and dried."

"No ma'am. I don't think anything. I'm a fact finder. My job is to conduct interviews and present the facts of the case. I have no opinion."

"If you have no opinion, you must lead a pretty miserable life. Mr. Loggins, I don't have anything to say to you about Dr. Montclair. And I want you to leave my property."

"Yes ma'am, I'll leave right now. But please think about what we've talked about. If you change your mind, you can reach me at the number on the card . . ."

"I won't be changing my mind."

". . . please understand that if you do not voluntarily cooperate with us, we can issue a subpoena and require you to attend a formal hearing."

Katherine closed the door, perhaps a little more forcefully than she intended. She leaned back against the door, trembling. It was at that moment that she understood that she cared about Jason more than she realized. She felt protective toward him. Perhaps because she was thinking about Jason, she had a sudden sense that the man was still standing outside the door. She turned around to see for certain. He was gone. In the distance, he saw him standing on the dock, getting into a boat.

With Bessie at her heels—she had eyed the visitor with a wary eye during their conversation—she went into the studio and found her cell and called Taylor's office.

"Taylor Prescott's office," said a familiar voice at the other end.

Katherine recognized the voice: it was his secretary.

"This is Katherine Summer. Could I please speak to Mr. Prescott?"

"Hi, Miss Summer—this is Miss Sweeny. How are you doing today?"

"I'm fine—how are you?"

"I'm terrific—it's a terrific day."

She paused a minute.

"I'd put you through, except he's not here. He and Todd are at the television station, where Mr. Prescott is doing a live interview. If you turn on your television, Channel 3, you can watch."

"Thank you . . ."

But before Katherine got off the line, Miss Sweeny said, "Let me give you Todd's cell number."

"Okay, that would be great."

Miss Sweeny gave her the number, speaking slowly, as if Katherine was a preschooler, and wished her a good day.

Katherine punched the number in and waited while it rang. She was filled with competing emotions, so that from one ring to the next, she went full circle from anger to hopeful expectation, experiencing everything in between.

Todd answered while in the soundproof control room; but still he whispered.

She couldn't tell whether Todd was happy to hear her voice or not, but she didn't really care, either, so it didn't matter. Once they got past the greetings, she asked Todd to give Taylor a message.

"Oh, sure," he whispered.

"Ask him to give me a call once the interview is over. If he's coming home tonight, I'd like to see him."

"Oh," said Todd, rolling the o-sound into several syllables. "A secret rendezvous?"

Damn, he's annoying she thought, but she said, "No—nothing like that. Just give him the message, please."

"Will do."

Katherine turned off the phone and put it down. Then she went into the den and clicked on the television. The interview had been in progress for more than five minutes. He looked better on television that he did in real life, and that was saying something because in real life he always looked like he was on television.

The camera came in close while he was talking. He had the whitest teeth she'd ever seen on a man. She wondered if his teeth were that bright naturally, or whether he had bleaching treatments. Either way, it didn't really matter. It was just something that jumped out at her during a close up.

Taylor looked very much in charge. The interviewer was earnest, persistent in his questioning, but he was no match for the master. Taylor reeked with charm. What cheap cologne was to some men, charm was to him.

"You seem to have a unique vision for where we should be headed as a nation."

Taylor smiled, flashing his teeth.

"I think the people of Canada have their own vision of where we should be headed. My job is to articulate that vision."

"You recently issued a position paper on casinos that I find interesting. You are in favor of federalizing the operation of casinos across the country?"

"That is correct. I think that provincial control of the casinos has created problems that only can be corrected by federalization."

"What kind of problems are you referring to?"

"As the situation now stands, each province sets its own rules and regulations—and establishes its own agenda. The provinces decide when and where casinos will open, and they set foreign trade policy that should be expressed at the national level. They also limit the amount of money that can be channeled back into the communities where the casinos are located. We think that the existing requirement to link casinos to charities is bad for the economy. Of course, we want money to go to charities, but we think that percentage should be reduced to a more realistic rate."

"What do you mean by foreign trade policy?"

"Individually, the provinces have decided to block American casinos from opening in Canada. That's the position of the Liberal Party. The Conservative Party believes in free trade and we think it is not in the national interest to block legitimate American business from opening franchises in Canada."

"I guess I never thought about it that. How do you reconcile supporting legislation that would enhance a business that your constituents find offensive?"

"Yes, the majority of my constituents are opposed to casinos, period. They would like to see them disappear, even though we have in my district a very successful casino at Gananoque. But that will not happen, at least not as long as the province is governed by the Liberal

Party. A federalized system would allow the Conservative Party to set standards for the casinos—and that would very much please my constituents."

He's amazing thought Katherine. *He can turn a negative into a positive without anyone noticing the sleight of hand. I'd better keep my eye on him.*

"Do you have the backing of the Conservative Party for your legislation?"

"Yes I do. I think it will pass without difficulty."

The interviewer looked into the camera.

"There you have it. Straight from the mouth of the man that many political observers think will be the next Prime Minister."

Katherine turned off the television. She was thinking *I made love to a man who may become the next prime minister . . . how crazy is that?*

When the telephone rang, she knew who it was without looking at caller ID.

"Katherine—" Taylor said. "I called as soon as I got your message."

"I just watched you on television. Very impressive."

"Thank you. It's all in a day's work."

"You believe strongly in your casino issue, don't you?"

"Yes I do. I think it's important . . . not to change the subject, but Todd said you mentioned getting together this evening?"

"Yes, that would be great if you will be in town."

"I'll make it a point to be in town. May I send someone to pick you up?"

"No, I'll drive myself. See you at seven."

"Can't wait," he said.

Katherine put down the cell. She had mixed feelings about seeing him. Every word that came out of his mouth, every action, only made him more endearing to her. Would it even be possible to find a more appealing romantic partner? However, Jason's problems were like a festering thorn in the relationship.

Katherine returned to her painting. She still wasn't sure what she'd do with it when it was finished, but she felt compelled to finish it. The hardest part was detailing the back of her feet and her toes. She looked down at the toes in her scandals.

Should she make them identical to the ragged toes she saw protruding from her scandals? Or should she idealize them? Make them the perfect accent to a less than perfect body?

She returned to the canvas, delicately shaping the toes into perfection.

Later, Katherine bathed, dressed. She looked in the mirror. Funny thing. She knew she was an attractive woman. But when she stood next to Taylor, she felt more attractive. She'd never been around a man who took her breath away. Not even Roger did that. She found it confusing. She loved Roger more deeply than she'd ever loved anyone. She didn't feel that way about Taylor. Yet he took her breath away. It made no sense.

When she arrived at Prescott Place that evening, Taylor was waiting for her at the door. When she parked her car, he walked over and opened the door for her.

"You look lovely," he said, taking her in his arms. He kissed her in a gentle way and pulled away to give her another up and down look. He was quick to kiss, she noticed. He didn't waste time with small talk. They walked arm in arm to the house.

When they arrived at the door, he paused to say, "I didn't have time to have my chef prepare anything. Do you mind if we eat out?"

"Not at all," she said.

"Would you like to come in for a drink before we leave?" he asked.

"Sure—that would be fine. Besides, there is something I need to talk to you about."

"Oh," he said, raising his eyebrows with mock concern.

They went into the den, where Katherine tried not to glance at her painting. Okay, she did—once. And it looked marvelous bathed in its own special light. But then she turned away, sitting on the edge of the sofa so that her back was turned to the painting.

"I had a very disturbing experience today," she said.

"Oh, really," he said, genuinely concerned.

"Remember I told you about my therapist, Dr. Montclair?"

"Yes, of course."

"And I told you about the investigation . . ."

"Yes."

"Well, today an investigator from New York knocked on my door and asked to talk to me about it."

"What did you say?"

"I told him I wasn't interested. He said that if I didn't allow them to interview me they would subpoena me. Can they do that?"

"Yes, I'm afraid so. We have an agreement with the United States. They would deliver the subpoena to the OPP and they would serve it."

"Isn't there something I can do?"

"You mean, to avoid testifying?"

"Yes."

"I don't think so. Would that be such a problem?"

"Yes."

"Because you're still seeing him?"

"I'm seeing him as a friend. Yes, that would create a problem. He's a wonderful therapist and a great friend. I would never do anything to hurt him."

"I really don't know what to tell you."

Katherine paused, carefully going over what she wanted to say.

Finally, she said, "We can't figure out how the board found about this. You're the only person I told. Did you happen to mention it to anyone?"

"Me?" He seemed offended. "Why would I do that?"

"You didn't call the psychology board?"

"No—I would have no reason to do that. Do you really think I would betray your confidence?"

Katherine looked deeply into his eyes, luminous orbs that oozed with sincerity. She felt enormous guilt for ever bringing the matter up. After a long pause, during which she hoped he would say something else, something to take her off the hook, she said, "I'm sorry. It was wrong for me to suggest anything like that."

"I understand," he said, taking her in his arms, kissing her first on the neck, then on the ear, softly.

She melted like butter beneath his touch.

*　*　*

In the dream, Bessie was one-third her actual size, nestled away in Katherine's purse that was slung over her shoulder. It was an expansive purse in which Katherine frequently carried painting supplies. Katherine looked into the purse and smiled.

"Where are we going?" asked Bessie.

"I'm taking you to work with me," said Katherine.

"Why are you doing that?"

"Because I love you."

Bessie looked perplexed.

"Does that mean that, on the days that you don't take me to work with you, that you don't love me?"

"No, no," said Katherine, brushing Bessie's fur away from her eyes. "That's not it at all."

"Are you sure?"

"I'm very sure. I love you all the time."

The early morning light filled the room with brightness.

Katherine opened her eyes, her first thoughts on Bessie. She reached for her purse, but it was not there. Still groggy with sleep, she raised up on her elbow and looked around, expecting to see Bessie sniffing one thing or another.

She heard a sound in the bathroom.

"Bessie, is that you?" she said.

Moments later, Taylor stepped into the doorway, a towel wrapped around his waist. "I'm sorry—did I wake you?"

"No . . . no . . ." she stammered. "I was dreaming."

"About me, hope."

"No, it was about Bessie."

"Your dog?"

"Don't tell her that. She thinks she's human."

Katherine discretely pulled the covers up around her neck and looked around the room. Directly across from her was an elegant rattan dresser, on either side of which were rattan chairs upholstered with a dark-maroon fabric. The lamps and accent items in the room all reflected a South Pacific décor.

"Where am I" she asked.

"The Tahitian Room," he said proudly. "It's one of my favorite rooms in the house. Since you are an island person, I thought it would be perfect for you."

Taylor lay on the bed next to Katherine and slowly pulled the sheet away from her, exposing her nearly perfect breasts. He spread butterfly kisses across her skin and then he propped up to look at her.

"You have the most beautiful skin I've ever seen. It's like fine porcelain."

She put her arms around him and pulled him in close to her, the scent of his cologne filling her nostrils. She whispered into his ear, "I have a question."

"What's that?"

"What did you do with Bessie?" she asked in mock seriousness.

He looked stunned at first. He didn't know what to say. Not until she cracked the beginnings of a smile did he laugh.

"Katherine Summer, you are a handful."

CHAPTER
23

The sun fell flush against her face, the warmth a welcome contrast to the coolness of the breeze. Fall was muscling its way onto the river. It wouldn't be long until all the trees were covered with golden and red leaves, a brief reprieve before the stark barrenness of winter.

Katherine sat on the edge of the dock and cried about her life, tears flowing down her cheeks.

The river was stilled, not a wave in sight; but beneath its mysteriously shadowed surface the currents ran deep, rushing headlong to the Atlantic, oblivious to her tears. Bessie crawled up beside Katherine, next to the fishing gear she'd brought from the house, and went to sleep, her sporadic snores occasionally sawing through the quietness.

Lulled by the river's sweet music, Katherine stared out across the water for almost an hour before she decided to fish. She cast a reddish spinner out into the river and slowly reeled it back in. Her dad had taught her how to fish, but Roger taught her the art of fishing. He was like that. Not so much a perfectionist as he was a connoisseur of life. He showed her, in myriad ways, that results are the child of effort.

Roger, I'm so sorry, she thought. *Sorry that I've moved on. Why do I feel so much guilt? Will it ever go away? What would you want me to do?*

Cloud shadows drifted across the water, the reflections distorting her fishing line.

In the distance was New York. She wondered about Jason. Wondered how he was coping with the assault on his career. That's what it was—an assault. He was a good man. Compassionate. Considerate. Devoted to helping others. How was it possible, in a rational world, for such a person to lose everything, simply because he expressed affection for another human being?

Katherine was glad she could make a living as an artist. It frightened her to think that she would ever have to conform to a regimented society.

Suddenly, her line jerked and she realized that she had a strike. She lifted her rod, only to see it bend sharply at the tip.

"Come on," she muttered.

She worked the line, pulling, lifting, reeling, slowly bringing the fish in the direction of the dock. Sensing that something was afoot Bessie awoke and sat up so that she could look out across the water at the spot where the line disappeared into the river.

Abruptly, the line moved south as the fish swam downstream. Then, when it ran out of line, there was a jerk—and the fish reversed direction, this time headed upstream.

"He's got a plan," Katherine said to Bessie. "But it's not going to work."

She could tell by the tension that it was a large fish. She released the line and allowed it to feed out about ten feet. Then she reeled it in again, working the fish. She became more aware of the sun, as if it had awakened from sleep and wanted to have its say about the fish. The rays felt good against her face. She took a deep breath. There was no odor in the air. Just the moist crispness of a good day. The way she liked it.

She pulled hard on the rod, reeling, lifting the fish toward the surface.

"Nothing personal," she said. "It's just that it's your turn."

The line darted to the left about twenty feet. Then it went to the right about ten feet. She lifted the rod, reeling in more line, relishing the moment she landed the fish.

"Yes," she said. "You are a monster fish."

She heard the faint murmur of a boat in the distance, somewhere behind her. It was the first boat of the morning, but she couldn't be bothered at the moment. She reeled the line tight and then she yanked hard with the rod, lifting the fish.

Suddenly, it leaped from the water. To her surprise it was a largemouth bass, a rarity in the river. It was gone in an instant, but the visitation was long enough for her to see that it probably weighed ten pounds or more. She wondered if the fish might have started out in Lake Superior or Lake Huron, and then made its way down the St. Clair River into Lake St. Clair, putting on a pound or two each year, and then into Lake Erie and Lake Ontario, finally making it downriver past her island.

The line went soft and for a moment she feared she'd lost her fish, but then she reeled, taking in line until it again became taut.

"You're still there. I know it."

It was at that point that she realized that the boat was close by. She glanced over her shoulder and saw the boat, an OPP patrol cruiser. She refocused her attention on her fish, reeling it without much resistance now, the fish weary of the fight.

Just when the fish was ready, she felt a thud as the boat gently bumped into the dock. She turned and saw the two police officers who'd brought her the bad news about Roger and Dedi. Seeing them, if only for an instant, brought back a flood of bad memories.

"Looks like you got a big'un," said one of the officers.

Katherine didn't respond. Instead, she worked the fish, reeling it right up to the dock. Holding the line tight, she picked up a long-handle net and lowered it into the water beneath the fish. Once she had it in place, she lifted the fish, by then too weary to be outraged, onto the dock. She reached into the net and removed the hook. Then she slipped her fingers beneath its gills and lifted it up into the air.

"Look at that!" said one of the police officers. "That's as pretty a bass as I've seen in this river in years."

Katherine still had not acknowledged the men's presence.

"That'll cook up really nice on the grill," said the second police officer.

Katherine looked at the fish one last time—leaned over and kissed it—and then dropped it back into the river. It hit the water with a big splash and quickly disappeared from view.

"Have a nice trip," she said.

"Why'd you do that?" asked a police officer.

Katherine looked at them for the first time. With a wicked grin, she said, "Because I can. Do you have a problem with that?"

"No ma'am," said the officer.

Bessie sat quietly and stared at the police officers. But when one of the men reached over the boat to pet her, she growled, not loudly, but the hands-off message was unmistakable.

"What brings you to my island today?"

The men looked at each other.

Then one of the men reached into a plastic envelope and withdrew a paper envelope. He handed the envelope to her. The envelope had her name and address on it, nothing more.

"What's this?" she asked.

"I'm afraid it's a subpoena," said the police officer. "It's for a New York civil proceeding. We have a treaty with the United States that requires us to deliver this to you. We're sorry to have to do that."

"I understand," she said, stuffing the envelope into her back pocket. "Is there anything else?"

The police officers hated that part of their work. No one ever got a happy subpoena. The parts of their job that they liked were when they saved people from the river, or saved someone from a kidnapper or rapist, or pulled someone from a burning car after an accident. Thus far neither of the police officers had ever done anything good for Katherine. They'd only brought bad news.

"We don't like to do these things," said one of the men. "It's our job."

Katherine nodded and headed for the house, Bessie at her heels. The police officers stood there a moment, speechless, and then got into their boat. They hoped that she would turn around and wave, but she didn't.

The boat pulled away and the motor revved up so that they could make a speedy exit. The men looked at each other, each shaking his head at the same instant. They wouldn't blame her if she hated them for the rest of her life. Lords knows, they hated themselves and each other.

Back in the house, Katherine returned to her studio. The room seemed to swim in a bath of pinkish-white light. She picked up her brush to resume work in her self-portrait, but then she paused and thought better of it and returned the brush to the solution that kept it soft. Instead, she walked over to where she had several paintings leaned against the wall and she withdrew the painting of Dedi and carried it over to an empty easel near the window. She placed it on the easel and turned it so that it faced inward, the backwash of light behind it creating a halo effect.

Oh, Dedi she thought. *How much we already have missed together. I looked at this image of you frozen in time and in my heart I know you already have changed, wherever you are. I ache all over when I think about the things we will miss sharing. I will never know what you will look like when you are ten or fourteen or twenty-one. Will you look like me—or will you look like Roger? I would like to think that he is with you now. Is that possible? And you, Roger—what you must think of me now? It wasn't that I made a conscious decision to move on. I never decided to put you aside. It didn't happen that way. I wish I knew more about what happens in whatever place you are now. Do you watch me? Would you be able to warn me of danger? Do you ever shed tears for me?*

Katherine looked at Dedi's angelic image. Never was sweetness so appealing on a child's face. She wondered if children were ever given a second chance for life. Was it even remotely possible that children could be snatched from earth, with no hope of ever having the opportunity to live a full life? What kind of God would do that?

As she gazed at the painting, there was a growing awareness of something else. It pressed against her from her back pocket. She ignored it for a while. But then it returned and she remembered what she had in her back pocket. She reached back for the envelope and opened it. The letterhead referred to the New York Psychology Board.

She saw her name typed into an inch wide white space, along with her address. Then she saw Jason's name and his address. In between the "hereby's" and the "whereas's," were words that directed her to appear in Albany tomorrow at 10 a.m. Further, it stated that refusal to comply with the order would result in her arrest.

"This is outrageous," she said, speaking to Bessie. "They can't order me to go to another country and testify against Jason. I live on an island, don't they know that?"

She tossed the subpoena onto the table next to her chair, and sat there, fuming, trying her best to ignore the letter. After a while, she picked it up again and re-read it, looking for some loophole, something that gave her an alternative, a multiple-choice solution that made the whole thing go away if she checked the correct box.

Incredibly, the subpoena did not ask for her opinion about any facet of the case. It was an order, not an invitation for a meaningful dialog. Once again, she slapped the paper onto the table, disdainful of its intrusion into her life.

Images of Jason paraded through her head. She thought back to the first time she met him. She was a nervous wreck, exhausted from days of unrelenting crying. She walked into his office and sat down, expecting an emotional procedure not unlike what happens in the dentist's office when needles and drills and sharp instruments punctuate the dentist's soothing words. She'd never been to a psychologist before, so she naturally assumed that it would not be an experience that she would ever look back on with fond remembrance. Just shows you how wrong a person can be.

When she sat in the chair across the desk from him, she was struck by how good looking he was. Somehow she'd gotten the impression that psychologists looked like Sigmund Freud or Groucho Marx. Dr. Montclair was a handsome man. He was well dressed, clean shaven. To her surprise, he made her laugh within the first five minutes of her visit.

Nothing disrespectful to her reason for being there. In fact, her laughter was enticed by his ability to laugh at his own foibles. He instantly put her at ease. Her instincts told her that he was a man that she could trust with her feelings.

Later, when their relationship changed from a professional one to a personal one, it was still the laughter that cemented the bond between them. He laughed at her. He laughed at himself. He laughed at the entire world, especially the entire world. All of which was why seeing him so upset over the threat to his livelihood was painful for her. He saw no humor in the board's intrusion into his life, and neither did she.

Katherine wanted Jason in her life. She needed him to make her laugh again. But she was fearful of what would happen if she attended the hearing. How could her presence there do anything other than destroy their relationship? If she thought she could lie and save him, she would do so. As it stood, there was no room for lies.

She could not deny being his patient—there was ample proof that she was. And she could not deny going out with him—there were plenty of people who could testify otherwise. As she saw it, the proceeding was lie proof. Her words would be used to destroy a man that she very much cared about. Her only options were either to not attend and hope for the best, paying the price for her loyalty if necessary—or to attend and utterly destroy his life.

Then there was the matter of Taylor's involvement in it. He denied telling anyone, but if he didn't, then who did? Was it possible that a waiter overhead their conversation? No, the only place she discussed it with him was at his house.

Was it possible that one of the housekeepers or cooks betrayed her? No, they were not in the house when she told him. Was it possible that he'd told Todd? Yes, but what would Todd gain by filing a complaint? That made no sense whatsoever.

Surely, it was the worst thing she ever could tell another person—the life-destroying truth about a man who trusted her to keep her mouth shut.

She couldn't blame Jason if he hated her for the rest of his life.

After twisting her emotions into a knot of self-blame, she revisited the possibility that someone on Jason's end had betrayed him. He was positive that his secretary had told no one, but how certain could he really be?

Perhaps he told someone else and just forgot about it. People forget things. Perhaps he told his barber. Or his doctor. Or his best friend, if he has a best friend.

Why does it have to be my fault?

CHAPTER
24

Margaret squared off against him, her feet firmly planted.

"I can't help it if I'm good looking beyond the ordinary."

Jason had ducked into the Quick-Mart to get a six-pack. There she was at the checkout counter, still pretty, but a few pounds heavier. As they waited in line, they got caught up on things. She asked about his practice; he didn't tell her about the investigation, instead blah-blahing about how great everything was.

She asked if he was dating anyone. He hesitated at first, pondering the definition of dating, but then he rallied and said, "Not really," knowing that she'd be pleased that he was without a woman in his life. The truth meant more to him than winning a post-marital scrimmage with his ex-wife.

"And how about you?" he asked.

It was a legitimate question. She had divorced the doctor that she had left him to marry and he had lost touch with her. Ogdensburg only had a population of twelve thousand, but that was plenty large enough for two people to avoid each other.

In response to his question, she'd answered, "Oh, yes—I'm dating a beautiful young man, a college man. His father owns the pickle factor over at Watertown."

It was when Jason commented about her dating a much younger man that she squared off and said what she did.

"I never said you weren't attractive. I was just commenting on his age."

"You've never dated someone younger than yourself?"

Jason paused, wondering what he could say to stop that line of conversation.

"I did once, but it didn't work out," he lied. "She died."

"Oh," said Margaret. She didn't really want to offer him sympathy, so she decided not to follow through. Instead, she asked him if he thought he'd ever get married again.

"I don't know," he said, instantly thinking of Katherine.

"I bet you will." Margaret leaned into him, so that they were almost touching. "Sometimes I regret we haven't stayed in better touch."

"What do you mean?"

"We obviously cared for each other, or we never would have gotten married. Once people care for each other they should hold on to some part of that caring, even if it is only a small part. Know what I mean?"

"I think I do."

"That's the part of life that's always confused me. How can a man and a woman share everything—every thought, every private moment— and then suddenly decide not to share any longer, as if the memory of it can be completely erased. I don't mean the sex. I understand how men and women can have sex and walk away from it without ever looking back. But sharing emotions is different, isn't it? How do you forget sharing?"

"You can't. Not completely."

"Do you never think about me?"

"Of course I do."

"When?"

"At odd moments. No particular times."

"Do you ever think about me when you're intimate with another woman?"

"No."

"Really?"

Jason nodded. "Why do you ask? Do you think about me during intimate moments?"

"Perhaps women are different in that way."

"So you do?"

"Sometimes."

"I don't know what to say."

"Don't let it go to your head or anything. You're a psychologist. Surely you understand that women are different in that way. If we experience something with a man during an intimate moment, something special, we hold onto it. That's nothing for men to crow about. It usually has nothing to do with their performance. It could be a song. Or a sunset. Or a movie. It's a female thing. If you don't understand, just don't worry about it."

Jason nodded, thinking that he had nothing to contribute to that line of thinking.

Margaret continued, "Do you ever regret we didn't have children?"

"Why do you think about things like that?"

"I think that's a normal thing to do. We shared a part of a life together. Everything we shared is gone now, as if it never existed. If we'd had a child, it would be a validation of what we shared. Don't you think?"

"You're right—and, yes, I do wish we'd had a child. Everyone should have a genetic connection to the universe. If we'd had a child, a small part of us would be there to live on past us."

Margaret thought about that a moment, her eyes welling with tears. She suddenly grabbed her package and headed for the door.

"Wait a minute!" Jason shouted. He slapped a ten dollar bill on the counter and told the clerk to keep the change. Then he hurried to catch up with Margaret before she reached the door.

"Listen," he said. "If you ever need to talk, just give me a call."

She nodded, but then as they went out the door, she said, "Oh, by the way, I hope your hearing goes all right."

Surprised, he asked, "How did you know about that?"

"Why, it was in the newspaper. Didn't you read it?"

"Bye," he said, and hurried to his car and tossed the six-pack onto the passenger seat.

The newspaper he thought. *Those bastards wasted no time. Couldn't the board at least have held the hearing before they released the complaint to the press?*

On the drive home, he thought about Katherine. That business about every couple having a child made him think about Katherine's loss. She not only lost the man she loved the most, she lost the validation of that love.

How does she find the strength to wake in the morning and then continue through the day as if she is ordinary and the day is ordinary, when there is nothing ordinary about her or her days? She's the most unordinary woman I've ever known.

CHAPTER
25

Jason debated whether he should call her. He hadn't heard from her about the hearing in Albany, and he had no idea whether she planned to attend. He thought about it from the moment he awoke, and then all during his shower and breakfast. His first instinct was to ask her to ride to the hearing with him, but he couldn't very well do that, considering the reason for the hearing.

The injustice of her being forced to travel all the way to Albany to testify against him made him nauseous. It was so unfair. It was in opposition to the healing goals of his profession. Since when did rules and regulations become more important than people?

After breakfast, he went to his closet and pondered the possibilities. What would a psychologist who was guilty of violating ethics regulations wear to a hearing, the purpose of which was to end his career? He chose a dark suit, white shirt and burgundy necktie (he'd once read a magazine article on power dressing and he seemed to recall mention of a burgundy or red necktie). He needed all the power he could muster.

He stood before a full-length mirror.

I look like I'm going to a funeral, he thought.

He sat in his favorite chair and pecked Katherine's number into his cell. But he didn't push send right away. Instead, he held the cell, thinking about whether he should call. That decision was not made until he looked at the clock and saw that it was time for him to leave for Albany. He pressed call.

"Hello."

The sound of Katherine's voice was tonic for his soul.

"It's me, Jason. I wasn't sure whether I should call or not."

"I'm glad you did. I've been thinking about you."

"I guess you know that today is, don't you?"

"I've been served with a subpoena."

"Really." He paused, his heart aching at the thought of Katherine being subjected to such an indignity *because of him.* "I'm sorry about that. I'm surprised they are so heavy-handed about this."

"It was delivered by the OPP, and they didn't look all that happy about it."

"I'm sure they felt they had better things to do." Another pause, this one more awkward than the last. "What time are you leaving?"

This time it was Katherine who paused.

"Katherine, did you hear me? I think the phone cut out."

"No, no," she said. "I heard you. I was just trying to think of a way to tell you that I'm not going."

"Not going?"

"I care too much about you to ever do anything that would hurt you."

He said, "But they'll issue a warrant for your arrest," but his thoughts were whirling around the phrase *I care too much.* What did that mean? She'd never said that to him. Perhaps it meant nothing. Perhaps it was just a figure of speech.

"Then I'll deal with that when it happens."

Jason looked at his watch. "Well, I guess I need to go. I'll call you after the hearing."

"Why don't you wait until tomorrow? I'm going to Ottawa to hide and I'm turning off my cell."

"I don't blame you."

"Good luck, Jason. I'll be thinking about you."

"Thank you."

It was 266 miles from Ogdensburg to Albany, a drive of about four-and-a-half hours. For most of the way, he thought about Katherine.

I care about you too much.

What does that mean when a woman says that? Did she say it as a friend? Or did she say it as someone who had romantic feelings for him? His lawyer gave him a list of things to think about on the drive to the hearing, but he couldn't focus on the list.

Jason didn't much care. His lawyer, Trevor Hall, specialized in labor cases. Jason pretty much figured he didn't have a leg to stand on when he asked his lawyer what his defense would be and he replied, "Defense—are you saying you are innocent?"

"Why no—it happened the way the charges say it happened."

"In that case, I'm afraid you don't have much of a defense. I've got two goals. The first is to take advantage of any procedural errors they make."

"So you'll try to make them screw up?"

"Yes . . . and the second is to lay groundwork to request leniency in the punishment phase of their deliberations."

"You mean, cut our loses?"

"Yes. A lawyer's first goal is to win. The second goal is to get the client the best deal possible. To be honest, I don't think winning is an option for you."

After his initial conversation with Trevor Hall, Jason considered getting another attorney; but then after he thought about it for a while, he realized it wouldn't make a difference. He was guilty as charged. Getting a new lawyer wouldn't change that fact.

When he arrived at the building where the hearing was to take place, by chance he ran into Trevor in the parking lot and they walked inside together. As they made their way through the corridors, they discussed the case. Eventually, Trevor brought up Katherine's testimony.

"I see she refused to be interviewed."

"That's what I understand."

"I wonder what she will say under oath."

"She's not coming."

Trevor stopped and faced Jason. "What do you mean she's not coming?"

"I spoke to her on the telephone this morning before I left. She told me that she had been served with a subpoena but she had no intention of respecting it."

Trevor released a soft, low whistle.

"They'll send the guys with handcuffs after her."

"She knows that."

"I see . . . you're quite the couple, aren't you?"

"We aren't a couple."

"If that's what you believe, then you are in denial."

Jason looked surprised.

"I don't know what I believe."

When they entered the hearing room, the five board members, three men, two women, were seated behind an elevated desk in the shape of a semi-circle. Heads bowed, each member thumbed through various manila folders, oblivious to their surroundings.

There was a small table to the left, where the clerk sat with all the parliamentary levers of power at her disposal. A larger table, used by witnesses, was centered in front of the board members. Jason and Trevor walked past that table and sat in the area directly behind the witness table. Within minutes of their arrival, the clerk announced that the hearing was in session. She read Jason's name and articulated the case number.

Jason whispered to Trevor, "I'm just a number to her, aren't I?"

Trevor didn't respond, but he thought *what did you expect?*

The board chairman instructed the clerk to call the first witness. The clerk called out, "Will Katherine Summer please be seated at the witness table."

Almost a minute went by.

The clerk repeated her summons, this time her voice slightly irritated, "Will Katherine Summer please be seated at the witness table."

When there was no response, the clerk said, "Witness Katherine Summer was issued a subpoena, which I understand was served by the Ontario Provincial Police. We have received no communication from her indicating mitigating circumstances."

The clerk sat with her arms folded, the stern look on her face an indication that she felt that Katherine Summer had prevented *her* from properly doing her job.

The board members huddled, speaking in low voices that did not carry as far as the audience. Everyone seemed to be in agreement. The chairman raised his head and instructed the clerk to issue an arrest order for the missing witness.

Then he asked her to call the next witness.

Going through the same motions, a routine she repeated many times a day, she stood and said, "Will Dr. Jason Montclair please be seated at the witness table."

Jason and Trevor got up and walked over to the witness table and sat next to each other. Trevor leaned forward and spoke into the microphone.

"My name is Trevor Hall. I am an attorney representing Dr. Montclair in this matter."

The chairman lowered his head and peered over his glasses at Jason.

"May I assume that you are Dr. Jason Montclair?"

"Yes sir, I am."

"For the record, do you stipulate that you are licensed to practice psychology in the State of New York?"

"Yes sir."

". . .and you have an office in Ogdensburg . . ."

"Yes sir."

“. . . and you had as a client a woman named Katherine Summer . . .”

“Yes sir.”

“. . . and at some point in providing counseling to her you instructed her to seek the services of another therapist . . .”

Trevor gently bumped Jason aside and said into the microphone, “Mr. Chairman, I don’t think it is proper for my client to answer further questions until the commission has established the facts that are in evidence in this case. It is a constitutional issue, I believe. He will be happy to testify once a foundation has been laid for his questioning.”

The chairman smiled and said, “Mr. Hall, I believe we have had occasion to work with you on previous cases, have we not?”

“Yes, I believe you have.”

“I am going to dismiss Dr. Montclair until such time as the witness, Katherine Summer, is brought before the board to testify.”

“Thank you Mr. Chairman.”

“You are dismissed.”

Trevor got to his feet and walked to the door, with Jason close behind. Once they got into the outside corridor, Jason asked, “What happened?”

“They can’t ask the accused to provide the foundation of fact. That’s what witnesses are for. I called them on that and they dismissed you.”

“Until when?”

“Until they locate Katherine Summer and transport her to the hearing.”

“Can they bring her against her will?”

“Yes, indeed.”

“She won’t like that—not at all.”

“I don’t imagine she will.”

“So what do we do now?”

“We wait until the hearing is rescheduled.”

“Do you think I should spend the night—or return to Ogdensburg?”

“I would spend the night if I were you. It won’t take them long to locate her.”

CHAPTER
26

No one would ever guess that Katherine was in the eye of a hurricane. She moved about the house with quiet determination, performing ordinary chores, tossing play toys to Bessie, opening and closing windows, turning on lights, turning off lights, preparing lunch: ordinary things in an unordinary day.

Once she finished her chores, she went into her studio and resumed work on her self-portrait. She was almost finished. There was only one thing about the painting that bothered her. She'd used a little too much pink in the coloration of her behind. A pink behind was cute on a baby, but not on a woman.

She took her brush and dabbed colors onto her palette, mixing them, until she found what she considered the perfect flesh tone. It only took a few brush strokes to de-pinkify her behind. This time, when she looked at the painting with a critical eye, she approved. She could see why women were eager to pose nude for the masters. They knew their images would endure, possibly for eternity.

Once she was done, she went through her paintings, choosing several to take to the Ottawa gallery. She looked at her portrait of Dedi and put it back. Then a few minutes later she revisited it. She put it on an easel and walked around the room, looking at the painting from different angles. Inexplicably, she had an argument with herself.

Why shouldn't I take it to the gallery?

Because Dedi is not for sale.

All paintings are for sale.

Not this one. This one is special.

Your choice is to ether hide it away, or send it out into the world for all to see. During your life, you may paint dozens of portraits of Dedi. Will you keep all of them hidden away—or will you share them and celebrate her memory?

Katherine sat in a chair directly across from the painting, one leg tossed over the arm of the chair. Dedi seemed to speak to her with her eyes, or perhaps it was her impish smile. She felt her presence in the painting. She knew that she would be with her, always. She lived in the moment, breathing deeply of its freshness, savoring the optimism that always accompanies love that is pure and unconditional.

Her mind made up, Katherine gathered her paintings, putting Dedi's portrait with the others she'd chosen to take to market.

Before leaving the house, she filled two bowls of water for Bessie and put plenty of food in her dish, all during which Bessie looked at her with great apprehension. She learned at an early age that Katherine went through certain motions before leaving the house. Two of them being pouring water into two dishes and setting out food for her, more food than she could possibly eat at one time. The next thing she listened for was the jingle of car keys and then the hurried steps to the door.

"Be a good girl while I'm gone," Katherine said, closing the door behind her.

When she pulled out on the road, she had the feeling that she was being followed, but when she looked in the rearview mirror she saw nothing. A bad case of nerves, nothing more. It was not easy for her to defy the subpoena. It rubbed against her grain to be so defiant of authority. Yet she felt that she had no other choice. She'd rather be a criminal than destroy Jason's life.

Ottawa was not a big city, but it was large enough to swallow up someone who wanted to disappear. She refused to think about tomorrow. Today she would be lost. She had some control over that. Tomorrow was a new day over which she had no control.

The gallery owner was delighted to get new paintings, considering how quickly they sold. Spotting the portrait of Dedi, she asked, "Who is this darling little girl?"

"An angel," said Katherine, not wishing to explain. She wanted the painting to be purchased on its own merits, not because of any story attached to it.

"Oh. A painting with a mystery. I like it. Why don't we title it 'Little Angel'?"

"You can title it whatever you like."

"You're *sooo* easy to work with."

"Some people wouldn't think so."

"I can't imagine anyone having a difficult time with you. You're such a sensible person. So many of the artists have airs about them. I don't like them very much."

"All artists are different, I guess."

After she left the gallery, Katherine drove directly to Attorney General Donald Kelly's residence, where she had an appointment to do preliminary sketches of his wife, Rose. The home was located in the Riverside South Community, in the southern part of the city along the beautiful Rideau River, a favorite playground during the winter months for skaters. Katherine found the house without difficulty—an elegant, two-story redbrick house that was totally without pretense, much like the Attorney General himself.

Katherine felt guilty about going to his home after defying the OPP, but doing the portrait was his idea, not hers, so she didn't worry about it too much.

To her surprise, Rose greeted her at the door.

"Did you have a nice drive?"

"Quite nice. The leaves are turning, and it made for a beautiful day."

Rose invited her into the house and suggested that they do the sketches in the den, a large room with skylights and wide windows. Katherine liked the room and told her that it was perfect. Rose sat in what Katherine surmised was her favorite chair, a well-padded recliner that was covered with a velvet-like fabric; but the lighting was all wrong there, so she asked her to move to a chair closer to a window.

She posed her on the edge of the chair, with her back arched and her hands in her lap. She wanted to sketch her face from different angles. It was a pose that allowed her to turn left and right without distorting the essential dimensions of her face.

She sketched her straight on, left profile, right profile, her chin tilted down, her entire head tilted slightly to one side. She was an excellent subject. High cheekbones. Full lips. Doe eyes. Flawless complexion. A nose that looked like it might have been surgically altered when she was younger. Square shoulders. Hair that fell past her shoulders.

"I understand you haven't done many portraits."

"This is my first on assignment."

"I'm honored that you chose me for your first."

"I thought you would make an excellent subject."

"Thank you. Donald has wanted me to do this for years. I was a dancer when we met and he liked my figure so much that it took a couple of years for him to acknowledge that I even had a face. You know how men are."

Katherine laughed. "Sometimes they seem to have a one-track mind."

Rose was pleasant enough, but Katherine wished she wouldn't tell her quite so much about her private life. Her comment did make her think, however. Men seem to fall in love with packages. She wondered what her face/figure ratio had been with Roger.

Was his attraction to her based on one more than the other? Did he love her face and tolerate her body? Did he love her body and tolerate her face?

See she thought. *That's why I wish people would keep their thoughts to themselves. Idle conversation raises more questions than it answers. Ignorance is sometimes a woman's best friend. If you must speak, please say something that will make me feel something, not something that will make me think myself into a corner.*

"Is your relationship with Taylor serious?" asked Rose.

More questions.

"When I find out, you'll be the first to know."

"Oh," said Rose. "Everyone thinks you make a great-looking couple."

"Looks are sometimes deceiving."

"What are you saying?"

"Only that Taylor and I only recently started going out."

"Most people at the luncheon thought that you looked like honeymooners, what with the sparkle in your eye and everything."

Katherine recalled the experience in the drawing room and blushed, a lapse that did not go unnoticed by Rose, who quickly added, "But you know how people are about gossip."

Katherine ignored the comment. Instead, she changed the subject and wrapped up the session.

"I think I would prefer to do the actual painting at my home, where I am the most comfortable when I'm working. I hope that you don't mind."

"Oh, not at all. Donald said you'd probably want to do that."

Rose walked her to the door, apologizing several times along the way.

After she left the Attorney General's residence, she drove directly to Taylor's office. Were they dating? Or were they going out? Were they a couple? What exactly was a couple? Does having sex make you a couple? Or is one's couple status based on something more substantial . . . like perhaps a shared vision for the future?

As she navigated the noon-hour traffic, she argued with herself over whether she'd made a mistake by going out with Taylor. If so, was it a bigger or a smaller mistake than going out with Jason? She despised conflict.

I should never have left the house she thought.

She parked on the street about a block away from Taylor's office. The sidewalk was filled with people. Women in tailored suits accented with stylish shoes. Men in assorted dress jackets, all worn with a necktie. Ottawa had a regimented look of its own, distinctive from Toronto and Montreal, where conformity was not so much an issue. She thought of herself more as an island girl, even if the island was in a river and not in an exotic location. She liked to dress up, but only for special occasions.

As soon as she walked in the door, Miss Sweeny called out in a loud voice, "Well, look who's here—it's Miss Summer!"

Papers rattled in the other room.

"How are you Miss Sweeny? Is Taylor in?"

Suddenly, Todd appeared in the room.

"What a surprise. We didn't know you were stopping by!"

Before she could respond, Taylor was in the doorway of his inner office, a broad smile on his face.

"What a nice surprise."

He escorted her into the office and closed the door behind them.

"I never realized that stopping by my MP's office would cause such a stir."

Taylor laughed. "You are what is called a very high-profile visitor."

They embraced and enjoyed a lingering kiss. Then Katherine tossed her purse into one chair and sat in the one next to it.

"I dropped more paintings off at the gallery and then stopped by the Attorney General's house to sketch his wife."

"So you're going to do a portrait of Rose?"

"Yes."

"She'll make a beautiful subject."

"Yes, she is very attractive."

Taylor glanced out the window, avoiding eye contact with her.

Katherine could tell that something she said was bothering him.

Finally, he said, "There's something I need to tell you before you hear it from someone else."

"What's that?"

"Rose and I were an item before she married the Attorney General." Katherine looked surprised.

"Oh . . . well, that's something good to know. I guess."

"That was a long time ago, of course."

"I don't know what to say. Why did you feel it necessary to tell me that?"

"If you are going to do her portrait, I assume you will spend time with her alone. In that situation, I can't imagine that she wouldn't tell you about our former relationship, human nature being what it is."

"In that case, thank you for telling me. Were you in love with her?"

Taylor squirmed. He was beginning to regret bringing it up. In politics, they call it damage control—an attempt to put out fires.

"I wouldn't say that . . . we went out a few times. People saw us and talked about it. Then it was over."

"Do you think she was in love with you?"

"How would I know?"

"Can't you tell when a woman is in love with you?"

"I think men and women have different skills when it comes to love detection. We never know when a woman is in love with us, and half the time we don't know if we are in love with a particular woman. It's a gender defect, I know."

Katherine laughed. "Oh, I feel so sorry for men."

"It's true. We know what we're doing when it comes to sports . . . or cars or planes . . . but when it comes to women . . ." His sentence trailed off into self-deprecating laughter. "Let's just say we have a lot to learn."

Taylor got up and walked around the desk. "How about lunch?"

"See, you know more about women than you think. I'm starved—and you picked up on that right away."

Going back through the office with Taylor was a little bit like running a gauntlet. Todd and Miss Sweeny were both extraordinarily protective of Taylor.

Do they see me as a threat she thought? *Someone who might upset the balance of power? Or do they see me as a partner in their quest to take care of Taylor?*

Once they were outside, Katherine was glad to feel the sun on her face again. They walked two blocks to a restaurant and darted inside. She could feel people looking at her, but she was getting used to that when she was with Taylor.

Power was not a quality that she ever associated with other relationships in her life. Roger was who he was—a loving, caring man whose dreams had nothing to do with the acquisition of power or wealth and everything to do with his unique talent of making something from nothing. With Taylor, it was difficult to separate who he was from the public perception of who he was. His talent was being Taylor Prescott.

They ended up having a two-hour lunch. Taylor had a knack for telling stories, and he told one after another, keeping her constantly entertained. Several times other diners stopped at the table to say hello to Taylor. He was always gracious, always brief in his interactions with them, responding rather than initiating conversation.

After lunch, Taylor looked at his watch.

"It's three o'clock. Why don't you give me a ride back to my house? We can watch the sunset and have a late dinner."

"What about your work?"

"I've done enough work for today."

* * *

The ride back to Brockville was her first long-distance road trip with Taylor, who sat in the passenger seat as she drove. When he initially suggested that he return with her, she wondered how he would deal with being merely the passenger and not in control of the vehicle. As the miles went by, she realized—*stupid me!*—that he was *most* comfortable when he was being catered to, and he did not feel the least bit diminished by her control of the vehicle.

Once they passed through Kemptville, he pointed out with great pride various developments that were built with national funding, a direct result of his political influence.

"The way the system works, people have only as much power and influence as their elected representatives can muster. All counties and provinces are not created equal in the eyes of the law."

"Why did you decide to become a MP?"

"Because I wanted to make a difference. And I think I have. Why did you become an artist?"

Katherine was surprised by the question. People often asked her how she learned to paint, or how she chose her subjects, but no one had ever asked why she painted.

"To be honest, it's not something that I've ever thought about. I never made a conscious decision to become an artist, not the way you decided to become a politician. From an early age, I *was* an artist, just like I was female and had red hair."

"That makes sense to me."

"We're very different people."

"Yes, but it's where we intersect that's important."

When they arrived at Prescott Place, the housekeeper let them inside and then made herself scarce when they went out onto the back patio. Katherine pointed to the river and said, "Now that you've lived on the river, could you possibly ever live anyplace else? The view from this ridge is spectacular. I have more of a river-level view."

"My view allows introspection. Your view allows participation."

"Do you always talk like a politician?"

Taylor laughed. "It is a hard habit to break. I guess I do sound a little stuffy sometimes, don't I?"

"But you've got a *real* side as well. I've seen it. And I think it's very appealing."

Taylor walked up behind her and wrapped his arms around her, kissing her once on the neck, causing her to say in a soft voice, "That's nice."

They stood like that for a long while, her hands on top of his hands, tenderly holding each other, watching the river shut down for the night as the shimmering light flickered off the water like a thousand church candles.

There was no denying the confusion she felt about her relationship with Taylor, but the nearness of him, the comforting sound of his voice, the scent of his cologne, muffled whatever doubts she had about him.

"Let's go inside," he whispered.

She followed, glancing over her shoulder at the river's watery constellation, dragging the final twilight glimmer, the final breath of river air with her. Inside, they were greeted by one of the cooks, who told them that dinner was on the table in the small dining room. Katherine liked the room more than she liked the formal dining room. It had the same impressive appointments as the larger room, but it was more intimate and made her feel more at home. She wasn't hungry, perhaps because of the lateness of their lunch, but she nibbled at the pork loin roast and the asparagus, using her fork to spear the smaller roasted potatoes on her plate.

She wondered what it would be like to take such a splendid home for granted—to awaken each morning with the knowledge that it belonged to you. Never in her life had she sought wealth, but that didn't mean she couldn't be influenced by its seductive trappings. What woman wouldn't? Nice things were a weakness.

They had coffee in the den and talked for a while; then they went upstairs to the Tahitian Room. This time Taylor didn't try to undress her as he kissed her, nothing so high schoolish this time. Instead, he stood on the other side of the room and slowly undressed, his gaze never leaving her eyes, not for an instant. He removed his shoes and socks. Unbuttoned his shirt. Slipped off his slacks. Then he got out of his briefs and stood before her, his gaze still strong . . . patient . . . waiting.

She stood on her side of the room as he undressed, watching his every move, her eyes wide with excitement. She waited until he was completely undressed and then she started removing her clothes, starting with her shoes which she slowly took off and neatly placed side-by-side on the floor.

Unlike him, she looked away, avoiding eye contact as if he were not even in the room, casting him in the role of the voyeur. Each time she removed an article of clothing, she folded it, neatly shaping it into a square that she put on a chair next to her shoes.

Once they got into bed, he cuddled her, wrapping his arms around her, kissing her first on the lips, and then all across her face, small kisses, the sum total of which left her breathless. She closed her eyes and felt herself slipping away to a peaceful place where there was no pain or memory of lost love.

CHAPTER
27

The ship's captain slowly turned in his chair, back and forth, as he doodled with a pen on his desk calendar. He was immaculately dressed in a spotless white uniform, complete with white shoes.

"Our medic feels that you are suffering from amnesia. That nasty cut on your forehead is our strongest evidence that it was caused by trauma. Do you not have any recollections?"

"None whatsoever."

"We examined your clothing and found that your slacks were made in America and your shirt was made in Canada. You could be a citizen of either country. Or you could be a citizen of most any English speaking country. Have you ever been to Australia?"

He shook his head.

"I just don't have a clue."

"If we turn you over to port authorities in Toronto, it will create a lot of problems for us. The ship will be searched. There will be tons of paperwork. We will be cited for taking on an undocumented alien. We could be held in port for weeks."

"What do you want me to do?"

"If you stay on board when we reach Toronto there will be no reason for authorities to inquire about you. If you are willing to do that, I can take you back to Cape Town and see that you receive the therapy that you need to recover your memory. Would you be agreeable to that?"

He shrugged. "I may not have a memory, but I understand your dilemma. Of course, I am willing to cooperate with you."

The captain smiled. "I was hoping you would say that."

After leaving the captain's office, he was allowed to go on deck, where he took a deep breath, the first fresh air he'd had in .   . . well, forever.

Standing next to him was Junior Officer Muller.

"What river are we on?"

"St. Lawrence Seaway."

"Runs between the United States and Canada, right?"

"Yes sir."

"And that's Canada on the right?"

"Yes sir."

He pointed to several islands in the distance. "What's that?"

"That's the last of the islands in the chain of land masses known as the 1000 Islands. We found you bobbing in the water near one of the islands further downstream."

"Really."

He starred at the islands ahead, a faint memory tugging at his recollection.

"Do those islands ring a bell with you, sir?"

He looked at the junior officer, a tear rolling down his cheek.

"No, nothing. But something about those islands makes me want to cry."

"You are crying, sir."

CHAPTER
28

When Katherine awoke the room was dark. She sat bolt upright in bed. *Bessie! What have I done? How could I leave you alone on the island?* She could not see Taylor, but she could hear him breathing next to her. She looked at the digital clock: 10:33. Staying all night was out of the question. What on earth was she thinking?

She half-crept, half-crawled out of bed, one foot after the other, careful not to wake Taylor, who lay face down on the sheets. Once her feet were firmly on the floor, she moved slowly along the bed and then turned left toward the closed door, her outstretched hand blindly moving from side to side like a blind person's cane. There was not the slightest sliver of light in the room.

After several steps, she got down on her hands and knees, searching for the chair that held her clothes. It was to the right, she knew that much. The first thing she came across were her shoes. Then the chair. She picked the shoes up off the floor and gathered her clothes in her arms and walked straight to the door, sliding her hand along the paneled wall until she located the doorknob.

Once she was in the hallway, she lowered everything to the hardwood floor, quietly, so that she would not awaken Taylor. Then, heart pounding, she quickly dressed and hurried along the hallway, shoes in hand.

Down the staircase. Out the front door. Closing the door behind her like a thief in the night. The night air was surprisingly cool. The leaves already were beginning to turn. Soon the leaves would be gone and there'd be a white carpet of snow across the land and, yes, across the river. She closed her car door without slamming it, pulling it toward her until the latch quietly clicked into place. She drove out the driveway with her lights off and didn't turn them on until she reached the road.

Brockville was almost deserted. The city's nightlife was pretty much confined to the suburbs, where the hotel lounges and shopping centers buzzed with nocturnal activity. The dating scene. Married men and women escaping the tensions of an unhappy home life. People alone deathly afraid of being alone.

The short drive from the city to her boathouse was remarkable for its lack of incoming traffic. She didn't encounter a single car on her way home. Once she reached the road that sloped down to the boathouse, she stopped and scoped it out to see if there were any cars parked on her lot. There were none.

She eased down the slope and parked. She waited a minute before getting out of the car, alert to anything unusual. As soon as she stepped out of her car, she was overcome by a cacophony of night sounds from the trees. Tree frogs, insects of all shapes and sizes, squirrels, myriad creatures, all sounding the alarm that fall was here. They were the types of sounds that you don't notice when you are with someone; but when you are alone, they are all you can hear.

Katherine went into the boathouse, after first turning on the light and sticking her head inside to look around. In no time, she was in the boat, motor revved, and on her way to the island. There was a brisk wind prowling the river, strong enough to create choppy waves three feet high. It was a moonless night, which made the river treacherous because of the logs that floated in the current.

She focused on the lights of her house. How many lights had she mistakenly left on all day? Two? Three? Four? She wasn't sure. It's so easy to overlook lights during the day, especially if the house is flooded with bright sunlight.

The beacon that was her house drew her safely to the dock.

Walking to the door, she saw Bessie inside the house, jumping up and down, running from side to side, overjoyed to see her again. *People have a lot to learn from dogs* she thought. Once she opened the door, Bessie was all over her, jumping up on her, talking to her in that special high-pitched bark that she used only for greetings.

Katherine left the door open and walked out on the deck so that she could see Bessie running and sniffing through the grass, overjoyed at being able, finally, to address her bodily needs.

Suddenly, Katherine heard a boat motor.

That's odd she thought. *I hardly ever see anyone on this part of the river at night.*

She walked down off the deck and peered around the side of her house.

In the distance she saw a boat headed directly to her house, a bright spotlight sweeping the river across the bow. She couldn't tell what kind of boat it was. Only that it was coming on fast with a purpose that was more compelling that the threat of floating logs.

It's them! she thought.

She ran out onto the grass, looking for Bessie.

"Bessie!" she screamed in her no-nonsense voice. "Come!"

Within seconds, Bessie burst from behind dense shrubby at a full run.

"Come on girl!"

She ran to the dock, motioning for Bessie to follow.

She hurled over a big slab of the dock and landed in the boat, wasting no time untying the bow and stern lines, and then starting the motor. By the time the first putter popped from the motor, Bessie was airborne, soaring from the dock to the boat—landing on the seat next to Katherine, her eyes wide with excitement.

Katherine cast off and pulled away from the dock, headed south at full throttle.

"Hands on, girl."

The waves rolled west to east. She took a strong jolt on her starboard side as a wave rose and struck as the boat was dipping. To keep from capsizing, she made a forty-five degree turn into the waves, still at full throttle.

Behind her the other boat closed in on her. It obviously had a much more powerful motor. Katherine glanced back over her shoulder just in time to see the flashing blue-green lights, identifying the boat, just as she suspected, as being an OPP cruiser.

Bessie got very agitated and crawled from the seat, down to the floorboard, where she curled up, her eyes glued to Katherine, who every now and then reached down to pet her in a reassuring manner.

Above the roar of the motor and the waves, Katherine heard a loudspeaker from the other boat.

"This is the Ontario Provincial Police . . . turn back to your dock!"

I'm in trouble now she thought, but she ignored the order and headed toward the international boundary. Once she crossed, the OPP would have to turn back. They could not pursue a boater into American waters.

Suddenly, she heard a loud pop.

At first she thought they were firing on her. Then she realized that they had fired a flare, sending a ball of light skyward, the burning ember lingering over her boat as it slowly drifted to earth. They could see her, but she couldn't see them, since the OPP boat was beyond the perimeter of light created by the flare.

Again, the voice electronically altered, sounding other-worldly in its diction: "Mrs. Summer, we know it is you—you are ordered to turn back!"

The thought never crossed her mind.

Katherine's boat rose and fell several times a minute, splashing angry water into the boat and against her face, which by then was wet, dripping with foam, smelling of the river. Behind her was the flashing light, that boat, too, tossed by the waves, the angle of the light changing radically every few seconds, bobbing up and down.

Ahead of her was pitch blackness, a bleak nothingness without horizon or sky, a sable wall of gloom.

Hang on she thought *just hang on!*

From nowhere appeared a lighted buoy, the end of the road for her pursuers, for it meant that she was about to enter American waters. She cheered when she spotted the buoy, bringing Bessie to her feet to see what was going on.

Once she saw that it didn't concern her, she curled up again on the floorboard, unhappy with the water that streamed onto her coat with alternating severity.

Then what she hoped would happen did happen. The OPP cruiser turned away, blinking lights now turned off, its spotlights slowly turning west in a wide arc that broadened into a northward direction, away from the international boundary.

Once she saw what'd happened, she turned west, taking the waves head-on as she bulled her way into the night, staying inside the United States, headed in the direction of Dark Island, where she and Bessie could take shelter inside Singer Castle, a five-story, twenty-eight room mansion built in the early 1900s by Singer Sewing Machine magnate Frederick Bourne, one of the wealthiest people in the world at the time of construction. Open for public tours during the day, it had a solitary watchman that she felt she could elude until morning.

This was not the kind of boat ride that Katherine enjoyed. When she wasn't worrying about being capsized by the waves, she worried about striking an uprooted tree. She held onto the steering wheel so tightly that her arms started to cramp. She alternated rubbing her forearms, never able to massage them for long, because no sooner did she release one of her hands from the wheel, than another wave struck and made the boat shudder.

About now they'll be calling New York she thought. *I doubt the New York state police will send anyone out at this time of night, not for something that's not an emergency. In the morning, I'll go back home and smooth things out with the OPP. By then the hearing will be over and there will be no need for me to testify. Jason is a good man and an honest man. Someone will recognize him for who he is.*

She thought about her house. About how she'd left the back door wide open.

That was stupid, she told herself—*what if someone steals all my paintings?*

Katherine had convinced herself that if she evaded authorities, the hearing would take place without her and everything would be fine. After all, she'd committed no crime. Jason's hearing was not a criminal matter. How angry could the OPP possibly be? She could always lie and say that she didn't see the OPP cruiser in the storm. How could they prove otherwise? Since she was in the right, she wasn't concerned about the consequences. The main thing was to stay absent until after the hearing.

Katherine had passed Dark Island during all hours of the day and night. She knew that there were outdoor lights along the pier at the entrance to the castle. A wall of bright lights. She counted on passing close enough to the island to see them.

If she missed the lights, she would be in big trouble, since west of Dark Island were dozens of small islands with stone embankments that would break her boat into hundreds of pieces if she blindly slammed into any one of them. She held a steady course through the open channel, the river pounding her boat with unrelenting repetition, one dip, rise, and slam after another. Several times she was knocked off balance and had to pull herself back up to control the wheel, the blistering wind burning her cheeks.

With no visible markers, it was impossible to judge her location. She pushed ahead, led solely by instinct. Time seemed to stop still. She knew about how long it took to get to Dark Island, but she had no idea how long she'd been on the water. Nor could she judge how fast she was traveling, since it seemed that for each ten feet that she gained she lost five feet. And, for all she knew, she was moving in a circle.

Then, when she least expected it, it came from nowhere. All of a sudden, she saw lights off to the left. It was the right place for them to be. She was positive that she hadn't slipped to the south side of the island. Her heart pounded. Was it Dark Island?

Just as quickly as the lights appeared, they disappeared. Unknown to Katherine, a giant wave had lifted her boat high into the air—it was the point at which she saw the lights—and then dropped her back into a trough in which the lights were blocked from view. She panicked, fearful she'd somehow been carried past the lights, but then she was lifted again and the lights returned.

She turned further south, taking a direct line to the lights. It was Dark Island, all right. Even with a night sky, Singer Castle loomed over her, a massive structure, dark and foreboding, without a single light in sight. Once she had her bearings, she turned east, skirting around the house to the south front of the island. There was a small cove there, where she and Rodger once fished in daylight hours. She could find it with her eyes closed.

True enough, with the island blocking the wind and the high waves, the waters calmed somewhat and she throttled back and made her way into the cove. She pulled up next to the rock embankment and leaped from the boat with the port and starboard lines in hand. She tied the boat off to a massive tree stump and then she helped Bessie out of the boat. That done, her legs wobbled and she sank onto a flat rock, trembling.

"Bessie, it looks like we made it," she said, running her fingers through her soaked coat. Bessie looked up at her, trying her best to understand.

After she'd rested for a while, she walked up the embankment and toward the castle. Off to the right was a well-lighted cottage, lights she'd not seen from the river, perhaps because the cottage was obscured by shrubs. She crept up to a window and peered inside. Sitting next to the window, was a uniformed guard, a stout fellow with a bald head, talking on a cell. He spoke loud enough for Katherine to overhear the conversation.

"No sir," he said, "I haven't seen a thing. If she comes this way, I'll notify you just as quick as I can."

So the New York police already have been contacted Katherine thought. *I'll have to be very, very careful until the sun rises.*

The guard took out a pen and took notes on a clipboard. "Red hair, you say . . . good looking . . . may have a cocker spaniel with her that answers to the name Bessie."

Katherine looked at Bessie and then kissed her on the top of her head.

"I doubt she'll come here, but I'll keep my eyes open, you can count on that . . . is she considered dangerous . . . well, okay, I still won't take any chances with her."

Katherine backed away from the window, Bessie at her heels. She walked down a steep incline, and then onto a well manicured lawn and over to the rear of the castle. In recent memory, wealthy Internet tycoons had build very large houses on the island that they called castles, but they weren't really castles. Singer Castle was the real thing. It had turrets and dungeons, and it had the *feel* of an old European castle, which was what Bourne had in mind when he built it.

She tried every window and door on the south side of the castle. All were securely locked. In the distance she saw the powerhouse, where electricity was generated for the castle. She remembered Roger once telling her about the powerhouse, how he'd learned while researching some old manuscripts, that there was a secret tunnel that ran from the powerhouse to the kitchen inside the castle.

As she approached the powerhouse, she saw that the door was open. That made sense. Why would anyone lock a powerhouse door at night? During the day, perhaps. Not at night, when quick access by the guard or maintenance workers would be critical.

She crept up to the door, hopeful that there was not another guard inside.

She leaned over and looked inside.

The room seemed empty. Slowly she made her way inside and looked around for anything that resembled a secret door. The generator was massive and the room was noisy as power was busily generated for the island's lights.

After looking into several closets, all of which had solid walls, she spotted something suspicious beneath a table on which sat a kerosene lantern. The table wasn't very large, so she easily moved it aside. Clearly visible was a trap door. She lifted it and saw that it contained steps that disappeared into a dark cellar.

She looked for a light switch, but she couldn't find one. Luckily there was a box of matches on the table. She lit the kerosene lamp and descended the steps, with Bessie at her side, closing the trapdoor behind her. If someone entered the powerhouse, she hoped they wouldn't notice that the table had been moved.

The passageway was not very wide, no more than five feet across and it smelled musty, as if the air had not been changed since the early 1900s. With the lantern held at arm's length she followed the passageway all the way to the end, where she discovered another stairway. She took her time going up the steps, careful to make no more noise than was necessary. Another trapdoor. She pushed it up about six inches and peered into a darkened room. She went higher with the trapdoor and reached up and put the lantern on the floor, revealing the room to be a massive kitchen.

Bessie hopped up into the kitchen and began sniffing with wild abandon, smelling no telling what on the marble floors. Katherine followed and made her way into the interior of the house so that the light from her lantern could not be seen from a window. She kept walking until she reached a staircase that took her to the second floor.

Again she stayed in an interior hallway, looking for a place to spend the night. The castle's furnishings were impressive—heavy, wooden pieces, offset by well-padded chairs covered in silken fabrics. The paintings on the wall were beautiful, all reminiscent of turn-of-the-century society, but none of the paintings she saw were especially valuable.

Not far from the staircase she found a library, with floor to ceiling bookshelves. There were several hundred books in the library, many of them apparently first editions; but they all were secured behind locked glass panels. She was surprised that there was no window in the library. At the other end of the room she noticed that there was semi-circle mark on the carpet near one of the bookcases. She closely examined the shelves, finding quite by accident, a lever that caused the shelf to open like a door.

It was a secret passage to another part of the house. She nudged Bessie inside the passage and closed the door behind them. She followed the passage, noting that every ten feet or so, steps appeared that took her downward, each series of steps taking her lower and lower into the house's interior.

Finally, the passage came to an end. Another door. She opened it, lantern outstretched, and saw what she immediately recognized as a medieval torture chamber. On the walls were chains and hooks and small hammers and pliers in various sizes. In the center of the room was a wooden table upon which leather straps had been attached. At the other end of the room was a small bed. Apparently, it was meant for the torturer so that he could take naps in between his tiresome chores.

"This is as good a place as any to spend the night," she muttered.

Bessie didn't look so certain, but she followed Katherine's lead and acquainted herself with the room.

"They would never think to look for us here. I doubt the guard even knows it's here."

Katherine put the lantern on a barrel next to the bed and she sat down on a rough, cotton-tick mattress that'd probably never been covered with a sheet. After looking around the room for a few minutes, she leaned over and blew out the light.

With no window, the room was pitch-black.

She stretched out on the bed and listened. The old castle made sounds from time to time, but nothing that sounded like footsteps.

Exhausted, she quickly dropped off into a deep sleep.

CHAPTER
29

The next morning Katherine woke to Bessie's gentle nudges against her shoulder. She sleepily reached out and caressed her, the familiar feel of her silky coat bringing a smile to her face.

"Bessie, you are a built-in alarm clock."

The room was just as dark as it was when she went to sleep. She groped around the room until she found the lantern. Then she pulled the matches from her pocket and lighted the wick. She looked at her watch: 9 o'clock.

"Oh, God," she muttered. "I've got to get out of here."

She considered going back the way she came, but then she saw a second door and she opened it wide. Another dark hallway. Unlike the previous night, the castle was filled with sounds. Doors opened and closed. Shoes scuffing against the hardwood floors. An occasional voice, directionless, genderless, muffled.

They've probably found my boat by now. How could I have overslept?

At the end of the hallway was a staircase that dead-ended at a closed door. She made her way to the top and put her ear against the door and listened. Nothing. She slowly opened the door and encountered another dark hallway.

With Bessie sticking so close to her that she often bumped into her legs, Katherine followed the hallway to yet another closed door.

She listened. This time she heard voices.

Sounds like a tour group. That could be a good thing for me.

She extinguished the lantern and immediately saw light bleeding around the door into the hallway. Ear flat against the door, she heard what sounded like a small group of people talking and murmuring, generating a low hum like a beehive. She waited until the voices tapered off and then she opened the door and stepped out into an enormous bedroom that was flooded with light from windows that faced the early morning sun.

She squinted at the white glare and followed the trail of chatter that led into a hallway, where about a dozen people ambled along, admiring the paintings that lined the wall. She and Bessie stepped up behind them and tried to blend into the group.

The tour guide droned on with a memorized spiel, her voice neither rising nor falling: "The architect was a man named Ernest Flagg. Besides designing Singer Castle, he designed the Singer Tower in Manhattan and the buildings at the Naval Academy at West Point. He was one of the most respected architects of his time."

As they walked along, a young man looked at Katherine and smiled.

"I don't remember you and your dog on our tour boat."

"That's because I wasn't on it. My boat left without me while I was on the back lawn walking Bessie. I thought I'd stick with you guys and go back on your boat."

The man nodded knowingly, accepting her explanation. How could he not? She had the face of an angel, though somewhat disheveled by a night in the dungeon.

One of the tourists asked, "Why does the castle have turrets? Did the castle ever come under attack by Canadians?"

Katherine grimaced when she heard that.

"No ma'am," intoned the guide. "The Canadians have always been quite friendly."

Not satisfied with the answer, the tourist turned to a friend and whispered, "Must be there because of the Indians."

The guide clearly heard the comment, but she ignored it and continued: "One of the things that make Singer Castle unique is the hidden passageways that connect nearly every room in the castle. When Mr. Bourne built his private study in one of the upper floors, he designed it so that the only way to enter was through a hidden passageway."

The guide stopped in front of what looked like a closet.

"Behind this door is a passageway that leads straight down to an underground tunnel that goes to the boathouse. Mr. Bourne was a very wealthy man who worried about kidnappers, which was why he wanted the secret study—some people now call rooms like this panic rooms—and why he insisted on having a secret way of leaving the castle."

As the tour group moved on, Katherine lingered behind with Bessie, pretending to examine one of the paintings. As soon as the last person in the group rounded the corner, she opened the closet door and peered down a dark stairway.

There was no time to go back for the lantern. She pulled the matches out of her pocket and counted them. Six matches. Not enough to make it all the way, but probably enough to go most of the way. She stepped into the closet with Bessie and closed the door behind them. She struck a match and descended the stairway, holding the match out at arm's length. The passageways were not ventilated so she didn't have to worry about a sudden gust of air extinguishing the match.

The flame flickered brighter than she expected.

Once she reached the bottom of the staircase, there was only one direction to go—straight ahead. The tunnel was remarkably clean, as if it had been swept on a regular basis—and perhaps it had—but it had a damp, moldy odor that left a brackish taste in her mouth.

She allowed the match to burn down until the heat against her fingertips was unbearable and then she struck another, going through all six matches faster than she'd anticipated. Just before the flame from the last match went out, she reached down and grasped Bessie's collar.

"Girl, I'm counting on you to lead me out of this."

Bessie pulled ahead, sniffing from side to side as her feet padded against the stone floor, taking Katherine directly to a light in the distance that was shaped like an inverted-L. At first, Katherine was baffled. Not until they were almost there did she realize that the light was coming around the top and side of a closed door.

She pressed her ear against the wood-frame door and listened.

All was quiet.

She cracked the door no more than an inch and looked inside the room. She saw and heard nothing.

Then she opened the door all the way, allowing Bessie to gallop across the floor and back. It was an office of some kind. One wall consisted almost entirely of windows that looked out onto the cove, where several large boats were moored.

The door that opened outside onto the lawn had a window in it. She peered outside, looking left to right. Nothing but grass and shrubs. Less than ten yards from the boathouse was a long row of thick shrubs and small trees. The river could be seen through an occasional break in the shrubbery.

That's my ticket out of here she thought. *I'll follow the shrubs along the river until I get to my boat.*

With Bessie at her heels, she dashed from the boathouse into the shrubbery. The footing was treacherous because of the ragged stone placements along the water's edge, but she picked her way across the rocks, sometimes sliding and hitting her knees, always catching herself with her hands, pressing ahead.

When she finally saw her boat it brought tears to her eyes. *I would have sworn they would have found it by now and taken it away* she thought. *Never in my life have I been so glad to see a boat.*

She jumped over the last few rocks and bounded into the boat, with Bessie clamoring in behind her. She put the key in the ignition and hit the starter, but nothing happened. She tried again and again.

Suddenly a voice came from nowhere.

"Miss Summer, I don't think the boat will start without this."

A New York State Policeman held up a twelve-inch starter cord. He walked down from the shrubbery that'd concealed him. Bessie barked, but Katherine told her to hush.

Katherine's heart sank. She'd been so close to getting away.

The police officer walked down to river's edge and extended his hand. Katherine took hold of it and stepped out of the boat onto the rocks, followed by Bessie, who needed no help getting out of the boat. The police officer was young and he had a sympathetic face, but his words cut her to the quick.

"You are under arrest for illegal entry into the United States. You have the right to remain silent. You have . . ."

Katherine listened to the whole litany of rights, wanting to ask him if she had the right to live her life without being hassled by other people. She didn't. She smiled and didn't protest when he slapped handcuffs on her wrists.

"What about Bessie?" she asked, concern in her voice.

"She'll be held at the customs office until there is a disposition on both you and the dog."

"And my boat?"

"It will be impounded until we work everything out."

"Great," she muttered under her breath, thinking *all this because I had dinner with a nice man who happens to be a psychologist.*

Katherine was taken back across the lawn to the front of the castle, where several police officers stood next to a boat with a New York State Police insignia on the bow. As they approached the boat, the tour group that she'd joined inside the castle walked by.

"Look!" said one of the tourists, pointing. "Wasn't that woman in our group?"

"I remember the dog. I wonder what she did!"

"She doesn't *look* like a criminal."

"If she wasn't a criminal they wouldn't be after her."

Katherine and Bessie were taken back to police headquarters, where they both were fed and allowed to perform bathroom duties. Katherine was shocked when she saw herself in the mirror. She washed her face and tried to do something with her hair, but without much success. She had on the same clothes she wore to Ottawa—a light blue cotton blouse and a navy wraparound skirt. The blouse had smudges on it and the skirt was torn in two places.

I look like I've been riding boxcars all day.

When she emerged from the bathroom, she was cuffed again and allowed to say goodbye to Bessie, something that caused her great pain because she wasn't sure if she'd ever see her again. She was taken to another squad car and instructed to get in the back seat. A nice officer put his hand on her head to prevent her from striking it against the door frame. Once she was inside the car, she asked the driver, "Where are you taking me?"

"To Albany."

"To that hearing?"

"Yes ma'am."

"That was yesterday, wasn't it?"

"It was recessed until you could be located."

"They stopped the hearing because of me?"

"Sure looks that way."

* * *

On the drive to Albany, all Katherine could think about was how all this would affect Jason. She thought that if she did nothing, it would be the right thing to do and his problems would disappear. Now she feared that she'd only made things worse for him.

"What if I refuse to testify when I get there?"

"You have the right to refuse to give testimony that could incriminate you."

"What if I refuse because I don't want to hurt a friend?"

"You can't do that."

"What would happen to me if I refuse to testify on the grounds you said?"

"You would be excused from the witnesses' table."

"And?"

"You will be arrested for illegal entry into the United States."

"They'd do that to punish me?"

"They'd do it to uphold the law."

"That's not fair."

The police officer laughed.

"I'm pretty sure that if you look through all the law books the only place you'll see the word 'fair' will be in the phrase, 'fair and impartial jury.' Justice has got nothing to do with being fair. It's about the law, not right and wrong."

Katherine got a sinking feeling in the pit of her stomach. Her nonviolent resistance had evolved into a nightmare. She said nothing for the remainder of the ride, not even when the police officer asked her direct questions.

When they arrived at the building where the hearing was to take place, she looked around the parking lot hoping to get a glimpse of Jason.

If only I could talk to him first she thought. *I need to know what he wants me to say.*

The police officer opened the door and helped her out of the car.

"When do you take these off?" she asked, lifting up her cuffed hands.

"Right before we enter the hearing room."

As they walked across the parking lot and up the steps of the building, Katherine felt she'd been kidnapped from reality and transported to one of those low-budget *Lifetime* movies that seem to run twenty-four hours a day on cable. People stared at her, wondering whether she was dangerous.

If they only knew she thought.

There was a strong order of pine oil in the corridors, as if they had been scrubbed and rescrubbed with disinfectant. The scent was so strong that it made her eyes water. Their feet struck the floor with staccato effect. She felt like a condemned person being led to the death chamber.

They stopped outside a door with a sign that indicated that a hearing was in progress. He unlocked her cuffs and said, "You are to sit next to me in the hearing room—and after you testify you are to return directly to me. Understand?"

Katherine nodded, longing to be back on her island.

Once they walked into the hearing room, the first person she saw was Jason. He rose to his feet when he saw her, but he didn't try to approach her, having already been warned by his lawyer to have no contact with her. The police officer led Katherine to the row of chairs directly behind the witness table.

Jason was shocked at her frazzled appearance. Her clothing was torn, stained, wrinkled. Her hair was a mess, though she obviously had tried to fix it.

Almost as soon as they sat down, the hearing was called to order.

Katherine expected a lot of talking, like they do on proceedings seen on television, but the chairman had nothing to say, other than to ask her to please sit at the witness table. She did as she was asked, at one point turning around to get another glimpse of Jason. He looked stressed, an expression she'd never seen on him before.

She desperately wanted to reach out to him.

After she was sworn in, the chairman asked if she'd been advised that she could have a lawyer present. She thought a minute. The police officers told her she had a right to see a lawyer when they arrested her, but they said nothing about her having the right to consult a lawyer before the hearing. She decided not to quibble. She was sure that the last thing that Jason wanted was for her to once again delay the hearing. She submitted to reality, not happily but with resignation.

"Yes sir," she answered.

"Have you ever been a patient of Dr. Jason Montclair of Ogdensburg, New York?"

"Yes, I have."

"When did that professional relationship begin?"

Katherine stated her reason for seeing a psychologist, briefly touching on the anguish she felt over her husband's and daughter's death, and she provided the date of their first session.

"Did you feel that your sessions with Dr. Montclair were beneficial?"

"Oh, yes—Dr. Montclair saved my life."

"What do you mean by that?"

"I don't know if you've ever lost a loved one, but I lost a husband and a daughter, everyone in life who was dear to me . . . and they were gone so fast. . . . I had a really difficult time coping with that . . . with the guilt of sending them off that day without me. Dr. Montclair helped me understand my grief, and he helped me . . . deal with my guilt. I don't know if I would have survived without him."

"If your therapy with him was so successful, why did it end?"

Katherine paused, gathering her thoughts.

"Dr. Montclair advised me to see another psychologist . . . he said it would be a violation of his ethics to continue with my treatments."

"Do you ask him why treating you would be a violation of his ethics?"

"I did."

"And?"

"He said it was because he realized that he had feelings for me."

"How did that session end?"

"We said good-bye and I left?"

"Was there ever any show of physical affection in his office?"

"What do you mean?"

"Did he ever hug you or kiss you?"

"Oh, no . . . nothing like that."

"Did he ever touch you in an intimate manner?"

"Of course not."

"When did you hear from him again?"

"He called to see how I was doing and I agreed to have lunch with him."

"Was that lunch the beginning of an intimate relationship with Dr. Montclair?"

"No, nothing like that."

"So you are testifying under oath that you did not go out on dates with him?"

"We went out. I don't know if you could call it dating?"

"What is your definition of dating?"

"My definition? I guess dating is what happens when a couple goes out to dinner, a movie, or whatever, and begin an intimate relationship."

"By intimate, do you mean a sexual relationship?"

"Yes."

"Have you ever had a sexual relationship with Dr. Montclair?"

"No."

"Would you say kissing is a factor in intimate relationships?"

"Yes. I would say so."

"Have you ever kissed Dr. Montclair?"

"That's a very personal question, isn't it?"

"You are under oath, Mrs. Summer."

Katherine gritted her teeth. *Jason is a wonderful man* she thought. *If I say yes, it could destroy his life. Do I dare lie?*

"Mrs. Summer? Would you please answer the question?"

Katherine felt a shiver cascade through her entire body. *He told me to tell the truth. If I lie, he will think less of me and I couldn't stand that.*

Finally, she answered, "Yes, we have kissed."

There was a murmur in the hearing room.

The commission members huddled and whispered, their hands blocking their microphones. Then the chairman sat up straight and said, "Mrs. Summer. Thank you for your testimony. You are excused."

As she got up from the table, she heard the chairman's voice again, saying, "Will Dr. Jason Montclair please sit at the witness table?"

Katherine and Jason met in the aisle. She wanted to say something, but she didn't dare. She wanted to ask if he was furious with her. She wanted to ask if he was all right. As they passed each other, he smiled, providing an answer to her first unasked question.

Katherine walked over to the police officer, expecting to sit next to him during the remainder of the hearing, but he got to his feet and directed her to the door.

"Can't I stay?" she asked.

"No, we have to get back."

Her last glimpse of Jason was of him seated at the witness table, his hand raised to accept the oath.

Outside the door, the police officer took out the handcuffs and snapped them in place around her wrists.

"Where do we go from here?" she asked.

"My orders are to take you to the Seaway Skyway Bridge at Ogdensburg."

"So I'm not going to be prosecuted for illegal entry?"

"No ma'am. They just wanted you to testify. You did—so now you're going home."

"What about my dog, Bessie?"

"She'll be transported to the bridge, where you can pick her up."

"And my boat?"

"It was turned over to the Ontario Provincial Police. You'll have to ask them what they did with it."

"They won't keep it, will they?"

"I wouldn't know."

CHAPTER
30

From the witness table Jason looked back over his shoulder, hoping to get a glimpse of Katherine. He was disappointed that she no longer was there. When he heard about her wild ride on the river and her capture at Dark Island, he didn't know whether to laugh or cry. He'd never known a woman capable of leading the police of two different countries on a chase . . . *and it was all because of him!*

There had never been much confusion about his feelings for Katherine, but not until now could he honestly tell himself that he was in love with her. He hoped that she loved him too. But she wasn't like any other woman he'd ever known, and he wasn't sure about her feelings for him. That she was willing to go to jail to protect him surely said something about her feelings for him. Still, he had doubts.

"Dr. Montclair . . ."

Jason had allowed his mind to wander. He'd never much cared for the chairman, who'd built a long career on the administrative and academic end of the profession. He'd never been in the trenches, dealing with people who had problems. Mostly, he created problems for psychologists who lived in the trenches.

Trevor, Jason's attorney, who was sitting next to him, whispered into his ear, snapping him back to reality.

"Yes, I understand . . . I was thinking about your question."

"Let me rephrase my question, then. You heard Mrs. Summer's testimony about the nature of her relationship with you. Is there any part of that testimony that you would like to challenge?"

Jason couldn't bear to refer to the chairman as "sir," even though he knew that was the proper way to address him. "No, I don't think I'd want to contradict anything she said in her testimony."

The chairman looked at him with disdain.

"I'm not sure I understand your position. You don't wish to challenge her statement that you told her you could no longer treat her because you had feelings for her?"

Jason shook his head. "No, I have nothing to add."

"And her statement that you asked her out on dates and engaged in kissing . . . you have no evidence to contradict those statements?"

"No."

"On how many occasions did the kissing occur?"

Jason was startled by the question, but he quickly recovered.

"I'm not sure. Two or three times."

"Was there any touching involved?"

"There was no intimate touching."

"What do you think the effect of the kissing was on your former client?"

"I really don't know."

"Dr. Montclair, you were her therapist. You must have some idea of the effect your actions had on her?"

"She seems happier now than before."

"Are you the reason for that happiness?"

"I don't know. I would hope so."

The board members covered their microphones with their hands and talked back and forth in low voices that did not carry beyond their desk. Heads nodded. Hands pulled back from the microphones. One of the board members, a woman in her thirties, leaned forward and asked, "Dr. Montclair, do you feel that you have shown poor judgment and demonstrated inappropriate behavior?"

Jason paused to ponder his answer, thinking *I just want this to be over.*

Trevor leaned over and whispered in his ear, advising him to deny using bad judgment.

Ignoring his advice, Jason said, "Yes, I did . . . in both instances."

The woman continued. "Where do you think you went wrong?"

"I don't think we can control whether we are attracted to another person or not. My attraction to Mrs. Summer was beyond my control. Under those circumstances, I think I did the right thing by telling her she needed to find another therapist. My mistake was in telling her my reasons. I should never have told her I had feelings for her."

"And your pursuit of a relationship with her? Was that wrong?"

"Ethically, I suppose it was. But what was I supposed to do? Walk away? Pretend that I didn't have feelings for her?"

"If you had, you wouldn't be here today, would you?" barked the chairman.

"I don't know—it just seems to me that we, as professionals, should make allowances for love."

"Yeah, yeah—love makes the world go around," said the chairman. "We're all in favor of love and babies and puppies. But the question remains, did you commit an ethical violation?"

"Yes—as the standards are written, I did."

"Are you prepared to take responsibility for your actions?"

"Yes."

"We will adjourn for our deliberations."

Jason and Trevor got up as the board members stood and then left the room.

Jason looked at Trevor and asked, "Where do we go from here?"

"We wait."

"How long do they usually deliberate?"

"In this case, I don't think it will be very long?"

"Why's that?"

"Because you pleaded guilty, though you didn't say so in those words. You hanged yourself—what they're trying to figure out is how long to leave you swinging in the wind."

"Oh."

"Next time, try listening to your lawyer."

"I hope there won't be a next time."

They moved back several rows to sit in the chairs reserved for spectators. Trevor wasn't really in a conversational mood, not after being rebuffed by his client, but Jason talked to him anyway.

"Did you see the way Katherine looked?"

Trevor nodded.

"She looked terrible—like she'd been through hell."

"I don't know all the details. But I'm pretty sure they captured her early this morning and brought her directly to the hearing. Those must have been the clothes she slept in."

Hearing that made Jason feel terrible. He'd put her through so much, and he didn't know how he'd ever make it up to her. *It's all my fault. She's totally without blame for any of this. She must really despise me at this point.*

After deliberations of less than ten minutes, the clerk entered the room, followed by the board members, each of whom avoided eye contact with Jason. The clerk went through the motions of declaring the hearing back in session. The chairman looked at his notes a moment before speaking. Then he looked up and looked Jason squarely in the eyes.

"Dr. Montclair, we are unanimous in our opinion that you are in violation of the ethics code duly adopted by the New York Psychology Board. We hereby suspend your license for a period of two years, after which we will consider reinstatement. This hearing is adjourned."

Jason sat in stunned silence as the clerk and the board members folded up their note pads, gathered their pens and pencils, and left the room. Trevor got up and waited for Jason to walk with him to the door. Trevor was a sore loser.

"What'd you expect? You ignored my advice and practically dared them to find you guilty."

Jason looked at Trevor, hearing his words, but not caring about what he said, instead thinking of Katherine, how devastated she would be that he'd lost his license.

"Jason?" said Trevor. "Did you hear me?"

"Yes—but it could have been worse, you know. They could have permanently barred me in New York."

"I suggest we get out of here before they change their mind and do exactly that."

Jason followed Trevor up the aisle, wondering if Katherine would ever speak to him again.

CHAPTER
31

The Skyway Bridge loomed in the distance, glistening in the sunlight. Katherine had crossed the suspension bridge that stretched from Ogdensburg to near Prescott dozens, no hundreds, of times, never giving much thought to it. Today it was the most beautiful bridge she'd ever seen in her life.

"Where's Bessie?" she asked the police officer driving the car.

"She's waiting for you at the customs office."

"U.S. or Canadian?"

"U.S."

For most of the way, from Albany to Ogdensburg, Katherine thought about Jason. Almost immediately after she did it, she regretted telling the truth at the hearing. *How can telling the truth be a good thing if it hurts someone you care about?*

It was a question that made her heart race. Did she care for Jason?

What about Taylor? I can't care about two people at the same time. Can I? No, absolutely not!

From the moment they turned in the customs office parking lot, Katherine's face was close to the window, looking for Bessie. The police officer parked the car a little too slowly and carefully for Katherine's impatient taste.

Katherine held up her wrists so that the cuffs could be removed, but the police officer didn't respond.

"Not yet," said the police officer. "They have to stay on until we turn you over to the Ontario Provincial Police."

Katherine didn't like the way that sounded.

The police gave her instructions on entering the building—straight ahead, take your first left, then right—and she stayed directly behind her, her right hand resting on her service automatic. The hallway was cool, sterile, like something you'd encounter in a hospital. Katherine turned left. Then right. The hallway dead-ended at a metal door. She turned and looked at the police office, who nodded for her to enter.

Before the door fully opened, she heard Bessie—that bark she has when she's happy, the scratch of her paws against the tile floor, the panting.

"Bessie!" she screamed, sounding more like a high school cheerleader than a respected landscape artist. "My little scrumpskins!"

Bessie jumped up on her, paws almost to her waist.

Katherine knelt to her knees and tried to pet Bessie, but the handcuffs made it awkward. Bessie sniffed the handcuffs and rejected them as insignificant. Then she looked up at Katherine with the biggest grin she'd ever seen on a dog.

"Bessie, I'm *sooo* glad to see you!"

Bessie responded by licking her on the face. As they moved away from the doorway, Bessie's wildly gyrating tail found a metal trash can, thumping it like a bass drum, causing one of the two customs officers already in the room to grimace and hurry over to move the can to a quieter location.

Katherine ran her hands over her coat—both hands since they were cuffed together—and looked her over, making certain that she hadn't been hurt in any way. Bessie nuzzled her, whimpering, crying, trying to scrunch her face under Katherine's arm in an attempt to escape the sight of her captors.

One of the custom officers said, "We didn't have any dog food, so I went by McDonald's early this morning and asked them to cook a couple of quarter-pounders for Bessie. I hope you don't mind."

"Oh, no," said Katherine, smiling at the officer. "I'm sure she loved it."

The police officer who'd transported her looked at his watch and said, "Well, I've got to be running along." He looked at Katherine, her eyes surprisingly watery. "Good luck to you."

He reached out and shook her hand. Then he quickly turned and left the room.

"What's next?" asked Katherine, looking at the customs officers.

"We're going to drive you and Bessie across the bridge and turn you over to Canadian authorities."

"And my boat?"

"We turned the boat over to the OPP. I understand that they have it at their dock facilities in Brockville."

Katherine nodded her approval. That all sounded good to her. As they walked back out the way she'd entered the building, she asked, "What about these cuffs? They aren't very comfortable."

"They aren't supposed to be. Our regulations require us to leave them on until we turn you over to the Canadians."

The customs officer took a few steps and turned around to face her. "Illegal entry into the United States is a crime. You're lucky to be going back at all."

"I know," said Katherine. "And I appreciate that."

When they got to the car, they put Katherine and Bessie in the back seat, a gesture that Bessie considered the ultimate treat, prompting her to lay on the seat with her head on Katherine's lap. Katherine took a deep breath and relaxed, allowing her head to tilt back to the rear of her seat. As they drove across the bridge, the sunlight slanted into the car, rhythmic blasts of brightness, alternating with shadows, putting a smile on her face.

It will be so good to get home. The first thing I'll do is call Jason. I hope he will forgive me for telling the truth.

She felt the car braking. She leaned forward and looked out the window. The Canadian flag had never looked so good to her. She ran her fingers over Bessie's head and grinned foolishly as the car stopped outside the Canadian customs building.

Waiting there were three Canadian officials, one of whom stuck his head in the driver's window and chatted with the U.S. customs officer, as the other two Canadian officers helped her and Bessie out of the car.

"I'm sure glad to see you guys," said Katherine, smiling.

Katherine held her wrists up for the U.S. customs officer, who unlocked her cuffs and stuffed them into his pocket. She turned her wrists from side to side, as if she were shaking off her bondage.

"Thanks," she said to the American.

The Americans and the Canadians shook hands, and then the Americans got in their car and drove off, turning to go back across the bridge.

As they were leaving, two OPP officers came outside and greeted Katherine.

Katherine said, "I hear you've got my boat."

One of the officers, a stocky man she'd never seen before, said, "Yes ma'am. We have it at the dock."

"Great," said Katherine. She nodded and started for the door.

"Mrs. Summer," said the other officer, a woman with bright yellow hair. "I regret to inform you that you are under arrest."

The other officer pulled handcuffs from a leather pouch on his belt.

"Please put your arms behind your back," said the officer.

Stunned, Katherine froze.

"I said, please put your arms behind your back."

Katherine did as they asked, confusion clearly showing on her face.

"I don't understand," she said. "Why am I under arrest?"

"You have been charged with refusing to obey a lawful order to stop. With flight to avoid prosecution. And with endangering the lives of police officers."

Cuffed.

"What?"

"Yes ma'am. I think you heard correctly."

"Where are you taking me?"

"To the Leeds-Grenville Jail."

Her head was spinning as they walked back through the building, passing through a public area, where someone called out, "Look—there's that artist from the island! I wonder what she's done!"

Katherine saw a man wearing a plaid shirt and plaid pants, a digital camera dangling from his neck. He raised the camera and snapped a picture of Katherine, an image that, upon later viewing, showed a distraught woman in handcuffs, a wild-eyed cocker spaniel at her side.

In the parking lot, Katherine was put in one car, Bessie in another.

"What are you going to do with Bessie?"

"She'll be taken to the pound until this is resolved."

"How long will that take? No longer than ten days I hope."

"I don't know how long."

"Won't the pound put her to sleep if she's left there longer than ten days?"

"I don't know their policies, ma'am."

The two patrol cars drove off at the same time, with Katherine's car in the lead. She turned around and looked out the back window. Bessie was a silhouette in the second car, a dark flurry of activity as she jumped up and down to see over the front seat into Katherine's car. *Poor baby* she thought. *How could I have done this to you?*

Going into Brockville, they passed Prescott Place.

She turned, straining to see how many of Taylor's cars were at the house. Over the hedge she saw the limo. The Maserati. She wasn't sure if she saw the Merdie.

Katherine hoped they would take her to the police station, since that would allow them to veer away from the main street; but when they got to that turn, they continued on to the main street, stopping at every traffic light along the way. More than once people on the street saw Katherine in the back seat and pointed. A few people waved.

Finally, they reached the boulevard that stretched two blocks to the courthouse. Katherine turned to see if the second car was still behind them. It was not. They stopped in front of the courthouse and Katherine was assisted from the car.

Before entering the historic three-story building, built in the mid-1800s but recently modernized, Katherine looked up to the roof to see the green-tinged statue of Sally Grant, a blind-folded woman holding the scales of justice out for all to see.

Katherine was led through a couple of corridors and then handed over to a jailer, a stern-faced woman in her mid-fifties. As the woman removed her handcuffs, Katherine asked her if she had a dog.

"What?" snapped the woman. "A dog?"

"I was just wondering if you were a dog lover."

"Missie, you got more to worry about than whether I like dogs or not. Don't you think?"

"Sorry—just trying to make conversation."

Katherine was taken to a cell that was about six feet by ten feet. No window. Mint green walls. Concrete floor. Stainless steel toilet and lavatory. Single bed with rough, stainless-steel frame. Katherine sat on the edge of the bed and heard the door slam shut behind her. She looked around the room. She'd never seen such a desolate room. It made the castle dungeon look like at a child's playroom.

Katherine heard another prisoner cough. She couldn't tell whether her neighbor was male or female. After the cough, the jail was as quiet as an abandoned church. Each time she shifted her weight on the bed, the sound echoed off the walls. After about ten minutes, a young female jailer brought her jail-issue clothing—orange shirt and loose-fitting pants, flip-flops. No bra. No underpants. "Sorry about the color," said the woman, looking at Katherine's hair. The jailer had a gold ring through her nose. "I'll come back in a few minutes and collect your clothing."

"Excuse me," said Katherine, as the woman walked away.

The woman stopped and turned, waiting.

"Don't I get to make a phone call?"

"As soon as you get dressed."

Katherine pressed her face against the bars and watched the woman walk away.

The lighting was bright in her cell. She didn't feel comfortable undressing there because she didn't know if she were being watched by hidden cameras. She looked up at the ceiling, inspecting it for something that could conceal a camera, but she saw nothing suspicious. Reluctantly she undressed, folding her clothing and putting it on her bed. Then she slipped into the prison attire. The soft cotton felt good against her skin, though the jailer was correct—she didn't much care for the color.

Twenty or thirty minutes passed. She wasn't a good time guesser. But finally the door opened again and the young jailer walked up to her cell and unlocked the door.

"Time for that phone call," she said.

"Thank you."

Katherine eagerly left the cell and followed the woman from the cellblock into a corridor with offices, many of which contained typists and people sitting at desks. The jailer led her over to a small room that contained only a wooden stool and a telephone mounted on the wall. Katherine entered the room and sat on the stool.

"You've got ten minutes," said the jailer. "If you're still on the phone when I knock, hang up immediately. Don't let me catch you on the phone when I open the door."

"I understand," said Katherine, thinking *how odd this place is!*

The jailer closed the door.

Katherine took a deep breath. Her tongue was dry as sandpaper. She quickly punched in the number for Taylor's Ottawa office. Each ring seemed to last an eternity. Finally, Miss Sweeny answered.

Katherine identified herself and asked, "Is Taylor in the office?"

"Oh, how are you Miss Summer," oozed Miss Sweeny.

Katherine heard the ticking of a clock.

"Oh, I'm just fine. Thank you for asking. Could I please speak to Taylor?"

Two precious minutes wasted.

"I think he's on another line."

"Ah . . . please break in on him. This is an emergency."

"Please hold," said a skeptical Miss Sweeny.

Two additional minutes passed.

Then she heard Taylor's voice.

"Where are you?" he asked.

Speaking so quickly that her words overlapped one another and sounded like a sustained machinegun burst she told him everything that'd happened. He listened in stunned silence, and then said, "You're where?"

"The county courthouse jail."

"They locked you up?"

"Yes—please come as soon as you can, but before you come to see me, please stop by the pound and pick up Bessie."

"She's in the pound?"

"They put her there."

"Don't worry. I'll take care of everything."

"By the way, I may have to end this call abruptly."

"I understand. How are they treating you?"

"Oh, they're treating me fine. The jail gives me the creeps. Just the idea of being locked up. Well, you know what I mean."

"Don't worry. I'll make some calls. I'll be there soon."

Suddenly, there was a knock at the door.

"Gotta go," she said, and hung up the telephone.

The door swung open.

Katherine manufactured a smile that caught the jailer off guard.

"Time to go," the jailer said.

They walked a few steps. She turned and asked, "Why you looking so happy?"

"Why not?" said Katherine, cheerfully.

She was determined not to let this get her down.

When the door closed behind her at her cell, she sat on the edge of the bed. There was no clock in the room. They'd taken her watch. *How do people stand passing time, when they can't tell the time? How can they live in the moment if they don't know when they've lost the moment?*

She didn't feel comfortable enough to stretch out on the bed, so she sat leaned over, her elbows propped on her knees, hands against her cheeks. Time went by. She had no idea how much. She heard the voice again. This time she knew it was a woman.

The voice asked, "What you in for?"

Katherine didn't answer right away. *Is she talking to me?*

Then the voice again. "I said, what you in for?"

"I'm not sure. It's all very confusing."

"Yeah, for me, too. They said I stole some things at the drug store. I didn't steal them. I just forgot I had them when I left the store."

"I'm sure things will work out."

"Work out? Yeah, they always work out some way or another."

The exchanged ended and the woman faded away.

Each time Katherine tried to think, it went nowhere. She stopped thinking. Simply cleared her mind and stared at the floor. She saw where the mop had left a swishing design on the floor. Patterns. Shapes. The floor resembled a canvas.

Three hours later, give or take thirty minutes or so, the hallway door opened again and Katherine heard the sound of footsteps.

"Katherine?"

The voice was familiar.

She looked up and saw Taylor standing next to the jailer.

"Are you all right?"

Katherine got to her feet and smiled. "I am now."

The jailer unlocked the door and allowed Taylor to enter the cell.

Taylor gave the jailer a stern look. "Could I have some privacy, please?"

"Yes sir," said the jailer, and she left.

Taylor put his arms around Katherine and held her tight. No one spoke for more than a minute. Then Katherine pushed away and asked, "What about Bessie?"

"I rescued her from the pound and sent her home with Todd."

"Thank God," said Katherine, tears streaming down her cheeks.

"Let's sit," he said, and they both sat on the bed. "I'm taking you out of here tonight. I called the Attorney General and he called the provincial attorney general, who agreed to drop all the charges against you."

Katherine's face brightened. "Really? You mean it's all over?"

"It's all over. As soon as you change, I'll take you home."

CHAPTER
32

Katherine awoke in her own bed, alone except for Bessie, who lay curled against her. Normally, Bessie slept at the foot of the bed, but last night she insisted that she should be allowed to sleep next to her. Taylor wanted to stay over, but she sent him home, explaining that she was tired and needed to be alone.

Bessie had watched her sleep for more than an hour.

The instant that Katherine opened her eyes, Bessie got to her feet, tail wagging so furiously that it made the bed shake. As soon as Katherine's feet were on the floor, Bessie leaped off the bed, shadowing her as she went downstairs and put on a pot of coffee.

Katherine looked out the window at the river. The sun had only been up for thirty minutes or so and there was still a blanket of light fog hovering over the river. A freighter passed not far from her island, upstream against heavy currents, its foghorn rumbling across the water with authority.

What they say is true: there is no place like home.

Katherine opened the door to the deck and smiled as Bessie ran at full speed across the deck and into the grass. The morning air was chilly, too cold for shirtsleeves. She put on a flannel shirt that hung year-long on a hook near the door and she stepped out onto the deck, noticing for the first time the warmth of her coffee cup.

She took in a deep breath. She felt clean again, the stark anguish of the cell jail no longer haunting her thoughts. *Why has all this happened to me? It was wrong of me to run away from the authorities . . . but it was wrong of them to violate my privacy and force me to testify against someone who has never done anything but be my friend. If Jason injured me by caring about me, then how much more did they injure me by forcing me to hurt him?*

Bessie was like a dog possessed. She ran and jumped and rolled on the grass and barked at everything, yet at nothing in particular, constantly in motion, her ears fluttering like flags in a high wind. The island was the only world she wanted, and Katherine understood that about her.

Not wanting to interrupt Bessie's revelry, she slipped back inside and sat at the table that contained her answering machine. She had more than a dozen voicemails. Five were from Jason. Four were from Taylor. The rest were from gallery dealers calling about her paintings. She listened to the business messages first and took notes about the calls she planned to return, someday. Then she listened to Jason's messages:

"Katherine, this is Jason. I've been trying to reach you. Your cell is turned off, so I called your land line. Please call."

"Jason, please call."

"This is Jason. I just wanted to let you know that they've issued a warrant for your arrest. I feel so badly about getting you involved in this. Please call so that I'll know that you are all right."

"Katherine. Jason. I looked for you after the hearing, but they said you'd already left. Please call me when you get home so that we can talk."

"This is Jason. I know you must be home by now. Please call so that I'll know that you are okay."

Then she listened to Taylor's messages:

"It's me, Taylor. Just wanted to make sure that you made it back to the island all right. Did you know that your cell is turned off? Call me."

"Taylor again. Please call."

"Katherine, I'm getting concerned about you not answering your phone. Give me a ring."

"It's Taylor. I just want to hear the sound of your voice so that I'll know you are all right."

"I was worried about you so I took my boat up your way and circled your island once to make sure you are all right. I saw your shadow against the curtains, so I assume you are all right and just don't want to talk any more tonight. Call me in the morning, please."

Katherine picked up her cell and turned it on. Then she went outside and sat in one of the deck chairs, amazed at how cool it was. The leaves on the island were golden, with thick patches of red scattered here and there. She hadn't done a fall landscape in several years. It was time, again. The very thought of it made her smile.

She took a deep breath and punched in Taylor's number.

"Hello—is this Katherine?"

"Yes, Taylor, it is. I'm sorry I didn't get back to you last night but I turned off my cell and the ringer on my land line. I just wanted to be alone. I'm sure you can understand that."

"Absolutely. I'm glad to know that you are all right. You sound just fine."

"Thanks. It's because Bessie and I are back on the island."

"You do like that island, don't you?"

"Now more than ever."

She paused to review the little speech she'd prepared.

"I want to thank you again for coming to my rescue, and for getting Bessie out of that pound. Please thank Todd for taking such good care of her."

"You can thank him yourself when you see him again."

Katherine ignored the comment, and continued, "The last two days were not the worst in my life, but they are a close second. I hope your relationship with me won't hurt you politically. I'm sure this will be written up in the newspapers."

"Don't worry about that, Katherine. I'm certainly not going to give it a second thought."

"You're kind to say that, but I know I must be an embarrassment to you. I know I'm an embarrassment to myself. I did some things that were wrong, and although I did them for what I considered a good reason, I doubt most people will see it that way."

"You did nothing wrong. You didn't want to hurt your therapist. You just wanted to get away to figure things out for yourself. I'm sorry that I . . . " His voice faltered.

"Sorry what?" It was the most pregnant "I" she'd ever heard in her life.

"Never mind. I was just rattling on. Don't mind me."

Katherine dropped it. By now she pretty much knew the rest.

"I want to thank you for everything that you've done for me. After Roger and Dedi died . . ."

"Katherine?"

". . . I'd lost everything important to me and . . ."

"Where are you going with this?"

". . . I lost touch with who I am. Without your help, I don't know if I'd ever found my way."

"I just did what any man would do. If he cared about a woman."

Katherine paused. She was almost there. She took a deep breath. The air went down dry, scratchy. *Be strong*, she thought.

"Taylor, I don't think we should see each other anymore."

"What did I do to deserve that?"

"You're wonderful. It's not you. It's me. I'm just not ready for a relationship. To be honest, I don't know what I want right now"

This time it was Taylor who paused. Rejection from a woman was a new experience for him. When he spoke, Katherine heard something new in his voice, anger: "Well, I really don't know what to say. Are you sure you want to do this?"

"Yes, Taylor. I am sure."

"I think you're making a mistake."

"It wouldn't be the first time."

"What? What did you say?"

"Can we stay friends?"

"Of course . . . well, I guess there's not much left to say, is there?"

He didn't wait for her to answer.

"Stay in touch."

Then he hung up his telephone.

Katherine leaned back in the chair and took a deep breath.

Then she punched in Jason's telephone number. He picked up on the second ring.

"Katherine—where have you been?"

"Hello, Jason. That's a long story."

"Why didn't you return my calls?"

"I was in jail."

"What?"

"The OPP charged me with a long list of offenses and I was hauled off to the jail in the courthouse."

"Unbelievable! How did you get out?"

Katherine told him the whole story, from start to finish, ending with, "Bessie and I are happy to be back on the island where we belong. I'm sorry I didn't return your calls, but both of my telephones were turned off. All I wanted to do was get a good night's sleep."

"Were you able to sleep?"

"Yes. The deepest sleep I've had since Roger and Dedi . . ."

Jason interrupted. "You probably shouldn't be alone right now."

"I think being alone is exactly what I need right now."

"I'd be happy to drive over and talk to you about it."

"I know that, Jason. You've always had my best interests at heart. I've never doubted that. What happened at your hearing? I wanted to stay but the police officer wouldn't let me stay. She drove me straight back to Ogdensburg. So what happened?"

"They suspended my license for two years."

"Two years? Really!"

"It could have been worse. They could have pulled my license permanently."

"What a nightmare! What are you going to do?"

"I don't know yet. Something will come along."

"I feel so guilty about this. I wanted to lie to them. I wanted to protect you. But you told me to tell the truth and I didn't want to disappoint you."

"You did exactly the right thing."

"Then why do I feel so guilty?"

"Because you are a good person. You will get over the guilt because you know that you are a good person, and because you know that you did what I wanted you to do. I made the mistake, not you. The rules of life are that the person who makes the mistake is the one who pays for the mistake. It doesn't always work out that way. But in this case it did, and I'll have to live with that."

"It's not fair. You are one of the best people I know. Your only crime was having feelings for me—feelings, I might add, that I don't deserve, at least not right now."

"Why don't we take Bessie on a picnic tomorrow? The weather is changing quickly now. Soon it'll be too cold for a picnic."

"I don't think so, Jason."

Katherine felt her heart thumping in her chest. The last thing she ever wanted to do was cause Jason any pain.

God, please give me the strength.

"I don't know any other way to say this, except straight out, but I don't think we should see each other anymore."

Jason said nothing.

But Katherine could feel his pain, and she continued, "I'm just not ready to deal with all the complicated feelings that relationships demand. To be honest, I really don't know what I want right now, other than to be left alone."

"I understand."

"I put you through so much hell. Do you hate me?"

The instant she said it, she knew she'd regret it.

"Hate you? No, on the contrary, I love you."

"See, that's what I mean by complicated feelings."

"You're right—I should have seen this coming."

"I need to go now. Bessie's dragging up something from the rocks."

"Just call if you ever need me."

"You know I will."

Katherine put down the telephone and ran out onto the grass, where Bessie was in the process of dragging a dead turtle toward the house. It was her trophy turtle.

"No, no, Bessie," she said, picking up the turtle by its hind leg. Holding it at arm's length, she walked over to the river and tossed it as far as she could, hoping it wouldn't again wash up on the rock. Then she bent over and stroked Bessie's head.

"You can't keep everything that washes up on the rocks."

CHAPTER
33

The therapist busily made notes on a clipboard.

After months of therapy they were no closer to a solution than they were when they began. All he wanted out of life was an identity.

"I'm discouraged," he said.

The therapist looked up from her notes and adjusted her eyeglasses.

"I can understand that," she replied. "But you have made some progress."

"When you have an identity you never think about it. You worry about disease. Making a living. Relationships. Making a car payment. But if you don't have an identity finding one is all you can think about."

"I understand. But you also must look at the positive things in your life. The South African government has granted you a passport. You have found meaningful employment. You are in good health."

"Believe me, I appreciate all that. But there is a part of me that is missing."

"Has the government done anything to find out if I am an American or a Canadian?"

"Yes. They have gone through the proper channels. But there is so little for them to go on. There were several deaths on the river during the time you were on board the ship, but there were no missing persons reports filed during that time. In other words, no one is looking for you."

"That means I don't belong to anyone."

"You must never give up hope. At the same time, you must come to terms with the possibility that your true identity may never be determined. You must look to the future. Only by doing that do you have any chance of re-establishing your former memories."

"Are you saying that by reaching out to the future I can possibly discover the past?"

"Yes—there is a fancy theory that explains that concept, but I won't bore you with the details. Your brain has millions of electrical connections. When you make new connections they reach out to the old connections to form a network. I think that you will find your past—and you discover that your memories were temporarily misplaced, not lost."

"I pray that you are correct."

CHAPTER
34

Third week in October. The first snow of the year fell, covering Katherine's island with two inches of dry snow, which accounted for how readily it was snatched up by the wind and whirled about in gusts that resembled cumulous clouds.

Bessie loved the snow. She loved to run through it, going no place in particular, just running from one side of the island to the other, taking great pride—or so it seemed—in her footprints. In the snow, she frequently barked for no good reason.

Katherine was gazing out the window at Bessie, thinking that she didn't know what she'd do if she ever lost Bessie, her best friend, when her cell rang. It was Rose Kelly, the Attorney General's wife. She was at the boathouse, eager for Katherine to transport her to the island so that she could sit for her portrait.

"I'll be right there," said Katherine.

Katherine threw on a jacket—the temp was in the high twenties—and she headed down to the dock, shouting to Bessie that she'd be back in a minute. Bessie paused to listen to her explanation and then resumed her activities in the snow.

Katherine started the boat and made a u-turn to go to the boathouse. There was no ice in the river yet, but by late December or early January the water would be solid ice and she'd have to travel back and forth to the boathouse in her iceboat.

Rose was waiting for her on the dock when she arrived, so she never had to turn off the motor. Rose seemed glad to see her. She smiled and waved, eager to begin the adventure of sitting for a portrait. On the ride back to the island, Rose shouted, "The air is pretty nippy today, isn't it," to which Katherine responded, "Oh, come back in two months and you'll see what nippy is all about."

Ottawa was further north than the river, but the moisture off the water made the river seem so much colder.

As soon as they docked, Bessie ran off to greet their visitor. To Katherine's surprise, Bessie didn't bark. She sniffed about Rose's ankles and waited for her to pet her. Then she was off again, stomping her way through the snow over to the other side of the island.

Inside the house, Katherine took Rose's jacket and waited for her to slip off her boots. On their way into the studio, Katherine said, "Please thank your husband for helping me out of that jam."

"Oh, you mean those trumped up charges," she said. "He was happy to do it. The very idea of them putting an artist of your caliber in jail. I don't blame you one bit. If it'd been me, I'd have given those police officers the chase of their life."

Katherine laughed. "Then you're not embarrassed for me to paint your portrait—a common lawbreaker."

"Listen, dear, I consider it a badge of honor, what you did. Besides, there is nothing common about you."

Katherine showed her around the studio, pointing out where she wanted her to sit.

Seeing the paintings leaned against the wall, Rose asked, "Do you mind if I take a look."

"Not at all."

Rose took her time looking at the paintings, frequently stopping to praise some she liked. Then she saw something that really caught her interest.

"Oh, how lovely this is," she said, holding up Katherine's nude self-portrait. "I didn't realize you did figure studies. Is this someone you know, or was it a professional model?"

"She's not a professional model, not by a long shot. And, yes, I know her quite well—it's me."

Rose looked at her with surprise, her eyes widening.

"It's beautiful—simply beautiful."

"Thanks—I have no idea why I did it."

"I know someone who'd love this painting."

"Who's that?"

"Taylor, of course."

"Oh, I guess you haven't heard. We aren't seeing each other anymore."

"What a shame—hope you didn't take it too hard. Short term relationships are the norm for Taylor."

Katherine shook her head. "No problem."

Rose carefully returned the painting where she got it and walked across the room and sat in the chair. "Have you thought about how you want to paint me?"

"I think a three-quarters profile, showing you from the waist up, would be tasteful."

"Hmmm," said Rose. "That would be very elegant."

She paused long enough to touch her index finger to her lips.

"What would you think about doing a figure study of me? Would you have a problem with that?"

"No, not at all. But would you like to discuss it with your husband?"

"Not on your life," said Rose. "I'm an independent thinker—like you! I'd like to surprise him with a figure study."

"Fine with me," said Katherine. "What do you have in mind?"

"You're the expert, but I think a portrait of me from the waist up, with my hips draped in velvet or something, would be perfect."

"Let's do it," said Katherine.

Rose undressed and sat in the chair. Katherine rummaged through her closet and pulled out a length of maroon velvet fabric that she fashioned into a drape. Rose folded her hands in her lap and smiled prettily for her. Rose didn't have a perfect face—her nose had a slight hook to it—but her breasts were perfect.

Katherine instantly realized that her biggest challenge would be to keep the focal point of the painting away from her breasts, otherwise it would resemble the typical *Playboy* centerfold.

"Do you want me to scout around for you?" asked Rose.

"What do you mean?"

"You know, find you another man. Another Taylor. I know scads of men."

"Thank you, but I'm on hiatus from men."

"Really. That's admirable. I would, if I could. Take a hiatus from men—but I'm married."

"That's hard to do when you're married."

"Not impossible. But, you're right, it is difficult. I'll tell you what gets to me the most about men. We say we're sick of men and can get along fine without them—but we can't. Men, on the other hand, when they say they can get along fine without women, they mean it. They'll go on hunting or skiing trips with their male friends and never look back."

"Oh, they look back all right. Not for relationships, but for sex."

"You're right. You're absolutely right!"

As she painted Rose, Katherine noticed something that she'd never thought about, and that was how utterly still women can sit when they want to, a quality that eludes the male of the species. For two hours,

Rose never once shifted her weight or asked to take a break. She couldn't imagine a man being able to do that, unless he was asleep.

The first part of the sitting, Katherine spent outlining her curves, especially her breasts, which were full but remarkably firm. The remainder of the time she worked on the lines of her face. She had beautiful skin and a seductive mouth, and Katherine wanted to capture both in the painting, making her mouth the focal point.

At the end of the session, Rose dressed matter-of-factly, as if posing for a figure study was something she did every day.

When Katherine returned to the studio after taking Rose back to the boathouse, she sat for a long while looking at the canvas. She wondered how the Attorney General would react to the painting. It was not what he told her that he wanted, but how could he possibly be disappointed? She guessed that the painting would go in their bedroom, but she didn't know that for certain.

* * *

Rose returned for two additional sessions, each time riding to the island with Katherine in the iceboat, a loud, rough-riding conveyance that was propelled by a gigantic fan at the rear of the boat. The first time they used the iceboat, it was in late November, when there was ice in the river, but not enough to support the weight of a human. Since the boat could travel on water or ice, they used it as more of an insurance policy than a necessity.

At the time of the final session in mid-December, the river was frozen solid, strong enough to support the weight of an iceboat filled with people. Rose had never ridden on an iceboat, so she found it thrilling.

Rose was extremely pleased with the finished painting. The first time she saw it, she sat and stared at it for thirty minutes before saying a word. Katherine was pleased as well. Not only did it capture the reality of Rose's face and figure, it elevated that reality to a high level of artistic vision. It was the human form, transformed into an inspirational landscape of human emotion, a tribute to God's handiwork.

After Katherine helped Rose load the painting into her car and then sent her on her way, she returned to the island experiencing a sense of loss. Releasing her paintings was like sending a child off to private school or college. Bittersweet.

She called Bessie over to her side.

"Bessie, how would you like to go on a hike?"

Bessie didn't bark, but she did look at her like she thought she was crazy.

Katherine looked at the sky. It was an even gray. No hint of the sudden snow storms, called white outs, that sometimes descended on the river. The water was frozen solid to a depth of three or four feet. Plenty firm to hold a couple of hikers.

Katherine went into the house long enough to fill a thermos with warm milk and her pockets with trail-mix bars. She wrapped a woolen scarf around her neck and stuck a hat on her head. Then, with Bessie running at her side, she hurried down the slope to where the island met the ice. At first Bessie was reluctant to venture onto the ice. She had been taught never to venture beyond the rocks into the river and now Katherine was encouraging her to follow her past the rocks onto the ice. Very confusing.

They headed south, with nothing but grayness ahead of them.

The ice was not slippery because of a thin layer of snow that covered it. The temperature was in the low-twenties, cold enough to keep the air crisp, but not cold enough to sting her lungs. Bessie loved the river when it was frozen because she could run far ahead and still see Katherine, something she could not do when they hiked in the woods.

Walking on the river, knowing that beneath the ice was up to two hundred feet of icy water carried along by strong, sometimes stampeding, currents, was an experience like no other. Sometimes local residents foolishly drove their cars out onto the ice, most often for a leisurely drive, but occasionally to drag race up and down the river. But there'd been enough instances of cars breaking through the ice to discourage Katherine from ever trying it. The horror of being trapped beneath the ice was something that she could never imagine experiencing.

After about thirty minutes of hiking, Katherine turned and looked back at her island. It rose out of the ice with a volcano-like presence, her most enduring anchor in life. It amazed her to think that she was now standing where ocean freighters traveled during most of the year. It was a humbling experience.

She and Bessie continued on until they came near the invisible dividing line between Canada and the United States. She briefly considered pressing ahead, but the thought of repeating her previous border crossing experience dissuaded her from continuing.

Instead, she turned west, headed toward the stretch of river that had the most concentrated placement of islands. Up ahead there was nothing but a gray slate.

After frolicking in the snow, her large feet padding in a circle around Katherine, Bessie suddenly cut through the circle and ran up to Katherine, whimpering.

"What's the matter girl?"

Bessie made a twisting motion, an indication that she was upset about something.

"Just tell me what it is, Bessie."

Bessie tried her best to talk to her, but when she realized that Katherine didn't understand, she turned and started back the way they'd come, stopping every few feet to turn around and look at Katherine.

"No, we're going this way," Katherine shouted.

Finally, Bessie relented and ran back to Katherine, staying right on her heels.

After about fifteen minutes, Katherine felt the wind pick up, the tiny bits of frozen snow strong enough to make her eyes blink. The sleeves of her jacket began to flutter in the wind. Still, she pressed on until she saw a wall of tumbling black clouds in the distance. It was not until then that she took Bessie's advice and turned around to go back the way they'd come.

Within minutes, they were overcome by the cloud. It was a dreaded white-out.

The wind howled all about her.

 Each breath was a chore that sucked miniature ice shards into her lungs. Visibility was cut to zero. Looking down, she could not see her feet. Looking ahead, she could see no more than a couple of inches.

"Stay close to me, Bessie!" she screamed.

Bessie needed no prompting to do as she was told.

Walking was like stepping flush into a giant balloon, your air passages practically smothered by the plastic folds, and then trying to press ahead, the weight of the balloon constantly pushing you back, until you pushed and pushed, the muscles in your arms and legs moving well past aching, into stinging cramps that brought frozen tears to your eyes.

Unknown to Katherine, they got turned around in the snow storm and turned west. If they missed all the islands, if their path took them on the route the big freighters took, they could go for a hundred miles without touching land again. There was three hours of daylight left, but inside the white-out all was dark.

She pushed on.

Several times she tripped over her own feet and fell into the snow.

After about an hour, thinking she was in the vicinity of her island, she veered north, only in her disoriented state, turning north was actually a southward turn. By then her face was caked with icy snow, which she had to continuously wipe from her eyes.

She was exhausted, but stopping was not an option. She could perhaps build a snow break for herself and Bessie, sort of a roofless igloo, but there was no guarantee that would be enough to get them through the night.

Once again, she stumbled and fell. Only this time, when she reached to push herself back up, her hand landed on a large rock. She explored with her fingertips, finding more rocks. At first she thought it was her island, but then she realized it was not when she discovered that she was at the base of a sheer cliff.

With Bessie at her side, she made her way along the base of the cliff, finally finding an indentation that could shield them from the snow and wind. She huddled with Bessie against the frozen earth, feeling Bessie's warmth as she drifted off to sleep.

When she awoke, the sky was still black and the wind still howled all around her, but she no longer hurt from the cold. She pulled the thermos and one of the trail bars from her deep pockets and drank a half-cup of still-warm milk. Then she filled the cup and put it so that Bessie could drink. She also shared the trail bar with Bessie, who devoured her share in one gulp.

For the life of her, she couldn't figure out where she was. There were few islands to the east of her home and none of them had sheer cliffs that dropped to water's edge. It couldn't stay dark forever, she knew that. It was just a matter of time before the mystery would be solved.

All she and Bessie had to do was ride out the storm.

For the first time, Katherine really understood what it must have been like for the early explorers who traveled the North Country during the winter months. It was a miracle that any of them survived the hardships.

She pulled Bessie in close to her, a gesture that was greeted with enthusiasm by Bessie, who enjoyed her warmth as much as she enjoyed

Bessie's warmth. With Bessie cradled in her arms, Katherine thought about where she was in life.

It wasn't where she expected to be, that's for sure.

I don't know if I was right or wrong to break off my friendships with Jason and Taylor, but I surely didn't see a future the way they were headed. I couldn't continue to sleep with Taylor and maintain a friendship with Jason, because I know that wasn't what he wanted, ultimately. And I couldn't sleep with Jason and maintain a friendship with Taylor because that wasn't what Taylor wanted. I either had to see neither of them, or chose one of them. For me, it's always been feast or famine.

Katherine wondered what Jason was doing. She hoped he was warm and safe. For some reason, she didn't worry about him recovering from the board's decision. He would land on his feet, she knew that much. She had confidence in him as a survivor.

So weary did she become from trying to figure out her life, that she dropped off to sleep again. When she awoke, it was early morning and the sky was bright blue and there was not a cloud in sight.

She nudged Bessie and got up and dusted the snow off her clothing.

Then she looked around. She recognized the island. It was a rock island on the northern end of the ship channel, about ten miles west of her island. She was relieved to know that she hadn't wandered over into the United States. Normally, that wouldn't be a problem, but her past experience with the New York State Police, if known by authorities, might have made her an undesirable alien.

Katherine headed east, back to her island, with Bessie in the lead. It'd take most of the day to get home, but it was a glorious morning and the air was bright with promise.

CHAPTER
35

Katherine and Bessie celebrated Christmas alone that year, though she had invitations from several friends to join their families—and, of course, both Taylor and Jason called to wish her a happy Christmas and to invite her to dinner.

She turned down both invitations and kept the telephone conversations brief. It was her second Christmas without Roger and Dedi, and she spent it preparing a lavish meal for herself and Bessie, listening to Frank Sinatra croon holiday tunes, one song in particular bringing tears to her eyes: a soaring orchestrated version of "I'll Be Home for Christmas."

She listened to that song ten times in a row, finishing off three glasses of wine. Then she made her way up the stairs, one step at a time, careful not to lose her balance. Once she reached the bedroom, she threw herself onto the bed, face down, arms outstretched, and cried herself to sleep. Bessie jumped up on the bed and curled up nearby, so concerned that she watched Katherine all night, never once closing her eyes.

The highlight of her Christmas did not happen in December, but in January, when the winners of the prestigious Governor General's Awards were announced. Katherine won the award for art, though she didn't hear the announcement on television and did not learn about it until the next day, when Taylor called to congratulate her. It was the highest honor she could receive as an artist in Canada, but there was more to the honor than a pat on the back—with it came with a twenty-five thousand dollar grant.

Taylor offered to be her escort to the award's dinner, held in early March, but she politely declined.

"I hope I see you there, Taylor," she said. "But I think I'd rather go unescorted."

"I understand," said Taylor. "Do you mind if I pick out a gown for you?"

"Thank you, but I already have something in mind."

"If you change your mind, just let me know."

"I will."

She didn't hear from Jason, but she thought he probably didn't know about the award since she doubted it was reported in the local newspaper across the river.

March rolled around in the blink of an eye. Looking back, she really couldn't account for January and February. She painted a landscape that depicted a white-out with islands barely visible in the distance, but the painting had too much white in it to satisfy her and failed to capture the terror of such a violent storm, and she ended up painting over it, this time doing a springtime portrait of Dark Island, a timeless castle surrounded by white wildflowers and thick gardens of pinkish-red roses.

To pick out a gown for the Governor General's Award dinner, she took the train to Toronto and shopped her way through the most exclusive shops in the city. Finally, she found what she was looking for in the heart of Yonge Street, a black silk sleeveless dress with a choke-collar. The sales clerk was delighted with her choice, pointing out that actress Nicole Kidman had once worn the same dress to the Academy Awards.

Katherine drove herself to Ottawa, though Taylor offered to have Todd take her to the event. Still no word from Jason.

Perhaps he's forgotten about me—moved on with his life. I wouldn't blame him if he has.

When she arrived at the Rideau Hall, she had to wait behind a line of Mercedes and BMWs for her turn, finally handing off the keys to her Jeep to a young valet who looked at her as if she didn't belong in such austere company.

She'd barely stepped in the main entrance when she was greeted by Taylor, who insisted on escorting her to the Ballroom, where a podium and several chairs had been placed for the speakers and the winners of the awards for fiction and film. Taylor literally walked her to her chair and then sat in one of the chairs close to the podium.

"I'm so proud of you," he whispered over his shoulder.

"Thank you."

Within minutes, the Governor General walked up to the podium and leaned over to the microphone and introduced Taylor to the audience of several hundred. He rose to his feet and stood behind the podium, a broad grin on his face.

"This is a proud day for me. The winner of the award for excellence in art is Katherine Summer, who lives down river from me in Brockville. On an island, I might add. Her paintings have lifted the spirits of an entire nation, and they have inspired us to look beyond ourselves—at the beauty that is Canada. I give you Ms. Katherine Summer."

There was applause, during which Katherine stepped up to the podium.

Taylor paused long enough for it to die down.

"Governor General."

The Governor General stepped forward with the award and presented it to Katherine, along with an envelope containing the check.

"Would you like to say a few words to our guests?"

Katherine moved over to the microphone and looked out at the audience. To her surprise, there was someone at the rear of the audience that she recognized immediately. . . *Jason Montclair!* She flashed a wide smile and thanked Taylor and the Governor General and everyone who turned out for the ceremony.

After a brief speech, there was more applause and she returned to her chair. She couldn't see Jason from where she was seated, but just knowing that he was there made her heart soar. During the remainder of the awards, surprising even herself, she kept thinking . . .*hurry up, hurry up, please!*

At the end of the ceremony, the Governor General announced that dinner would be served shortly for the invited guests in the dining room. Taylor walked over to her, grinning like a silly schoolboy.

"May I escort you to dinner?" he asked.

"I'm sorry," she said. "There's someone I need to speak to. I'll meet you there."

She reached out and touched his arm—"Thanks for everything"— and then hurried away, leaving him at the podium looking a bit stunned.

Katherine picked her way through the crowd, stopping every few steps to shake hands with people that she didn't know, until she saw Jason standing off to the side, hands in pockets. She rushed up to him and hugged him.

"I'm so glad you came. How did you even know about it?"

Jason returned her smile, feeling a little foolish because he couldn't control his enthusiasm about seeing her again.

"It was in the Ogdensburg newspaper."

"Why would they print a story about a Canadian award?"

"Well, that wasn't exactly the focus of the story. The headline was 'Border Buster Rewarded by Canadian Government.'"

"You're kidding, right?"

"No kidding. You are quite the celebrity in Ogdensburg."

Katherine laughed and then said, "Bring me up to date. I want to know everything that's happened to you since I saw you last."

"I got a job at the high school coaching the football team."

"Really?" she asked, trying to visualize him with a whistle around his neck.

"And it's been really great. It brought back a lot of fond memories."

"But you can get your license back soon, can't you?"

"Yes, but I'm not sure if I want to start up another practice."

"So you plan on coaching for the rest of your life?"

She tried to hide her disappointment.

"Oh, no," he said. "I've handed in my resignation, effective the first of June."

Katherine looked baffled. "Why would you do that?"

Jason broke out into the biggest grin she'd ever seen on him.

"I got this idea for a book that I titled *Last Woman Standing*. I sent the idea off to a New York publisher and they gave me a huge advance. I've still got six months to go on the book, but they've already sold the movie rights for two million dollars, and I get half of that."

"So you're going to be a writer now?"

"Looks like it."

Katherine hugged him again. "I'm so happy for you."

"I came today because I have a favor to ask."

"What's that?"

"I'd like for you to go skating with me on the Rideau Canal. I read something about it once, and it seems irresistible."

"When?"

"Right now."

"But I can't skate in this dress!"

"Sure you can."

"I didn't wear a winter coat. I'd be too cold."

"I have a warm jacket you can wear."

"But I've got a dinner to attend."

"Do you have the check yet?"

"Yes." She showed him the envelope.

"Problem solved."

"That would be so bad of me to leave before dinner."

"It'd be so bad that it'd be good."

Katherine grabbed him by the hand and started for the door, saying, "You're such a bad influence on me. What am I ever going to do with you?"

Thirty minutes later, their feet laced into rental skates, they glided across the ice under a starlit sky, Katherine wearing Jason's winter jacket over her gown. The jacket-gown combination brought a few stares, but Katherine didn't care.

The downtown canal was filled with young couples, most of them holding hands as they skated among Ottawa's most beautiful buildings. The air was cold and crisp, and the ice was smooth and silvery. It was, at that precise moment, the most romantic spot on the planet.

After skating separately for a while, they whizzed by each other, reaching out, so that their hands found each other and clasped, sending them hand-in-hand across the ice. After making a sharp turn that was too much for Jason, he tripped and fell into her, pushing both to the ice.

Katherine laughed as they struggled to get to their feet. They stood there for the longest time, face to face, laughing uncontrollably, until Jason took her in his arms and kissed her.

For a moment, Katherine lost herself in the kiss. Eyes closed. Savoring the touch of his lips. She was on fire for him. It was that forbidden feeling that rattled her back to reality. She pushed away, her hand lingering on his chest as their eyes interlocked.

"Jason, I can't do this."

Her voice was strained, tearful.

"I'm sorry. I just can't."

Suddenly, she skated away, calling out, "I've got to return to the dinner."

Jason stood on the ice, swallowing hard as she moved away from him. He shouted after her, "But I love you!" Though he doubted that she heard him.

CHAPTER
36

After a long hard winter, spring typically tiptoes into the St. Lawrence Seaway in the dead of night and appears suddenly, without advance warning: warm breezes, sunny skies, flowers sprouting up everywhere, all seemingly overnight.

That was the way it happened this year for Katherine. There was a chill in the air when she went to bed, cool enough that she slept beneath a blanket; but the next morning she discovered that she had kicked the blanket off the bed and onto the floor.

Had spring arrived?

She hurried downstairs, taking two steps at a time, Bessie a blond blur as she ran past, her feet clamoring for traction, so that when Katherine opened the door and Bessie bolted onto the deck and then out across the lawn, Katherine was almost blinded by the bright light. She took a deep breath. The air was warm, mildly fragrant.

She went back inside and put on a pot of coffee.

Spring and fall were her favorite seasons. Within a week, the banks of the river would be covered with wildflowers and the maple trees would become giant green balls of fluttering leaves. Her head filled with ideas for new paintings. Landscapes that spoke to the heart. Sunrises that inspired and offered new hope.

Suddenly, the telephone rang.

She looked at caller ID. It was Taylor.

She reached for the telephone. Hesitated. Then pulled her hand back.

It's too early in the morning. He can leave a message.

She listened to three more rings and waited to see the message light turn red and blink. It didn't. Taylor didn't leave a message.

Must not have been important.

Katherine would be the first to tell you that she knows next to nothing about dating. As a young woman, the relationships she had with men were all very unstructured. Nothing like dating, where you have to see each other on certain days at certain times. Lots of rules. Expectations. What are we doing this Saturday, Honey?

Nothing like that happened with Roger. Their premarital and post-marital relationships were exactly the same: sort of a free fall in which they were each their own person. No expectations. No rules. No problems. No disagreements.

She was baffled by the inability of both Jason and Taylor to understand why, if she said she needed space, they couldn't understand that. Why did they continue to call? What part of "don't call me, I'll call you" did they not understand? Their calls were always pleasant—and always ended with, "if you need anything, just let me know"—but they were a distraction that came at a time in her life when she wanted clarity, not confused persistence. She once told Jason that he should date Taylor, that the two of them would be perfect for each other. It was a flip statement, a meaningless joke, but Jason analyzed it to death and drove her crazy for several days after she said it.

"No, Jason, I wasn't saying that I thought you're gay," she explained. "It's about personalities."

"Oh," he responded.

After her shower, Katherine put on jeans and a T-shirt and walked out to the dock and sat on the edge so that she could dangle her legs over the side. She saw three freighters, two to the west of her and one to the east. The river was filled with boaters, taking advantage of the first spring day. She imagined many of them were office workers who called in sick so that they could go out on the river.

She'd been on the dock for about an hour, when she saw a boat headed her way from the east, traveling along the Canadian bank. She didn't think much about it. Boats often seemed to be headed for her island, only to veer to the south and into the shipping channel that usually tumbled with waves from the freighters. Only this time, the boat didn't change course. It headed straight for her dock.

Oh, no she thought. *Not another OPP cruiser. What have I done wrong this time?*

She looked for the tell-tale flashing lights but saw none. Not until the boat was about fifty yards away did she recognize it as Taylor's boat. When he saw her looking his way, he stood from behind the windshield and waved. She waved back, wondering if she should run back to the house before he got there. She didn't.

"Good morning, Katherine," he shouted, pulling up to the dock. "I called earlier and you didn't answer. You must have been outside."

"Must have been."

She hated lying. She rationalized that it was a white lie. A very white lie.

The boat coasted in flush against the dock, but he made no effort to get out.

"What have you been doing this morning?"

"Not much at all. Mostly sitting out here."

"Where's Bessie?"

"She's around somewhere."

"Great dog."

"Yes, great dog. Definitely."

"Do you have anything planned for the rest of the morning?"

"Not really," she conceded, knowing it was a mistake to tell him that.

When I'm around men, I've got to learn to think faster . . . in a devious way.

Taylor reached back toward the housing that contained the inboard engine. On top of the cabinet was a basket.

"I packed us a picnic lunch. Why don't we go for a ride and see how the islands made it through the winter?"

Taylor smiled broadly, flashing his best imitation of a Clark Gable grin, something he knew she would like because she'd told him many times how much she liked his old movies. Taylor was proud of his ability to remember everything that women ever told him. The way he saw it, a woman's opinions are the way to her heart, because it's her opinions that reveal her vulnerabilities. His favorite come-on line with women was, "why don't you tell me what you think?" Works like a charm.

Katherine hesitated. She didn't really want to go on a picnic with Taylor, but making up a lie to explain why she couldn't go seemed like way too much work on such a beautiful day. Instead, she said, "Can Bessie come, too?"

"Absolutely—it wouldn't be a picnic without Bessie."

She called out for Bessie and saw her raise up out of the tall grass on the other side of the lawn. In an instant, she was lopping toward Katherine.

"Is there anything I need from the house? Do you have anything for us to drink?"

"You don't need a thing. Todd packed everything we'll need, and then some."

Katherine got into the boat and coaxed Bessie onto the seat next to her. Taylor pulled back on the throttle and the boat lurched forward, quickly building speed to cross over the channel waves into quieter water. The spray turned into mist and gently dampened her face. Within seconds, she was glad she'd gone along for the ride.

Taylor didn't have all that much to say, a rarity for him. He asked her if she was working on anything new and when she said no, he replied, "You will—and soon. You won't be able to resist the allure of spring on the river."

"You know me pretty well, don't you?"

"Not as well as I'd like."

Katherine smiled, not falling for the bait.

One good thing about boating on the river was that it was so noisy that it left room only for sporadic conversation. You can only shout back and forth so many times before it becomes tiresome. They continued west at high speed, past Stovin Island and the Brockville Narrows, on across a long expanse of open water, to Amateur Islands, where the river nearly tripled in width and took in dozens of islands, some small, some large to contain an entire village of cottages.

Going the opposite direction was an uprooted maple tree that had lived its life in relative obscurity on the banks of Lake Ontario, only to be uprooted last spring by a relentless rainstorm, the winds of which caused the tree to tumble into the lake.

It slowly made its way east, following the currents, losing first its leaves and then its limbs, its rich sap leached dry by the water, so that by the time it weathered the summer storms and drifted into the St. Lawrence River, it was little more than a stripped down log, nicked and scared by sharp rocks and passing freighters, a mere shadow of its former self. It spent the winter frozen in the ice around Wellsley Island.

When the thaw came it pulled loose and sought out the main currents that flowed all the way to the sea, and freedom.

Taylor and Katherine had ventured south into American waters, just north of Rabbit Island, when they slammed into the log at full throttle. They never knew what hit them. The boat splintered into a thousand pieces, the impact throwing them both into the water, with neither of them wearing life preservers.

They felt like someone had yanked the river out from under them.

Katherine struck her head on a rock in a finger-like shoal that extended from Rabbit Island out into the river. It didn't knock her unconscious, but it dazed her for a moment, so that all she could see were light flashes and random streaks of color that made no sense whatsoever to her.

The river water tasted bitter in her mouth, tainted by gasoline from the boat's ruptured tank. The currents were strong and they pushed her away from the shoal, away from the island itself.

"Bessie!" she screamed, swimming in no particular direction. "Where are you?"

"Katherine! Katherine! Where are you?"

She heard his voice, but she felt herself slip-sliding away.

"Taylor—where are you?"

Taylor had been tossed in a different direction. Somehow he'd injured his arm in the accident. It ached and he could barely move it. He struggled to stay afloat, propelling himself upward with frantic, flapping like motions, to see above the waves that rose above his head and pushed him away from the island.

Once he heard Katherine's voice—and had a direction to follow— he fought against the currents, struggling to find his direction.

"Keep talking to me!" she shouted. "I'm coming!"

"Yes!" he called out, his voice ricocheting off the foamy waves. "I'm over here!"

Katherine's head bobbed in and out of the water. She half-swam, half-floated, half-hurled herself, trying to recover enough to think what to do next. Her arms and legs ached from the thrashing, and her body felt heavy as lead.

Somehow she was able to snatch enough breaths to stay alive and afloat, her head spinning. She heard Taylor's voice again and she tried to see above the waves, but all she could see was water.

"Taylor?" she screamed, twisting and turning, head bobbing.

"Katherine!"

Then she was next to him, talking to him, telling him to relax, not to fight the water. She was going to swim for the two of them. She turned him in the water and looped her arm under his neck, holding him tight as she swam south, paddling with one arm. He struggled at first, but then he let go, allowing her to drag him through the water.

The waves got smaller and smaller, and the roar of the water faded somewhat, so that after about ten minutes they were in water shallow enough for them to reach down and touch solid ground, which they did— pushing, pushing, pushing their way to a sandy beach, where they collapsed and rolled over on their backs, their chests still heaving for air. After a moment, Taylor said, "Are you . . . all right?"

"Yes. How about you?"

"Yes."

They lay in the sand, arms and legs trembling, sucking air.

Katherine looked up and saw the same beautiful, blue sky she'd seen from the dock. It brought her back to reality. She raised up on her elbows and looked at Taylor.

"What did you do with Bessie?" she asked in an anguished voice. "Where is she?"

Taylor turned his head so that he could look her in the face.

"I never saw Bessie," he said.

"Bessie!" she screamed. "Bessie, where are you?"

She looked from side to side, seeing nothing but sand and beyond that, trees. She struggled to her feet and started toward the trees, calling out, "Bessie! Bessie!"

Taylor got to his feet and followed after her, the both of them staggering into the trees, pushing through the branches until they were confronted by a man in a uniform.

"Are you people all right?" he asked. "I'm a ranger at Cedar islands State Park."

"Is that where we are?" asked Taylor. "In the park?"

"Yes."

"In America?" asked Katherine.

"Yes."

"Oh, God," she muttered. "Not again!"

The ranger overlooked her comment, thinking that she probably was dazed, which she was, and he told them that he'd watched the whole thing from an observation tower.

"You need to be checked out by a doctor," he said.

"We've got to find my dog, Bessie. Have you seen her?"

"No ma'am," said the ranger. "I haven't seen a dog."

The ranger suggested that they follow him back to the ranger station so that he could get medical care for them and get them a ride back home; but Katherine would have none of that, insisting that they stay on the beach to look for Bessie.

The ranger acquiesced and the three of them returned to the beach. They walked the length of the sandy beach, calling out for Bessie, looking out across the river for any sign of her. Not until the sun started setting did Katherine agree to go with them to the ranger station.

"You will report her missing, won't you?" asked Katherine. "I mean, you can notify the residents of the other islands that she's lost."

"Yes ma'am, I'll do everything I can."

Taylor put his arm around Katherine and said, "I never saw her or heard her, so the chances aren't real good that she made it ashore."

"Don't say that! Of course, she made it!"

After they were examined at the ranger station—Katherine had a small cut on her forehead and Taylor's arm looked like it might be broken—they were taken to the state police station at the dock so that they could be taken back across the river.

Before they left, Katherine pleaded with the police officer to make a sweep past Rabbit Island, where the accident occurred. At first the officer said no, pointing out that it was already dark.

"But you have a spotlight," she pointed out.

"Yes."

"Could you take us along the north side of the island and shine your light along the water's edge? Bessie could be there, all alone, looking for me."

Reluctantly, the police officer agreed. They spent nearly an hour cruising back and forth past the island, looking for Bessie. Finally, it became obvious that it was a waste of time. The police officer was polite but firm.

"Ma'am, I've got to take you home now."

Katherine nodded, saying nothing.

Taylor sat next to her on the ride home, his good arm around her shoulder.

"I'm so sorry this happened," he said. "They'll find Bessie. I know they will."

Katherine didn't answer. Her mind was reeling. *How could this happen to me? Again? What kind of world is this?*

When they pulled up at her island, Taylor asked if she wanted him to stay the night with her. "No," she answered, looking away so that she couldn't see his face. She was thinking *There is nothing I'd like more tonight than to lie in a man's arms, there's comfort in that, but not tonight, maybe never.* "Thank you—but maybe some other time."

She stood on the dock as the boat pulled away with Taylor looking more than a little bewildered. He got to his feet and waved with his good arm. She waved back.

Then she went inside the house and closed the door on the world.

CHAPTER
37

For two weeks Katherine went from island to island, looking for Bessie. She walked the waterfront, both the elevated rocky areas and the sandy beaches. She hiked through the forests. She went door to door on those islands that contained cottages. She flagged down boaters and questioned them about their whereabouts on the day of the accident.

On one of the islands, she came upon an elderly woman working in her garden. The old woman was friendly enough, but she never put down her spade, clutching it as if it were a potential weapon. In fairness, Katherine did have a desperate look in her eyes.

"Pardon me for interrupting your work, but I'm looking for my dog—a blond cocker spaniel that answers to the name Bessie."

"What were you doing walking your dog on my island? This is private property."

"I wasn't walking her. We were in a boat that broke up just south of here. And Bessie got away from us."

"That was you, was it? I could smell your stinky gasoline for two days. I'm surprised you didn't burn up. Gasoline will burn on top of water, you know."

"Yes, I've heard that. Have you seen any dogs on your property?"

The old woman looked at her, eyes squinted, not sure if she should answer. Reluctantly, she said, "Yes, I did see a dog."

"Was it a cocker spaniel?"

"I'll tell you the same thing I told that fellow that came through looking for a missing dog. I don't know what kind of dog it was."

"Where is the dog now?'

"Gone. Chased it off into the water. It could have had rabies or something. Dogs are filthy creatures."

Ignoring that comment, Katherine said, "Do you mind if I look around?"

"Wouldn't do any good. I chased it off clean into the water."

The old woman pointed to the south, her index finger twisted with arthritis.

"Going that way the last I saw."

Katherine's heart sank. She had no idea if the woman really saw a dog, or, if she did, if it was Bessie. Just in case the old woman was right, she spent the rest of the day exploring islands in the direction that the woman said the dog swam.

Back at her island, Katherine sat on her deck until sunset, watching the sun fizzle on another day. As darkness crept across the water, slip-sliding over treacherous shadows, she went inside and closed the door and took a deep breath. The house was unbearably quiet without Bessie, not that she was ever a noisy dog. She seldom barked inside the house, unless someone was at the door.

But her footsteps around the house were a constant reminder to Katherine after losing Roger and Dedi that she was not alone in life. Now she truly was alone—and the pain was a constant in her life. Like a dripping faucet.

She lay in bed for the longest time, tossing and turning, unable to sleep.

Finally, she pulled a blanket and a pillow from the bed, and trudged downstairs and then outside onto the deck, where she made a bed for herself on a lounge.

That night she tossed for hours before finally dropping off to sleep.

There was a ship's horn not so very far away. Forlorn and deep, it rumbled through the fog, skipping across the water onto her lawn.

She tried to wake, but sleep pulled her away from the sound of the ship's horn.

It was a nice place. It was filled with sunlight, but she wasn't even there. She was looking in from the outside.

What she saw took her breath away.

Roger appeared in the distance, walking in her direction. He stopped only a few feet away but he didn't acknowledge her presence.

Why can't he see me, she thought? What's wrong?

She called out his name.

He didn't respond. Instead, he reached out, his other hand clutching something to his chest, a bundle of something she couldn't quite make out.

She called out, more desperately this time.

Roger looked straight into her face, without recognition.

It was as if she were viewing him through a camera's viewfinder.

She was detached. So very detached.

Roger looked off to the side and laughed.

What did he see?

Then, out of the mist, a dog's paw reached out and touched Roger's hand.

She strained to see the owner of the paw.

Suddenly, Katherine woke with a start. The T-shirt she'd slept in was soaking wet. Her heart pounded. Her mouth was dry. She sat up and looked around the deck. She'd dreamt of Roger and Dedi before, even Bessie, but never anything like this. It was like she'd crossed over to the other side and returned, only she was invisible and the people on the other side couldn't see her. She gathered up her things and went inside the house.

After breakfast and a shower, Katherine went back outside to sit on the deck. The morning mist lazily rolled, fog-like, across the water. She spent most of her time now on the deck, her eyes riveted to the river, looking for Bessie.

In her heart, she knew she would never look out across the water and see Bessie paddling toward her, but something inside her wouldn't allow her to stop thinking that it was possible. As a child she felt that something bad would happen if she ever stepped on a sidewalk crack. Now she felt that nothing good would happen if she ever stopped looking for Bessie.

In the space of an hour four huge freighters glided past, along with dozens of boaters, most of them overflowing with laughter. A time or two she was tempted to shout out that they were laughing *too loud* but each time she thought better of it, realizing that her annoyance was more a reflection of her than the people doing the laughing.

She could only see a portion of her dock from where she sat on the deck, but she heard something that made her think that a boat had stopped at her house.

I hope it's not Taylor she thought. *It'll be a long time before I'm ready to talk to him again. Maybe never.*

She listened and heard nothing more.

Voices, boat motors carried across the water all the time, distorting their location.

As she gazed out across the lawn, she saw something coming toward her out of the mist. Walking upright. It was an eerie sight.

"Who's there?" she shouted out to the intruder.

No answer. Whoever it was continued up the hill in her direction.

"Who is it?"

It's a man, judging by the shape of him, the way he walks, she thought, her anxiety rising. *And he's got something in his arms.*

Suddenly, the blurred image took shape.

Could she believe her eyes?

Roger was walking toward her—and in his arms was Bessie!

Katherine froze. Then she screamed and ran across the lawn.

Once she reached him, she threw out her arms and hugged the two of them, practically wrestling them to the ground.

"Roger!" she exclaimed, "How is this possible? Is this a dream?"

Bessie barked and lunged for her, Roger barely able to hold her in his arms.

Bessie kissed Katherine's face over and over again as Katherine ran her fingers through her coat, saying, "Sweet Bessie! I can't believe it's you!"

Soon Bessie pulled loose and hit the ground, running in ever widening circles across the lawn, across *her* lawn.

Katherine took Roger's face in her hands, smothering him with kisses. Roger held her in his arms, tears streaming down his cheeks.

Minutes later, Katherine pushed away and lovingly gazed at him.

"What happened? Where in God's name have you been?"

"It's a long story," he said, shaking his head. "I don't know where to begin."

"I thought you drowned in the accident."

"I was picked up by a freighter. I had amnesia. They took me to South Africa?"

"What?"

"Yes. When my memory returned, I got back as fast as I could."

"Where on earth did you ever find Bessie?" she asked.

Before he could answer, she wrapped her arms tightly around him. Then she looked up at him, kissing him on the lips once she saw the tears in his eyes.

They stood for what seemed like an eternity, arms intertwined, each afraid to turn the other loose, fearful that what they were experiencing was nothing more than a dream that would evaporate if the wrong series of words were spoken. They had one foot in heaven, the other in hell. They held tight, gently rocking.

Finally, when he was able to speak, he said, "It's a long story."

"Come—let's go sit on the deck. I want to hear everything."

As they walked back to the deck, Katherine said, "I didn't know life's sad stories ever had a happy ending."

Not realizing she'd said it she repeated it twice before they sat next to each other on the deck. She reached out and took his hand and held it, tightly.

"Now—tell me about Bessie."

Roger paused, looking at the house.

"Aren't you forgetting something?"

"What do you mean?"

"Where is she?" he asked.

"Who?"

"Dedi, of course."

"Oh, God," Katherine sighed. "I don't know"

"She's all right, isn't she?"

"Oh Roger . . . "

She felt his body wilt in her arms.

"You mean . . . are you saying?"

"Yes, in the accident. I thought I'd lost both of you. It was horrible. I miss her so much. Sometimes I hear her voice and turn around and no one is there."

Roger slipped his arms over hers.

"I'm so sorry."

Suddenly, Katherine felt something wet on her dangling hand.

Bessie was licking her.

Katherine turned loose of Roger and leaned over to pet Bessie.

"What I don't understand is why you are surprised to see Bessie?"

"That's another long story," she said, smiling. "Two weeks ago I was in a boat with a friend and Bessie, and we cracked up on the rocks. Bessie was tossed into the water. I've been looking for her for two weeks. How in the world did you find Bessie?"

Roger laughed. "Like so much of life, like my homecoming itself, finding Bessie was entirely serendipitous."

"So?" she asked impatiently.

"I came back on the same freighter that'd rescued me. The plan was for them to anchor directly across from our island and transport me in a launch the rest of the way home. Only when we lowered the launch I saw something familiar on the bank, not very far away. It was Bessie. She was just sitting there, looking out across the water. She obviously knew exactly where you were. She just didn't know how to get back home to you. I called out her name and she started jumping up and down. They were kind enough to take me to her. Right before we reached her rocky perch, she jumped over into the boat and started pawing at me like I was a piece of raw meat. She was so happy to be discovered. I couldn't imagine what she was doing there."

Katherine looked out across the lawn, where Bessie was still running in circles, so happy to be home again.

She reached out and picked up Roger's hand, holding it a moment before bringing it to her lips. She gently kissed his fingers.

"Thank you so much," she said, her eyes glistening.

"For what?"

"For coming home."

"Believe me, once I regained my memory, it was all I could think about."

"Why didn't you call?"

"I thought about it. But I didn't know the truth until recently—and I was afraid to explain this to you on the telephone."

"Afraid?"

"Yes. Afraid you would not understand. Afraid it would be too much of a shock. Afraid you might have met someone else and moved on with your life. I was afraid of a hundred different things. The unknown mostly."

Katherine sighed. If only he knew.

After a moment she said, "Would you do me the honor of having breakfast with me tomorrow?"

Roger looked puzzled.

Katherine smiled and shook her head.

"What does it mean if a woman asks you to have breakfast with her?"

"Is this some sort of a test?"

He paused, a slow-burning look of recognition creeping across his face.

"Oh," he said.

Then again, "Oooh!"

"Roger, we lost everything. But we have been given much in return."

"No one has ever been loved as much as I love you today."

Katherine wrapped her arms tightly around his neck, weeping with joy for the first time in a long while.